Psychological Breakdown

Other David Owain Hughes Titles

Novels, Novellas and Short Story Collections:
All-Wound Up
Wind-Up Toy
Wind-Up Toy: Broken Plaything
Wind-Up Toy: Chaos Rising
White Walls and Straitjackets
Escapees and Fevered Minds
Choice Cuts
Walled In
Man-Eating Fucks
The Rack & Cue
Collision Course
Granville
Home Improvements

Anthologies:
Shadows and Teeth Vol.3
Trapped Within
Hell of a Guy
Unleashing the Voices
Rejected for Content Vol. 4, 5 & 6
Crossroads in the Dark Vol.1 & 2
Fifty Shades of Slay
How to Cook a Baby
Madame Movora's Tales of Terror
Big Book of Bootleg Horror Vol. 1, 2 & 3
Shopping List
Depraved Desires
Easter Eggs and Bunny Boilers
Bah! Humbug!
Slashing Through the Snow
VS Vol. 1 & 2
Black Candy
Into the Abyss

Compiled & Edited Anthologies:
What Goes Around
Man Behind the Mask
Fuck the Rules

Psychological Breakdown

By

David Owain Hughes

A HellBound Books Publishing LLC Book
Houston TX

A HellBound Books LLC
Publication

www.hellboundbookspublishing.com

Printed in the United States of America

Cover and art design by Kevin Enhart for HellBound
Books Publishing LLC
https://art-kevinenhart.blogspot.fr/
https://www.facebook.com/kevin.enhart/

Edited by Brandy Yassa

Acknowledgements

A Mirror Never Lies – **Unleashing the Voices Within In** (Anthology) 2016

Blackout: **Shopping List** (Anthology) 2017

Dacchas: **Hell of a Guy** (tribute anthology to Guy N. Smith (Anthology) Note: the characters and settings within this tale are property of Guy N. Smith – permission has been granted for this story to appear in a collection of work belonging to me.

Dark Woods: **Rejected for Content 4** (Anthology) 2016

Picture Not So Perfect: **Shadows and Teeth Vol:3** (Anthology) 2017

*Filial Cannibalism: **How to Cook a Baby** (Anthology) 2017

For the Love of Shakespeare: **Rejected for Content 5** (Anthology) 2016

Recognition: **Big Book of Bootleg Horror 2** (Anthology) 2017

Sleigh Sisters: **Slashing Through the Snow** (Anthology) 2016

Techno Tendencies: **Big Book of Bootleg Horror 1** (Anthology) 2017

Thighs Maketh the Woman: **Depraved Desires** (Anthology) 2017

Dedication

I'd like to dedicate the collection to my children, Gethin David Hughes and Ruby Storm Leigh Hughes.

Psychological Breakdown

Foreword
By
Jim Goforth

In a world where we no longer have any new material to look forward to from the likes of the late, great Richard Laymon, it's a delight to know that there are writers such as David Owain Hughes who can ably step into the void.

The sort who pull no punches, leave no stone unturned, and have no qualms about delving into the darkest of corners. The sort who go places others wouldn't dare, and then continue to go beyond that. The sort who understand that the clue to horror is all in the label itself; it's supposed to be horrific, disturbing. It's meant to engender certain feelings in a reader, and I'm not talking warm and fuzzy ones. It isn't something to be watered down and censored.

There are a whole slew of emerging horror writers who are starting to make their mark, and rise above the crowd, and they write raw and debauched, undiluted savagery, yet never eschew story in favour of mere shock value. Hughes is among these fearsome newcomers, and is one of the most unrestrained, unapologetic, and gleefully brutal exponents of modern horror fiction.

Lacing his work with dark humour, threading it deftly amidst horrific scenes that can strike a blow like a gut punch from a wrecking ball, Hughes has the ability to craft a storyline, sometimes simple, sometimes far more complex, and then drench it in a deluge of blood and other bodily fluids with sadistic abandon. He plies his trade in the extreme end of the spectrum, but he knows the value of storytelling and you'll never find that sacrificed in his sanguinary scribblings.

I've encountered many a Hughes tale, most notably through the likes of the Rejected For Content anthology series, and I'll tell you this for free. If there ever was a writer born to be a perfect fit for that particular line of books, then David Owain Hughes is your man.

Granted, extreme horror is much more acceptable than it once was, more readily likely to be published by places that might have given it a wide berth previously, but all the same, Hughes pens some pieces that would have once seen some of these, let's say, *discerning* publishers running for the hills, screaming. Which is why we love him over at RFC; the guy knows how to knock out a tale that blends old school horror sensibilities with modern power, but shies away from none of the content that might otherwise get it rejected, and he's doing so with his own unique voice.

Now, I won't promise that you'll have a good time with what you encounter in these following pages, because that might well be a lie. It would probably be more appropriate to say you'll end up having a disturbing time, which is swiftly followed by myriad nightmares and countless hours of therapy.

After all, you should have been aware of what you were signing up for. Horror isn't about making one comfortable, and David Owain Hughes is here to ram home that point in unrelenting fashion.

Jim Goforth, 2017

CONTENTS

***

Psychological Breakdown

Psychological Breakdown

Picture Not So Perfect

"Always forgive your enemies—nothing annoys them so much." —Oscar Wilde

Adam sat with his back to the sun, his easel standing firm and erect on the uneven ground. He loved to paint his pictures here in the garden, nestled among the four apple trees his mother liked to call an orchard.

Behind the trees, and surrounding the garden, was an old wall with bricks amiss here and there, allowing the neighbour's daughter and local scallywags to hop the partition and thieve their apples. Not that Adam's mother minded, as the children normally lifted the fruit found on the ground, which were bruised and useless to her.

"Nothing worse than battered apples," she would say. "You can taste their badness in my pies! The rot will cause moss to line their stupid stomachs!"

Remembering this, Adam shook his head. "Silly woman!" he muttered, setting his pencils out in readiness to draw.

"I can't see why they don't ask us!" his father would add, peering with sobriety over the top of his broadsheet. "When they struggle to hop the wall, they end up toppling more bricks! Not just that, they trample my flowerbeds, snap my runner bean stalks, and squash my tomato plants." His father thought himself a logical, intelligent, and diplomatic man. "I should have strung them up by their balls after Adam told me who they were!"

Adam rolled his eyes, tutted, and set his empty pencil case to one side. Before sitting on his stool in front of his easel, he checked to make sure he'd brought everything from the house he would need: brushes, pens, eraser, palette, A2 pad of paper and pots of paint.

Dad wouldn't give them apples even if they asked! he thought.

He finished setting up and approached the wall. Placing his hands on the top bricks and pulling himself up to peep into his neighbour's garden, Eve, the daughter, was nowhere to be seen.

Maybe she's gone to play at a friend's house today? After all, it's such a lovely day! I can't expect her to hang around here all the time to keep me and my ugliness company!

"You're not *ugly*, but beautiful!" Eve would reassure him.

"Maybe I'll see you later..." he whispered, lowering himself from the wall and returning to his easel. A light breeze rustled his paper and rattled his pencils, causing him to look up at the clear blue sky, which had been filled with stormy-looking clouds early that morning. "No chance of rain," he smiled, happy the weather wouldn't be an issue.

Adam sat at his easel and picked up a sketching pencil. "Okay, Dorian. Let's see if we can get you picture perfect today." He put the pencil in his mouth, like a dog would with a bone, so he could tie his long hair into a ponytail. Then he wriggled his arse on the stool until he was comfy, and removed the HB from the clutches of his teeth.

"Okay, inspiration time!"

Adam put a hand in his trousers pocket and withdrew the small mirror he had there. Before braving a look, he drew in a slow, deep, and shaky breath. When he released it, he felt like crying.

Come on, the poet needs the pain! His hand flirted with the mirror, tilting it this way and that, the sun catching in the glass and shining in his eyes. *It's now or never...* he thought, bringing the mirror up close. Adam forced himself to look at his reflection.

"Ugh!" he gasped, drinking himself in. "I'm like the son who gets locked in the attic. I'm like Quasimodo's uglier brother." He poked his tongue out at his mirror image. "You're hideous!" he proclaimed.

Except there was no twin brother, *or* sister.

His parents hated him. He'd always thought this was all in his head, until the night, recently, when Dad got drunk and told Adam how much he damaged his mother's insides when he was ripped from her at birth.

"You were a nineteen-pound Rottweiler!" he said now, echoing his father's slurred words. "You almost tore your poor mother asunder, you repugnant little fuck! You're nothing but an unsightly monster!"

Words hurt, no matter what the rhyme said.

Where were those good looks Eve could see? He slanted the mirror this way and that, trying to seek out the beauty beneath his beastly image in the glass's edges, middle and corners.

The "monster" stared back.

With his scant, patchy hair pulled into a ponytail, Adam could see the ungodly lumps on his forehead, around his temple and peeking through his thinning locks. Bulges of unequal size and measures graced his back, arms and legs. Some of them wept, but caused him no pain.

His eyes were a total mismatch: one looked as though it belonged to a snake. The pupil was slender and beady, matching that side of his scaly, thick-as-a-Panzer's-armour skin. His other peeper glowed a majestic green, giving credence to his face, overall, as one that belonged to a human man.

One of his arms was shorter than the other, his hands and fingers normal. His left foot was slightly cleft, V-shaped and missing toes. However, he had no problems walking on it, suggesting it was not club-foot.

His organs were intact and functional.

His speech, which Adam found to be his one redeeming feature, was soft and child-like.

"I am a monster with a poet's tongue."

He lowered the mirror and absorbed the grief by swallowing it down with the mucus that had built at the back of his throat.

Adam set to work.

"I'm going to be a famous painter!" he'd once told his parents, who had scoffed, mocked, and cowed him.

"They only bought me my art equipment to shut me up!" he muttered, starting his sketch of Dorian Wilde—the character who Adam believed lived inside him. "I *will* perfect you on paper this time, my angelic Adonis!"

In his mind, Dorian was a golden-haired warrior from a forgotten age.

The person I should *have been!* he thought, feverishly etching his character's face and body with immaculate precision. Before he knew it, Adam was adding the finishing touches to Dorian's outline. His persona's fiddly details, colour, shading and everything in-between, would be added next, as he continued to build his perfect Dorian.

He was in no rush.

Rome wasn't built in a day. Besides, I'm happy to be out here, with the sun—

Raucous cawing broke his concentration.

Adam snapped his head up and squinted at the murder of crows nestled on his father's sprouting vegetables. Another group of black birds settled themselves in his mother's apple trees.

He sighed. His father's cruel words flooded his brain.

"If you're in the garden, you know it's your duty to scare the birds away, boy. *You* are my little scarecrow!"

Adam's shoulders slumped. As he stepped around his easel, he turned and looked up at Eden Hall, the "country home," which had loomed large over him since nappies. His father was standing at one of the top windows.

I'm tending to it, Dad, he thought, feeling his father's eyes burn a hole through his forehead. *Bloody "country home," as mum calls it! It's a semi-rural house with two acres of land. They think they're heir to the throne, with their tweed clothing, hunting rifles and afternoon tiffin. What's next, cucumber sandwiches on the lawn? A spot of croquet in the outer field?!*

He kicked the ground and particles of dirt found their way into his mouth and up his nose. Like his dad, the crows eyed him suspiciously. Their beady orbs and small heads darted this way and that. Their wings fluttered, their feathers ruffled.

They cawed to each other as he neared.

If he's *watching, he's going to expect a spectacle.*

"And make sure you put effort into it!" he imagined his dad saying.

"Yes, *Daddy*!" he spat before throwing his arms in the air and screaming. "*Argh*!" His limbs thrashed. He opened his mouth and let his tongue flap wildly in the warm breeze as he ran to the birds. The crows around the vegetables took to flight immediately, but the ones in the trees remained until his oversized body crashed into one of the trees, causing its branches to shake violently. Apples and leaves rained down as though a B-52 bomber, laden with fruit, twigs and foliage, had dropped its cargo. An apple flew off his head. Adam's nose crunched against the hard, pale timber.

"*Oof!*" he cried, falling backwards and hitting the compacted ground with force. Tears blurred his vision. He could almost hear his father's laughter.

He sat up, and felt warm trickles of blood or snot escape his nose. He shook his head, stood, red mucus running from his face as he made his way back to his seat, cheeks flushing. He didn't dare glance up at the window.

"Bloody birds!" he said, nasally. He wanted to stomp, kick and cry. Instead he looked at the textbook image of Dorian, and it brought a smile to his hurt face. "Let's get you finished!"

His drawing, and Eve, were the only things that kept him from taking his father's shaving blade and slashing it across his lumpy, malformed throat.

She must *be out for the day,* he concluded, wiping fresh blood from his nose. *Eve would have been here scoffing apples by now, unless her dad has scuppered her plans. He's worse than my father!*

"I don't want you bothering with that monstrosity!" Adam had heard Mr. Evans say one day, whilst standing close to the wall picking apples. "They should have drowned the ogre at birth!"

Eve had defended his honour bravely, telling her father that she would bother with whomever she pleased. Her insubordination had earned her a slap, along with a promised taste of her dad's belt, which Adam had heard being unbuckled and then ripped through the loops on his trousers.

Luckily, she had escaped his wrath by hopping the wall and landing close to Adam. She'd smiled and placed a finger to her lips.

"You can't hide forever, you little bitch! The leather will be awaiting your return, as always!"

The man was nothing more than a dangerous drunk, corroded by failure, envy and hurt.

Eve had confided in Adam that her father used to beat and rape her mother, and that she and Eve had both been too scared to stand up to him. Her mother had eventually packed up and left in the middle of the night, leaving Eve alone with him.

That day by the wall, Adam held her tight, wiped her tears away and soothed her burning cheek.

All he could do was comfort. He wasn't good for anything else.

He took a deep breath, cleared his mind, and then broke out the pencils he liked to use for shading and creating fine detail. Within minutes, Adam was absorbed in his work.

* * *

The sun had begun to set when it was finally time for Adam to pack his pencils, brushes, and other bits and pieces away. He looked at the almost-finished picture. Dorian Wilde was a giant of a man: six-feet, eight inches. The drawing's long, black hair flanked his faultless, unblemished face, setting off his high cheekbones and unnaturally sultry lips. Sure, Adam had envisioned him as his blond Adonis, but such were the limitations of HB pencils that anything they rendered was in shades of grey and black. Dorian's mouth was set in an impressive half-smile, exposing impeccable teeth and healthy gums.

Adam lowered his gaze to Dorian's bull-like neck, bulging pecs and extraordinary eight pack. Draped over the man's arms and shoulders was an old leather jacket, which looked cracked and tired, the buckles worn. Around his chest was a strap, which held in place the acoustic guitar on his back—part of the fretboard, neck and headstock could be seen over Dorian's shoulder.

His massive thighs rippled with muscle, the veins protruding. On his feet were primitive-looking boots made from animal fur, which rode his calves and were kept in place by old cord.

A spiked mace hung from his left hip, a holstered Colt graced his other. A Bowie knife was tied to his right calf, with the bottom of its sheath disappearing into the boot.

"You're a warrior!" His dick started to harden the longer his stare lingered. It wasn't that he desired his own sex. But this man was just too perfect. "Why haven't I been able to draw you to this impeccable degree before now?"

Suddenly a noise in the distance caught his attention.

"Voices..." he whispered. He left his work and walked to the wall. "*Eve*?!" A smile grew across his face, which soon faltered, when he realised those voices belonged to boys.

He pressed himself flat to the wall and listened.

"...Let's see if their retarded son's around," someone said.

"*Yeah*! We can kick his backwards arse!" a second voice said. "I mean, we did say we'd pay him back! Dad went fucking nuts on us!"

"Aye. I can't believe that fucker ratted us out to our parents."

"We can fuck the garden up whilst we're at it!" a third person said.

"Fucking goddamn right!"

"You really think he's the by-product of his dog and mother?" a fourth chirped.

"Bah-ha-ha! Totally!"

"Ha! What is the mutt and mother called?"

"Cain and Mabel!"

"These pricks talk like its nineteen-seventeen or some shit!"

"Seen the way they dress? Fucking losers. Maybe someone should tell 'em it's the twenty-first century!"

Adam pushed off the wall and went to his things. He tried to gather everything as quickly as possible. He knew these boys—Matthew, Mark, Luke and John—all brothers, all savagely mean.

"*Hey*! Shit for brains!"

Adam dropped his brushes and pencil case. His eraser tumbled along the ground and nestled among his father's plants. The voice belonged to John. Timidly, Adam turned.

"Yeah, that's right—I'm talking to you, freak!" John continued. His brothers were in the process of scrambling over the wall and laughing.

"*No*!" Adam cried, watching helplessly as Matthew, Mark and Luke started to trash the garden. "Don't, please! My dad—"

"Your dad what, pencil dick?!" John said, getting in Adam's face. Their noses pressed together. "Are you going to piss yourself, chicken shit? Are ya?!"

Adam was much bigger than the boys. "I won't tell. *Leave*!" He tried to sound as strong as he looked, but his voice cracked.

If Eve were here, she'd tell them where to go!

Adam felt himself shrink.

The others laughed as they continued to take the garden apart, ripping out his mother's petunias and stamping on the vegetable patch.

"You told on us!" John prodded Adam in his chest. "We've been waiting to repay you, *pal*!"

"I *had* to tell! My dad asked. If I'd have lied—"

A robust fist ploughed into Adam's jaw, sending him to the ground. He looked up at John, who stood over him. He was now flanked by the others. "They're just *apples*! Take what you want, and get out! *Please*! I won't—"

One of the lads kicked him in his ribs, hard. Adam howled.

"Come on, let's do the bastard!"

A hot glob of spit landed on Adam's face.

"I—" he tried to protest. A flurry of kicks and punches rained down on him, taking his breath away. "*Argh*!" He flipped onto his stomach and tried to crawl away. Kicks turned to stomps. A set of hands found a spade and clobbered Adam about his back and legs.

Blood burst from his mouth and nose.

"Dad!" he screamed. "*Dad*!"

"Shut him up!" John said.

Adam was roughly turned over, his head held in place. A hand was clamped over his mouth as the boys took to his stomach and privates.

"Ugh-*argh*!" Adam cried a muffled cry. Tears mixed with blood. Through a red blur, he caught sight of his dad at the top window, watching.

"*Daddy*!" he grizzled, briefly ripping the hand off his mouth. Words and mucus caught in his throat when one of his tormentors kicked him in the balls. "*Ugh*!"

They let him go.

Adam lay there, panting. He felt like one of his mother's bruised apples. "My ribs..." he sobbed. He looked towards the house and saw his mother by his dad's side. He reached a pleading hand towards them, blood dripping from the ends of his fingers.

"Let's strip the pussy!"

"Fuck yeah!

"N-n…" Adam tried; it hurt to move his swelling jaw unable to work his jaw.

He felt their rough hands on him again as they feverishly ripped at his clothes. Within seconds, he was cold and naked. He could only watch through partly swollen eyes as John and his siblings pranced around the garden and threw his things into the trees and bushes.

"Ugh! *No!*" he gasped, seeing John lay hands on his painting.

"What's this, faggot? Been drawing pictures of your boyfriend?"

"*Ha!*" One of John's brothers shrieked, picking it up and throwing it on the ground. He danced on it, scuffing the image and tearing it.

"Dorian!" Adam yelled, mindless of the pain.

"Oh. My. Fuck! He's got a name for it!" John said, snatching the portrait from the ground and ripping it in half.

"*Nooo!*" Adam cried. Tears flowed down his cheeks. When he crawled closer to the vipers, they again laid into him with kicks and punches. His blood spewed into the air and splattered his face. "Mum… Dad…" he moaned.

"What ya doing, Luke?" John asked.

"Going to piss on him, man!"

The boys laughed to the chorus of zippers and splashing urine.

Adam's world tilted and turned black as he slipped into unconsciousness.

* * *

"You awake down there?" a new voice asked. Adam felt someone prodding his side. "Are you alive?"

"*Help!*" Adam gasped weakly. "Get me... *home!*" He felt cold, his body shivered. "Where am I?"

"Outside, in the garden of your home, I think."

Adam's eyes fluttered open. The person standing over him had long, blond hair, which blew in the fierce night breeze. Moonlight spilled out around the figure's hulking form. "Are you an angel?"

"A fallen one, you could say."

"You're a male angel?"

"What is this, forty questions? Yes, male. Do you want my help or not?"

"*Yes!*" Adam's eyes roamed deliriously.

The man wore a leather jacket. There was something stitched on the coat. *A patch*... With a squint, Adam read what was written there: "Devil's Tribe, South Wales," he mouthed.

"Who did this to you?" the man asked.

"Bullies."

"What's your name?"

"Adam."

The man nodded. "My friends call me Cobra, Adam. I don't like seeing people get pushed around. I can help you, friend."

"Help me home..."

"I can do more than that." Cobra leaned close to Adam's face.

"Are you an Indian, or some kind of gypsy?"

"I told you—I'm an angel."

"Mystery man..." Adam let his words trail off. He didn't know what he was saying. His head throbbed. "I need water."

"You'll have water." Cobra's face disappeared.

"Where have you gone?"

"Fetching you water. I have some in my saddlebags."

"You have a horse?"

"A steel one, friend. *Drink*!"

A plastic bottle was placed to Adam's mouth—cool water spilled from it. He drank greedily, until it was pulled from him.

"That's enough," said Cobra at last. "We need to move you."

"Go to the house. Get my parents! They must be worried sick."

"There are no lights on inside the house."

"They don't love me, do they?"

"Don't cry, friend."

Adam lifted his head—the world spun. What's covering my body?!" he shrieked. "Get them off me! *Argh*!"

"Calm down. Some leaves have blown onto to you. If you ask me, it's a good thing—your modesty has been covered." Cobra chuckled. "What's this?"

"I don't know. What are you looking at?"

"A sketch. It's been ripped."

A fresh lump developed in Adam's throat and he felt his cheeks burn. "That's Dorian Wilde. I'm not a faggot, I swear, it's just—"

"You see yourself as this person?"

"N-n-no, but—"

"There's no need to be embarrassed, boy. Like I said, I can help. Do you trust me? Do you want my aid?"

"Y-yes!" Adam said, nervously, not knowing what he was agreeing to, or what was being asked of him.

"Here, hold on to your soul!" Cobra said, placing the shredded A2 paper in Adam's hand. "I'll carry you home."

"I'm too heavy!" His eyes rolled like marbles. He felt on the verge of blacking out. "Where am I?" A fever seemed to be engulfing his body, driving out the shivering shakes he'd had upon waking. "Who are you?"

"Rest, friend."

Adam felt a hand on his eyes. "B-but…"

"Shh!" Cobra grunted. "Let's get you home."

Adam's limp body was scooped off the ground floor with apparent ease, as though he weighed as much as a pillow. The bouncing motions he felt as Cobra carried him to the sanctuary of Eden Hall were almost soothing, though his bones ached and creaked. "Am I dreaming? Are you a flaxen-haired maiden who has come to take me away? Is that you, Eve? What am I saying? Where am I? Who are you?"

Sweat beaded his scalding forehead. Adam fancied he could hear it boiling.

"*Stop*! Put me down. I need to—" A stream of searing, multi-coloured spew burst from his mouth. "Oh, God! I'm sorry…" Chunks of sick slid out.

Then he heard footfalls on steps.

We're on the front porch.

Hard knocks followed. "Open the fucking door, you inconsiderate pricks!" Cobra yelled.

How is he knocking? I'm in his arms.

"I'll kick the fucking door in! Come on!" More hard thumps. "Fucking arseholes. How can you treat your boy like this? I have a good mind to report you bastards!"

Adam swayed in and out of consciousness.

"Bring the retch in here," his father said.

"If I hadn't have come along, he'd be dead by now, you cold-hearted fuck!"

Adam felt his body being pulled this way and that. His ears then filled with the sound of intense clicking.

"I should blow your fucking head off!" Cobra sneered.

"*God*! I don't want any trouble!"

"Well, trouble's here, pal! Now, get your boy in bed, or I'll fuck you up!"

"Don't hurt him!" Adam wheezed, trying to stay awake.

"Always forgive your enemies—nothing annoys them so much!" Cobra whispered in Adam's ear. "Your new way will drive them wild with jealousy, obtaining revenge and giving you a new lease on life, friend."

Then there was a loud bang. It was the last thing he heard before the darkness overcame him.

* * *

"*Dad*!" Adam screamed, sitting bolt upright in bed. The early morning sun pushed through the cracks in his bedroom curtains. "What the—?" he gasped, looking down at himself. "How did I end up here? Where're John and his brothers? Cobra…?" his words trailed off.

The house was deathly quiet. He looked at his alarm clock.

"Almost ten a.m.," he murmured. "The servants should be busying themselves about the house—I'd have heard them by now. Where is everyone?"

He flung the bed covers off and instantly noticed his naked body covered in what appeared to be golden glitter. "Is that… s*and?*" he blurted, putting his fingers to the tiny particles that clung to his chest. Instinctively, he raised his hands to his hair and tousled it. More came out of his thinning locks, coating his thighs and sprinkling the mattress. "Was I at the beach yesterday?"

Adam's brow knit in confusion.

Of course I wasn't! I had seven shades of hell beaten out of me.

"*Dorian*!" Adam felt pained when he remembered how his portrait had been destroyed. "Bloody yobs!

How could they? And after I'd captured him so perfectly…"

He wanted to cry. He rubbed his eyes.

"Hang on," he said, his fingers pressing his eyelid. "How—?"

His eyes were perfectly fine; no swelling, no pain.

He threw his legs off the bed and stood up, arching his back, rotating his neck and shrugging the knots out of his shoulders. "I feel fantastic! Refreshed, too. What's going on? Was yesterday a dream?"

Adam was prone to vivid night terrors and daydreams, and so he could not discount yesterday as the product of his imagination. He walked over to the full-length mirror screwed onto the back of his door.

"It felt so real, though! Maybe I caught sunstroke?" He put the back of his hand to his forehead. "Feels like I may have a slight temperature. It's nothing to cause a mass hysteria over, though."

His face looked fine in the mirror—no cuts, no extra lumps or bruising.

"Strange. I could have sworn… *Nah!*" His dad was mean, but not so cruel that he'd watch Adam take a beating and leave him outside like a mangy dog. After all, he was annoyed with those boys. Surely he would have come to his son's aid and shooed them off. Adam raised his fingers to his face and allowed them to roam his lips, cheeks and forehead.

He turned from the glass and threw his curtains open. It was a glorious morning, with the sun high in the sky. "Maybe it was a premonition?" He smiled, knowing if that were the case, there would be no need to be upset over a portrait that never was—better yet, the thought that he'd be creating that fine piece of artwork today made him grin wider.

With a renewed vigour, Adam turned to his walk-in wardrobe where he kept his art gear, and pulled the doors open.

Confusion twisted his face.

"What's *this*?" He bent to retrieve what looked like a large piece of folded paper. As he began unfolding it, he heard footsteps proceeding up the stairs outside his bedroom door.

China rattled.

Adam looked at the scrap of A2 sheet in wide-eyed wonder. "*Dorian...*" he whispered, looking at the image. "So it *wasn't* a dream! But how—how are you intact? Well, not completely intact, but still."

He traced his finger down the split in the paper, which ran perfectly through Dorian's face and body, marvelling at how the paper had managed to knit itself back together. Boot prints graced the filthy image, with three corners out of four missing.

"I can trace the image! All is not—"

"Are you awake in there, young man?" his father asked. He sounded annoyed.

"Just a second, Dad!"

"Open up this instant!"

Adam tossed his portrait back into the wardrobe and closed it. He opened his bedroom door, allowing his father entry. He strode in with a tray in his hands. When Adam spied the teapot and mug, he knew what was in store.

Punishment.

"Feeling better, are we? *Good*! Once you've had your medicine for allowing those thugs to smash my garden up, you'll be made to go out there for the next four weeks! You'll eat and sleep out there. Do you hear me?"

"Yes, sir."

"With a bit of luck, those louts will have kicked some sense into that thick head of yours! Today, I want you to stand in the centre of the garden and stay there. When you need to pee or poo, you can do so where you stand. But *only* on permission."

"I'm to come—"

"*No*! You will not move. You will call for me until your throat is raw if you have to! And if I don't hear you, then you may soil yourself."

"Yes, sir..." Adam's head lowered—his chin touched his chest.

"Your mother and I see it as a fit enough punishment."

"What if the boys come back? They might kill me!"

"*Good*! One less ungrateful mouth to feed!"

Tears stung Adam's eyes. "Yes, sir. Permission to take my artwork outside?"

"*No*! Not ever! As soon as you leave this room, I will be burning your art stuff! Now, sit on the bed and drink this. All of it mind you!"

He did as instructed and watched as the tray was placed in front of him. Adam put the back of his hand to the teapot, feeling for its temperature. He could smell the hot vinegar from inside the pot.

"Come on, pour yourself a mug!" his father urged him.

"B-but it's boiling! It'll roast my insides."

"Pour! Or I'll call your mother up here to deal with you, Adam, and you know how much she likes to thrash you with that broom handle of hers. Is that what you want? Maybe you secretly like it? Do you crave spanks from mummy?"

"No, sir!" Adam lifted the pot and tilted the spout. Clear, scorching vinegar filled his cup.

"Come on, to the brim! That's it. Now, *drink*!"

Adam placed the mug to his lips but couldn't bring himself to do it.

The pain it will cause. Oh, Jesus!

"Do I have to nail you up and make you drink?" his father roared.

He took a shaky breath and tipped some vinegar down his throat. Adam screamed. His leg thrashed, causing the garnish to spill and splash his thighs.

"All of it!" his father screamed, knocking the mug out of Adam's hand and placing the spout of the teapot to his mouth. "*Drink!*" He yanked his son's head back by his hair, and poured the scalding liquid down his gullet.

Adam gagged.

He tried to scream and plea, but all he could do was thrash his limbs and think of how wild his father looked.

How gleeful!

And then he couldn't swallow. The vinegar started to fountain out of his mouth as he threw up. However, his father continued to pour. The spout was rammed violently into his mouth, chipping teeth. He felt something pop inside his body, causing him to shake violently.

The teapot was removed from his mouth.

"Oh, *Christ!*" said his dad, his tone changing from rage to anxiety. "Adam? Adam!"

His vision started to fade. The space about him turned a blinding white. Before his body shut down, Adam saw a strange vapour in the air, like a cloud.

* * *

Where am I? Adam thought, opening his eyes. From above, he watched his father try to resuscitate him with chest compressions. Adam wasn't certain, but he got the impression his father was wasting his efforts. It was too late for that now.

"*Mabel*! Get up here, now—I think I've killed him!" his father screamed. "We need to get rid of his body! Hurry, woman! Quick! God, I'll rot in a cell for this! No, it won't happen. I'll get shot of him. Put his remains in the garden. Bury him beneath the plants and flowers…"

For the first time in his life, Adam felt furious. He wanted to scream and spit and lash out at his father with his fists, but he couldn't.

"Up here! *Now*!" his father screamed.

His mother answered with an unintelligible yell. She was still too far away for Adam to make out what she said, but judging by how the sound of her voice was growing stronger, she was drawing nearer to them in a hurry.

Adam was then yanked away. Everything became a blur.

It felt as though he were being shoved into something too small for—well, for whatever he was now. Adam screamed until he was able to reopen his eyes.

Everything was dark, his breathing erratic.

"For God's sake, woman! Shift your fucking arse!"

"I have legs!" Adam cried out in alarm. He stood. "Arms! A body, too! But whose?"

He shifted, still uncomfortable in this new skin, assuming that was what it was. He brushed into something and it fell to the floor, clattered about him.

"Who's there?" his father demanded. "Come on, show yourself!"

"It's me, Adam. Your son!" His feathery, childlike tone had gone, replaced by a strong, forceful voice. "What have you done, *Daddy*?" he intoned with fresh menace underpinning his words.

"I don't know you! Come out from hiding!"

"Sybil?" his mother called out to his father. She was closer now, and Adam could hear her clearly. "Who are you screaming at, Sybil?" she went on.

Dad's got a girl's name! Adam thought, chuckling.

"Stay where you are!" his dad said. Then, addressing his wife: "Woman—there's an intruder in the house!"

Adam stepped forward, pushing the door to his wardrobe open a sliver.

"Get out here! Come on. You're all shadows and teeth. I want to see your face!"

Adam stepped into the brightness of his room.

His father's eyes grew wide as saucers when they crossed Adam. "*Argh*! Who are you? Get away! Get out! Mabel, call the—"

Adam towered over his father. He grabbed the man by the throat with his newfound strength. "Look what you did to me!" Adam said, forcing his dad to turn and look at the carcass on the bed. "I was but a simple boy."

"*Urgh*!" Sybil choked, his eyes bulging. "L-l-let... *ugh*... go!"

Adam held his father in place with a hand, whilst his free one reached for the spiked mace that dangled at his side. He unsheathed it, and raised it overhead.

"Goodnight, Daddy!"

Adam shoved his father backward onto his bed, and then sent the medieval weapon crashing down on his face. Blood spurted up a wall in jets, spattering Adam's new body. He retracted his mace, bits of skin, bone and hair clinging to its spikes, then drew it back and set upon his father with a rapid-fire pounding.

Adam's mace hammered his father's head, destroying his face, smashing him again and again and again, his mother's rushing footfalls serving as the background score to the rattle of chain and smashing of bone. Adam stopped when there was nothing left of his father's head but a squashed, mangled mess. One of his eyes had popped out and rested on his cheek. His tongue lolled out of a toothless red maw.

"*Argh!*" Adam roared, turning to face his bedroom door, which was closed. When he spied himself in the mirror, his mouth sagged. "Impossible..." he mouthed, sheathing his blood-soaked mace. "*Dorian!*"

And yet, something was off.

Adam stepped closer to the glass and brushed his blond, blood-splattered hair out of his vision. "My cheek!" he said, turning his head to the left. It was paper white. A part of his chin, too.

Realization crashed down upon Adam that instant.

"I never finished colouring *me* in!"

He then noticed more colour missing from his clothes, chest and stomach. "No-one will notice. Besides, look how handsome I am!"

"What's going on in there?" his mother yelled.

His hand crept to his holstered gun. "Come and get some, *Mummy*."

When the doorknob rattled, he drew his gun like Billy the Kid, and fired four rounds through the door.

"*Argh!*" Mabel screamed, as the bullets splintered wood and ploughed into her.

He opened his door and stepped onto the landing. The wall was splashed with red, the banister broken. He looked down at his mother's twisted body, which lay in a heap on the stairs.

She stared up at him. "*Help!*" she whispered, coughing up black, stinking blood.

Adam started down the plush-carpeted stairs. "Oh, I'm going to help you all right!" he said, drawing his Bowie. "Help you to the other side!" he sniggered.

"No!" she bleated. "*Help!*"

He could see three out of his four shots had found their target: two had punched through her left shoulder, the third had penetrated her thigh.

"Who... who are you?!"

Adam grabbed his mother by the ankle. "Probably your worst nightmare, cunt!" He dragged her down the remaining steps, giggling to himself. He'd never used such language before! He could feel himself harden.

Mabel screamed. "*Wh*-what are you going to do to me?"

"I'm going to see if my friend and I can find your inner beauty, *Mother*!" he said, pulling her into the living room and holding his knife up. "Daddy dearest didn't appear to have any!"

"No, please! I don't know you! What have I done?"

Adam scooped her off the floor and slammed her down onto the dining room table. He put his knife to her face. "You were a bad mummy, Mummy!" he laughed. "I'm not so weak now, am I? I'd love to see you push me around, and smack me with that brush of yours now!"

"But, but—"

"I think I'll start with your face!"

"No, no!"

He pierced her cheek with the tip of his knife and sawed through her flesh. When there was a gap big enough for his fingers to fit beneath the flap he'd created, Adam withdrew his blade and set about peeling her skin away with his hand, merrily whistling. The leathery strips came away cleanly—it was just like stripping wallpaper.

She kicked and thrashed.

A pool of blood gathered slowly beneath her head as it ran freely from her skinless face.

"No beauty there! All I see is ugliness. Let's try a little lower, shall we?"

Mabel didn't respond. It appeared she'd gone into shock, her eyes lifeless, her body spasming. Adam used his knife to cut through her dress, bra and kickers. "Wow, *Mother*! What a body. It appears you *do* have some beauty after all. Come on, let's dig a little deeper. Where shall I start, hmm?"

He cut her in several places, and then placed the knife to one side. He flensed her skin off her breasts, stomach and about her groin, watching with satisfaction as it stretched and came away like broiled chicken skin.

"I'm not seeing any beauty!" he said. "Maybe you have some in your heart?"

"Argh-*urgh*!" she coughed, spitting blood into the air.

"Don't you fucking die on me yet, *whore*!" Sneering, he stabbed his knife into her chest, shattering the breastplate, and cut around her heart. He dug his hand inside her and felt around. He couldn't get a grip on the thing with all that bone and rib in the way.

Mabel sputtered as at last her body went slack with death.

He kept his hand inside her for a while, enjoying the warm, squelchy meat swaddling his fist.

* * *

Adam sat, cross-legged, in front of his bedroom mirror and stared at himself—at the phenomenon—open-mouthed. His lips formed a perfect O.

"If I finish the painting, maybe it'll fill in my details too?" he wondered out loud, poking a finger at the white patch on his cheek. "*Meh*, not that it matters. Look at me! I'm god-like!" He tensed the muscles in his gut, making his eight-pack protrude and ripple. "Wait until Eve… Eve. *Shit*! How am I going to explain all this?"

Reality kicked in.

Playtime with Mummy and Daddy was over.

"How in the hell did this happen?" Adam looked at his corpse. God, he was an ugly bastard. Good riddance. He scrambled to his feet and opened his wardrobe. He unfolded the paper and found it to be blank, apart from a few running colours. "What on *earth?!*"

A sizzling sound caused him to jerk his head in the direction it came from. His carcass was smoking like burnt pork on a barbecue. Slowly, he folded the paper and placed it in his back pocket, his eyes not leaving his old body, which was now melting into his bed. Within seconds, nothing remained.

He walked over to his bed and touched the area where the corpse had lain. No trace remained—the duvet was dry, except for the places that had been splashed by his father's blood.

"I need to figure out what in the hell I'm going to do." He ran his fingers through his thick hair. People would talk. *Eve*. She'd know what to do. She wouldn't push him away. She'd help him…

"Help a killer?"

He shook his head to dispel his doubts. Of course she'd help him. She knew how abusive his parents were. Hell, how many times had they planned to run away together?

"Calm down. Think. I have all the time in the world."

He paced the room to steady his racing mind.

"I can't very well go over there, can I? What happens when Eve comes to the door and says she doesn't know me?"

The answer came at once—she'd call her dad, and he knew what her dad was like.

Adam glanced at his own father and his mashed up non-face; he didn't want to have to kill anyone else today.

"The *phone*! Of course. I'll call her and tell her to come over."

He rushed out of his room and down the stairs. When he got to the living room, he picked the house phone up and dialled Eve's number. He was in luck. Eve answered.

At first, she sounded dubious.

"You don't *sound* like you, Adam!"

"I'm not feeling well. Please, come over—I have something very important to tell you."

"Okay, I'll try and slip away. I wanted to come and see you yesterday, but my dad's been watching me like a hawk!"

* * *

The phone call had taken place a little over an hour ago.

Adam was starting to get impatient. Anxious, even.

"Come on, Eve!" he said, peeking out of the curtains in the living room. He looked at his watch. "It's been ages!"

After his conversation with Eve, Adam had carried his mother's remains upstairs and dumped her with his father. He'd then returned to the living room, where he spent the next twenty minutes cleaning the blood and guts off the dining table, walls and floor.

"I should have taken care of this *before* calling her!" he'd scolded himself whilst scrubbing, not expecting to finish before her arrival.

Shall I ring her again? he thought, parting the curtains a little wider. Nothing. *Her dad's probably— Wait, what's that?* His ears perked up to a noise. *Is that someone shouting? I can't see anyone.*

Adam opened one of the windows and poked his head through the gap. Over the light breeze, faintly, he could hear a female voice.

"Eve?" he muttered, straining his ears. She sounded distressed.

The voice, which turned into voices, moved closer, until Adam was able to hear what was being said.

"Let go! You're hurting my arm, Dad! *Please!*"

"You're off to see that troll, aren't you? What did I tell you would happen if I caught you going to see him?"

"He's my friend! And I told you, I wasn't! I'm off to see someone else!" she cried. "Stop hitting me!"

"Then don't lie, you little whore! I know you're off to see him! Want to suck his deformed little cock, don't you?"

"You're sick!" she said, and then let up another pained yelp. "You *bastard*!"

"You *cunt*! You little tease! Come back here!"

"Oh, no!" Adam gasped, watching Eve scramble over his garden wall. Before she had a chance to drop to the other side, her father grabbed her top and pulled himself up onto the wall with her.

In her struggle, her flimsy t-shirt ripped off, her bra falling askew. She wobbled, unsteady, and dropped to Adam's side of the garden.

"*Run!*" Adam yelled, but she didn't hear him. She got to her feet and raced toward his house, her father giving chase.

"Come back, you little slut!" her father yelled, catching up to her.

Adam's breath hitched in his throat as Eve was taken down like a gazelle in the jaws of a lion. "Now you're going to get it!" her father screamed in her face, pulling his belt free.

"*Adam!*" she screamed.

He silenced her with a hard crack across her face with his belt. "That fucking window-licker isn't going to help you!"

Eve brought up her hands to claw at his eyes. "*Adaaaaaam!*"

"Stay still!" her dad screamed.

Adam reached for his mace and bolted from the house. By the time he got outside, Eve appeared unconscious. Blood was spattered all about her father's face.

"You're developing fast, child," he said, grabbing her bare breasts. "I should have taken—*Oof!*"

Adam cut him off, planting his boot into her dad's chest and kicking him to the turf.

"Get your hands off her!" he roared.

The man rolled like tumbleweed, coming to a halt a few feet away.

Adam looked down at Eve. Her nose was crooked—clearly broken—and gushed blood. Her left eye was bruised and rapidly swelling.

"You sick fuck!" Adam yelled. He gave the mace a twirl, lassoing the spiked ball at the end of its chain, then brought it down on the small of the man's back.

"*Argh!*" he screamed, trying to reach a hand around to pull the spikes free of his flesh.

"Let me help you!" Adam sneered, pulling on the weapon. It ripped down his back and through his jeans. The mace came free, bringing with it flesh and a fountain of blood.

"*Ugh!*" he sputtered, choking on the pain.

Adam couldn't help but snigger when he noticed the mace had shredded the man's buttocks. "You won't be sitting for a while." He prodded the man with the toe of his boot to get him to turn over onto his back. Once he was face-up, he hammered the mace through his chest and stomach, dousing Adam in his blood.

When finally he was winded, he sheathed his weapon. His eyes fell squarely on the man's belt. He picked it up and kicked the man in the ribs until he was on his stomach again.

"Glutton for punishment, aren't we?"

Adam straddled the man's back, which creaked under his mass, and wrapped the belt around his victim's throat. He pulled on the leather strap as though it were a set of reins belonging to a horse-drawn coach.

"Ye have heard that it hath been said, an eye for an eye, and a tooth for a tooth: but I say unto you, that ye resist not evil: but whosoever shall smite thee on thy right cheek, turn to him the other also," Adam recited.

The man's body bucked as Adam tightened his grip, choking the life out of him.

"But where would the fun be in that?" he jeered.

He gave the belt one final, vicious tug, breaking daddy's neck.

"*Adam*!"

Eve's voice made him jump. The belt loosened in his grip. *She recognises me!*

"Is he dead?" she asked.

He let go of the leather and turned to face her. Eve's long hair flanked her face and covered her small breasts. Her blackened eye caused a lump to develop in his throat. "How do you know it's me?"

"What do you mean?" she asked.

Her question took him aback. "What do—*Look* at me! I'm completely different."

"I'd say! You just killed someone. What the hell are we going to do about my father? I'm scared, Adam."

Words failed him. *What is she seeing?* He couldn't fathom how she could be so blasé. *There's no time to argue over it now.*

"My parents are also dead..." he began, cutting off when he saw her expression change to one of horror. "It was self-defence!" he protested.

"Oh, Jesus!"

"My dad attacked me. I fought back." Shame burnt his face. "I'm going to fry in hell for this!"

She looked down at her father. "He was going to... *rape* me!"

"Let's get him in my house," Adam said. "We can work things out from there. I have something to tell you, regarding my new... *form*. I hope you can believe me."

"Adam, what are you talking about? Has something happened?"

"How can you—?"

"Hey, princess! Who's your faggotty boyfriend?" Adam heard someone call out. He knew the voice. When he looked up, he saw John and his brothers approach.

If it doesn't rain, it pours. What next, a shower of toads? Rivers of blood? A plague of locusts?

As John grew closer, Adam could see the look of bewilderment on the lad's face. "You're the homo from the drawing!" he said.

"Holy shit!" one of his brothers piped up when he saw the corpse of Eve's father lying in the dirt. "This guy's fucking dead!"

"It's not how it looks," Eve said. "He tried raping me! If Adam hadn't come to my rescue—"

"Shut up, *slut*!" John said, striking Eve across her face.

Adam towered over John, causing him to back up and bump into his siblings. "I suggest you leave."

"Fuck *you*!" the boy on John's left shoulder said, producing a flick-knife.

The others did the same, including John. "I think we may have a prize for taking this killer in! What do you think, lads?"

"We're with you, John," Left Shoulder said.

"Get to the house!" Adam told Eve, turning from the boys briefly. That moment of carelessness cost Adam—the boys set upon him, slashing at his body and face. "*Bastards*!" he hissed, stepping away from their swiping blades and drawing his gun. "Eat this!" He fired the two remaining shots, the slugs finding Left Shoulder's face and rupturing his head like an overripe cantaloupe.

"*Fuck*!" John screamed, hitting the dirt.

"Let's get out of here, Mark!"

"Fucking right!"

Adam stepped forward, unhooked his mace as he did so, and cleaned out both departing youths with two powerful, clobbering swings. Adam didn't take time in finishing them off. *They're not going anywhere!* he thought, turning his attention to John.

Their leader had pissed himself.

"I'll kill you!" he said, holding his knife out in front of him with a wobbly arm.

Adam drew his Bowie. "Mine's bigger!" He knocked John's blade out of his hand, grabbed him by his hair and yanked him to his feet. "Look how shiny it is!"

"*Don't*!"

Adam put his hand around John's pencil neck and held him in place. Then, with the blade level to the crown of John's skull, Adam sawed through the boy's scalp. When he was halfway though, he tossed him to the floor and then gripped his hair and ripped it the rest of the way off by hand, causing as much pain as he possibly could.

John bucked and screamed.

"How does that feel, big man?" Adam jeered, pulling John's trousers off and thrusting a knee into his back. "You're going to enjoy this." He placed the tip of his Bowie to John's anus and started to work it in slowly, inch by inch. Blood oozed out as John thrashed his arms and kicked his legs. When the knife was to its hilt, Adam gave it a slow twist before yanking it out with force. He then repeated the action again, and again, until John's body went limp—passed out or dead, Adam could not care less.

Adam stood and flipped John over, turning his attention to John's cock and balls, which he grasped in his free hand and squeezed. This did little to rouse the unconscious boy. "You won't be needing these again! Maybe I'll give Eve the nuts as a gift? She could make earrings out of them," he laughed, cutting through the genitals.

Adam spent the next fifteen minutes dismantling John's body. He removed the limbs, eyes, tongue and organs in his search for inner beauty. When he didn't find any, he looked for it in the other lads, but came up empty.

In the distance, he heard the grumble of a motorbike. He sought out the machine, but couldn't see it. "Cobra..." he whispered, at last spotting the man and his steel horse coming to a stop by the entrance to his garden. "So, he *is* real. Well, of course he is. I didn't get like this through wishing!"

He watched as Cobra killed his bike's engine, lowered the kickstand, and got off his machine by leaning it to one side. Cobra removed his helmet and gloves as he approached with a smile on his face.

"*You* did this!" Adam said. "You've turned me into a killing machine. Dorian and Adam are good people. They're not monsters!"

"You wanted the Devil's help, right?" Cobra said, pointing at his patch.

"I didn't know what you meant! Hell, I was half out of it!"

"Adam, Adam, Adam…" Cobra tutted, wagging his finger. "All I did was help in transforming you. I thought you wanted to be beautiful? Handsome, even. Well, you've got it! I didn't tell you to kill these people. Always forgive your enemies—nothing annoys them so much, remember?"

"No, I don't! You tricked me! I murdered my parents and Eve's dad…" He hung his head in shame. "Why can't Eve see the monster I've become?!"

"Because she sees your inner beauty. Only the ugly saw you as repulsive. What do you see when you look in the mirror now, Adam?"

"Dorian."

Cobra shook his head. "No, you're still Adam. It's only in your head."

"And in the heads of the haters, I guess?" Cobra nodded. "So what will I do about what I've done? Eve is going to hate me!"

Cobra smiled. "Well, I can help you there, too. But it's going to cost…"

"How much?"

Cobra raised an eyebrow. "Your soul. Murder was not part of our original deal."

"But there was no deal!"

"Fine. Go to prison, see if I care." Cobra turned to walk away.

"*Wait!*"

"Yes?" he said, looking over his shoulder.

"What happens to me *if* I give you my soul in exchange for help?"

Cobra turned to face him with a smile. "My deal is this, take it or leave it. I'll help you get rid of this mess, erase it from Eve's memory and yours, and make it look as though you had nothing to do with it. For that, I will claim your soul after you die a long, rich life with Eve as Adam, the boy you once were."

"And after I die…"

"Eternal damnation, Adam," he sighed as though it were a trifling formality.

"How long from now?"

Cobra smiled and whispered Adam's time, date, and age of death in his ear. "That's my trade."

Adam looked over and saw Eve standing close to his house. She was eating something. *An apple?* He yearned to be with her. "Deal!" he said, not taking his eyes off his girl.

"As you wish!" Cobra said.

"And you—" When Adam turned to face Cobra, the man had gone. *"Huh…?"* Then he heard a sizzling sound, much like he'd heard earlier. He looked about him and saw vapour escape the bodies lying at his feet. They melted into the ground and vanished. When he looked back at Eve, he saw the same type of smoke rising from an open window of his house. "Mum, Dad…"

Hold on to your soul! he thought.

Adam fished the portrait out of his back pocket, unfolded it, and saw the image of Dorian on the paper. "My soul," he whispered, feeling his face. "My imperfection has returned." He smiled, but it didn't last.

Hell awaits, he thought, letting the picture of Dorian flutter to the floor.

Blackout

Slamming the door shut behind her, Jennifer closed out the cold October evening, with its slanting rain and blustering wind. Auburn-coloured leaves managed to whistle their way into her passageway, causing her to mutter under her breath.

"Oh, well. They can stay there until the morning," she huffed, slightly out of breath. The trek from the car to her house had been somewhat challenging, due to the strength of the wind.

Before removing her shoes, she swept some strands of her hair out of her face that had been blown into a raven-coloured shock. Free from the partial blindness, she sighed, letting her bag slip from her shoulder and hit the floor, before removing her coat and locking the front door.

The heating clicked on, just as her second heel came off and plopped crashed to the floor next to the first. Staying bent over she pulled a thick book out of her bag, before sighing again, and made her way down the short passageway, and into her living room. A small lamp was aglow next to her reading chair.

As always, she left a light or two on in the house during the winter months, hating to return to a dark house after work. It was awfully lonely these days, she thought, ever since Daniel left.

"Stan," she called out. "Staaaan!" she tried again. Then listened.

Not a sound crept through the house. All she could hear was the murmur of the wind outside, which reminded her of a stranger's whisper in the night. She shivered.

"Hm," she said aloud, rerouting her thoughts. "He's probably still outside roaming around, the dirty Tom!" she tittered.

Moving into the kitchen, she flicked the light switch on and made for the kettle. Popping the button down, Jennifer went to the fridge and drew the milk out. After placing the plastic milk bottle by a mug, which she'd stuffed with a teabag, she went to the bathroom and used the toilet.

After urinating and wiping, she heard the kettle rumble to a boil, then click off, just before she flushed. Finishing using the bathroom, she went back out to the kitchen, poured her tea and made her way back into the living room.

She put the hot mug on the table next to her lamp and reading chair, along with the book she'd been holding in her other hand. It hit the table with a loud thump. Cover up – *In The Dark* by Richard Laymon – her all-time favourite author.

This book had managed to avoid her for quite some time, so she was shocked to see it turn up this evening at the library where she worked. It was lying on a desk near a book aisle. On inspection, Jennifer knew it didn't belong to the library, so she took it, thinking nothing of it.

Looking at the book now, she muttered, "Well, It's my book now, and on the shelf it will go with the rest of my Laymon collection." Shrugging her shoulders and grinning stupidly, Jennifer dropped onto her chair with a "*Humph*". She couldn't even be bothered to change out of her clothes and into her PJ's. She just wanted to read, to lose herself in fiction as she did every Friday evening.

It took an empty mug and a crick in her neck for Jennifer to realise she was two hundred pages into the book, and the best part of four hours had slipped by. Putting the open novel on the arm of the chair, she rubbed at her eyes, picked up her mug, and headed for the kitchen.

Laymon's at his best, she thought, smiling. Parts of the story had made her skin and scalp prickle, and had her feeling as though her blood were freezing over... As she passed the phone, it rang loudly. A seemingly angry ring, as it jangled in the cradle, startling Jennifer. Her grin faded.

"Who the heck would be ringing at this hour?" she thought out loud, scanning the clock on the wall. It read eleven forty-five. "If this is another bloody Indian order, I swear to God," she said, snatching up the phone. She snarled down the line, "Hello."

No greeting came back.

No breathing.

Just static and dead air.

"Hello," she tried again, pricking her ears, thinking she could hear the screech of a bird, or a small child, which seemed a great distance away. The sound was lost in the persistence of the static.

She thought her heart was going to pulsate its way through her chest.

The line went dead.

"Damn it," she said, trying to sound as courageous as she could, whilst slamming the phone down.

It rang again.

Instantly.

Startled, she delicately picked it up again and whispered down the line. "Who is-"

"Hi," the voice said, in a jovial tone, which somehow made it sound more sinister than if the person had bellowed out a grotesque laugh.

"What..." she started, but the line went dead for a second time, just as the lights to her house suddenly failed, casting her in darkness. Throwing the receiver to one side, she screamed once, then again on hearing a thump from upstairs crash to her ears.

Jennifer searched in the darkness for something, anything that she could use to defend herself with, but found nothing.

Making her way to the hallway with hands out in front of her for aid, Jennifer's breathing came in ragged, ripping sounds, as she screamed up the stairs, "Who the hell's there? I have a knife, you *bastard*. Get out. Now!"

Tears began to slide down her face as she saw a pair of glowing eyes at the top of her stairs. They began to descend, causing Jennifer to whimper, and press her legs together. Before she could turn and bolt for the door, Stan leaped into her arms.

"Damn it, cat!" she said, her voice somewhat lost in the blackness of the hallway. "You scared the be-jiggered out of me, you daft thing."

Letting go of a pinched breath, a nervous laugh escaped her, as she felt the roughness of Stan's small tongue lick her cheek. "Okay, I forgive you," she told Stan, keeping him close to her chest.

Maybe I should go outside, or knock next door? she thought. What, over some silly phone call? What if he's in the house? Who? It was only someone saying hello, for Pete's sake. The storm probably knocked the phone out before they could say anything else. Yes, but that voice..."Tut," she said aloud. "This is not a horror novel."

But to the front door she went, opened it, and saw that the streetlights were out. See, she told herself. It's a power outage. She closed and bolted the door again. Satisfied.

Whilst at the door, she heard a fat rumble of thunder roll, which rattled the door in its frame, causing Jennifer to shriek and giggle. Then she heard something else whilst standing there in the dark – a faint scratching on the wall to her right, as though someone or something were trying to burrow its way through to her home.

It was coming from the direction of the *empty* house next door.

Her flesh went Arctic cool.

Thunder boomed again, but she was sure she heard a drawn out whispery screech of her name penetrate the walls – "Jeeeeeennnnniferrrr..."

My mind's playing tricks, she thought. What with the storm and... her thoughts trailed off, and her hand went to the door handle.

The scratching continued. The noise reminded Jennifer of wallpaper being torn. She put her ear closer to the wall; still thinking her name was being hissed out.

Flickers of lightening lit the house every so often, which was followed by grumbles of thunder.

Jennifer swore she could hear something come from next door, and pulled away from the wall, laughing it off. "What a silly Billy I'm being. That book sure has set me on edge," she said, letting Stan go, and making her way out to the kitchen with the aid of her hands. "I'm sure there are some candles under the sink, maybe even a flashlight."

Making it to the cabinets in the kitchen, Jennifer dug a torch out of one of the cupboards and used the beam to look for candles, but found none. "The torch will do," she said. Turning around, her beam caught a movement out in the hallway. She stifled a scream, turned around, and tore the butcher's knife out of the wooden block on the counter.

Shining the light in the direction of the hall again, she could see a figure in the gloom standing close to the door, blocking her escape route. "Shit."

Rain pelted the windows behind her with a deafening sound, as the thunder and lightening persisted.

The shadowy form remained still. Unmoving. She noticed what looked like a weapon of some sort, dangling from its right hand.

"I have a mobile," she called out. "I'm calling the police right now, so you'd better get out."

Keeping the beam trained, the intruder kept still, not adhering to her warning at all.

He knows I'm bluffing, she thought.

Raising the knife, she moved forward. "Don't make me stab you," she said with a quiver, holding the blade up to be seen. As she edged closer and closer, she could see coats and umbrellas hanging off her so-called 'intruder'.

"Ha-ha," she blurted. "It's the bloody coat stand."

She was relieved that there was no one around to see how flushed her face was. *Not that they'd be able to see my embarrassment in the dark*, she reminded herself.

Jennifer got to the couch, sat down, and giggled. "God, what an eventful night it's been," she said aloud, laughing some more. "Best I try and get some sleep. It must be way past midnight and there's no way I'm reading by torchlight."

Grabbing the woolly blanket from off the back of the settee that she kept there for wintery snuggles on the sofa, she lay down, feeling Stan jump up and curl between her legs. Jennifer liked to sleep downstairs often since Daniel had left her. She found it somewhat comforting, not having to sleep in the bed they shared.

As she drifted off to sleep to the rhythmic sound of the rain, she startled at the feel, or so she thought, of someone gently stroking her hair. She didn't jump; instead turned the torch on, scanned the room, and found no one.

Waking the next morning to the sound of the TV blasting and the lights all on, Jennifer was thrown into confusion, as she raised from the sofa. She hadn't turned anything on. No lights, no TV. So how...

Her thoughts derailed as she spied the Polaroid on her mantelpiece, the '90's relic very much out of place.

Stepping close to it, she plucked it off the wooden shelf, and saw that it was a photo of her, asleep on the sofa.

Jennifer's mouth fell open, no words coming out. Her skin prickled. She flipped the snapshot over and read what was written on the back in rough red lines, as though a three-year-old had done it.

"To a great blackout. Let's do it again some time."

Rooms for Rent

Co-written with Alice J. Black

Tina entered the bathroom and groaned as she threw her towel down on top of the toilet's tank. The water pipes were banging once again which was starting to drive her mad. They'd even begun rattling and slamming in the dead of night, keeping her awake.

No matter how many times she reported it to Kenneth, her landlord, the problem was never sorted. "Bloody hell!" she huffed, putting the rubber plug into the plughole. "I've had a flamin' 'nough of this shit," she muttered to herself, starting the hot tap.

As the small bathroom started to fill with steam, Tina was forced to open the pokey window, which was a task in itself. The frame was cracked almost in two, meaning it couldn't be fully opened just in case the whole thing collapsed in on her.

"The place is a hovel!" she mumbled, tying her hair back into a ponytail.

When Kenneth had showed her the house at first, four weeks ago, she had been of two minds whether to take it. A few things had swayed her decision: the cheapness of the rent, how close she was to the university she attended, and the sparseness of neighbours.

Five, to be precise.

The lack of neighbours meant the area was quiet, which was perfect – Tina needed peace when studying books and papers for her university classes.

However, there were downsides, such as the place itself – it was filthy, and no matter how much, or how hard she cleaned, the house never seemed to get any better. The wallpaper was peeling in every room, the sinks were blocked constantly, the stains on the toilet didn't come off, electrical wires in certain rooms were exposed and the carpets were shabby.

The list was pretty inexhaustible.

She also felt that Kenneth *may* have been watching her when she was in the flat but she had no evidence to support that.

There were a lot of rumours about the scrawny man but she wasn't one to listen to hearsay. Instead, she liked to find things out for herself. Apart from her own creeping suspicions about the landlord, he hadn't, in fact, done anything, aside from look dubious whenever she saw him. He had a constant 'I-know-what-you're-up-to' look on his face and a shit-eating grin that made her want to vomit, and set her on edge whenever she ran into him. *Thankfully, I don't see him that often.*

But not only was it the inside of the house and Kenneth's weirdness that bothered her, but also the surrounding area. Just behind her house was a building, which looked a lot like a chemical plant. Every now and then, green smoke could be seen billowing from its huge chimneys. She kept her windows shut when she saw that, but it didn't stop the smell that seemed to permeate the very air in the area.

In between her house and the plant lay a marshland.

Tina had heard plenty of horror stories about that, too. Other students and members of the teaching staff had told her that there had been many more houses around the one she currently occupied. However, it was rumoured that they had been claimed by the quagmire many years ago.

She knew it was idle talk by people who should have known better. Tina put the stories down to others trying to scare her and the growth of the urban legend about the marshland, but it wasn't going to work; she didn't spook easily.

After adding a few of her own touches to the house, Tina had learned to live with the place. It was a hovel but it was hers and she liked that. Plus she would only be living in the house a few months a year as she planned to travel home during midterms.

Looking down at the bath, Tina noticed the water level was pretty high, and decided to shut off the hot tap. She then started the cold, which came out at a trickle. She tried not to let it bother her, as she lowered her knickers and sat on the toilet.

"Just one crappier thing about the place!" she said, looking at how the cold water came out of the tap at a snail's pace. "Only I could have picked such a palace to live in. Maybe I'll change accommodation next year. Maybe I'll be lucky enough to get a flat on campus? Yeah, fat chance!"

Breaking off a few sheets of toilet paper, Tina relaxed her bladder and started peeing. As she waited for the bath to fill with enough cold water, she continued to sit on the toilet with her knickers around her ankles.

"Come on!" she said, swishing the water from where she sat. It was still a little too hot to climb in yet. From where she sat, Tina slipped her t-shirt and bra off as she waited. The slight breeze that came in through the window prickled her flesh and stiffened her nipples. "Oh, that's nice!" she said, putting her head back.

She realised the heat inside the small room had become stifling.

Suddenly, a thump from above caused Tina to look up sharply. The ceiling had a very odd décor – it wasn't decorated white like normal. Instead, it was painted a sickly brown colour. It looked as though someone had covered it in gone-off stew.

"Hello?!" she called, instinctively covering her breasts.

She shuddered as she remembered what she had heard at university a couple of days ago. Apparently the attics to the houses connected. What if Kenneth had drilled holes in the ceilings? She wouldn't put it past that man.

Listening hard above the trickle of water, she couldn't hear anything.

Shaking her head, she huffed out a laugh.

"I'm becoming a wimp as I get older!" she uttered, and then laughed some more.

She was just about to get off the toilet when she felt something brush against her pussy. With a shriek, she leapt up and looked down into the water, which rippled as though it had been disturbed.

Her heart thundered like a racehorse's, as she stood frozen to the spot.

I definitely felt something, she thought, putting a hand to her privates – her thin covering of pubic hair felt slimy.

On inspecting her hand, she couldn't find a trace of anything. She put it down to imagination and bad pipes, hoping that it had been a splash of water from the bowl rather than anything else and quickly moved away from the toilet.

Stepping into the bath she felt the hot water envelope her feet, ankles and calves. She sank into it, enjoying the complete bliss the moment brought as her entire body submerged. That was the only good thing about the place; she could get a really decent bath, as it was big enough to cover her whole body whilst in water. Suds rocked up against her shoulders and the nape of her neck as she settled against the back of the bath and closed her eyes.

Studying English Literature was proving harder than she'd first thought, with a novel a week to read on top of everything else. It wasn't that she struggled with the reading; it was that some of the books were so damn boring that she couldn't stay focused and then when she got called on in a lecture she had nothing to say. She sighed. She hadn't told her parents any of this. They didn't know where she was living, or how she was living. Hell, hardly anybody did. She was embarrassed by the place and wouldn't bring anyone home, not even her closest friends.

Maybe next year, I will find somewhere a bit nicer. She knew she couldn't stick this place out for three years.

She took a deep breath and coughed as the balmy smell of sulphur hit her nose, causing it to wrinkle. She opened her eyes. That meant the plant was on and the pipes were billowing smoke again. She was as used to that smell as she was her own body odour but she had to say she would never like it. It came up through the drains and filled her entire apartment some days.

Her moment of bliss had been spoiled. With a sigh, she sat up in the bathtub, the water sloshing around her chest in an angry torrent. She grabbed the body wash and scrubbed herself clean—as much as she could in that place—and stood up. Droplets of bubbles and water dripped from her naked form and back into the tub as she grabbed her cosiest towel and wrapped it around herself. *Thank God for small comforts.*

Stepping from the tub and onto the mat on the floor she reached back and pulled the plug. Instantly the water formed a whirlpool as it was sucked down the drain and into the depths below. She was hit with another smell of sulphur, stronger this time and again she wrinkled her nose. *This place is gross.* She turned and made for the bathroom door when something flicked her wrist.

With a yelp she spun around, eyes darting around the bathroom looking for whatever it was. Of course she was alone and she knew that. She glanced down and saw that on her wrist lay several strands of hair. With a grimace, she pulled the slimy fibres from her skin and took a closer inspection. They were blonde, not at all like the colour of her hair, which was brunette. She glanced at the bath again and realised the hair came from there. She wondered whose hair it was and how the hell it got into her tub. She was the only one living in the hellhole—the only one stupid enough to pay for it.

Flinging the hair back into the tub she decided she would scrub it later but for now, she wanted out of there. As she left and closed the bathroom door behind her, she was met with the coolness of the apartment on the other side and some fresher air. The sulphur smell was stuck in the bathroom and she would leave it there.

In the bedroom she got ready as quick as she could and pulled on some warm clothes before settling in front of the TV. She knew she should be reading, after all, she had half a novel to read in two days but all she wanted to do was chill out. Her feet were up on the sofa and she flicked the channels with the remote. As she lay there, her eyes began to close. *Maybe I'll shut them for a minute.*

*

She was sinking deep and fast. Screaming, she struggled to keep her head above water, but it was no use. The stinking water of the marshland filled her mouth, overwhelming her with its stale and sour flavour. She gagged and kicked her legs. Her heart hammered. She would not go down like this. She fought for her life. She went under again, the water spewing over her mouth and up her nose. She propelled herself up and broke the surface, gasping for air with her mouth wide open. She could see the shoreline and her own house. Circling her arms, she tried to swim through the murky water.

It was thick and heavy. It wasn't normal water; there was something about it. The top was covered in a slimy film that she didn't want to think too much about. No matter how hard she pulled her body, she didn't move. Couldn't. Panic set in as her head dipped below the surface again. She was caught unaware this time, so her eyes were still open, and in the gloomy water she barely made out anything except the debris floating down there.

But, there was something in the distance. Something moving. It shot towards her. She screamed and kicked towards the surface. She broke it one last time. She gasped for air, screaming for help at the same time. This was it. She had to get out. She kicked hard and propelled her arms. Just as she felt she was beginning to get somewhere, something grabbed her foot. It yanked her back under with a hard jerk, yanked her head back. The vile water filled her mouth and sank down her throat. She thrashed, trying to turn to see what had her ankle. Everything went black.

*

After previewing Tina's upsetting episode on the toilet, and then in the bath, Kenneth crawled along the attic with a smile on his face.

It's waking up.

Soon it would rise from the deep of the marsh and feed. But, that was okay, since Kenneth had a row of houses filled with food for it. It always left him alone as long as it was kept satiated and he had done his job well for years now without suspicion.

The old beams creaked as he moved along them – *I must put some more planks down.* When he was directly above the bathroom to the second house, Kenneth squatted and peered through the drill hole he had created many years back. He knew from being down in that very bathroom that the hole was near impossible to see from down there. He rubbed his hands together as he was greeted by the sight below. He was in luck!

Lucy, who had moved in a few weeks back, just like Tina, was taking a bath. She was lying down, with the suds covering her completely. All that could be seen, were parts of her face and hair.

Unlike Tina, who was very athletic looking, Lucy was full-figured.

Voluptuous, some would say, he thought, licking his lips as he got closer to the peephole. Music could be heard playing somewhere in the distance. "Come on, let's see them tits," he whispered, his breath disturbing some of the dust close to his mouth.

He held his breath but Lucy didn't move.

When he'd first clapped eyes on her, she'd been wearing a short skirt, which had barely covered her arse. Her legs were long and lean – not like toothpicks. She'd also been wearing an ill-fitting blouse, which struggled to contain her massive knockers, as if two bald-headed convicts were busting to be free. Still, he couldn't say he cared too much, whatever they were willing to show, he was willing to spy on.

About to give up on his voyeurism and move on, the pipes started to bang once again. A grin broke out on his face. The show was about to start. This was always the best bit. Hurrying back to the peephole, he noticed the sound had disturbed Lucy from her relaxing soak. Lucy sat bolt upright, causing waves of water to crash over the side of the bath and soak the bathmat.

"Who's there?" she squealed. Smiling, he continued to watch, as her tits and glistening legs were on full display.

He felt his hardness push against the attic flooring, as the pipes continued to groan, thump and bang. Kenneth was tempted to unzip himself and play, but not this time.

"Fucking pipes!" she spat. "If I have to tell that retarded landlord once—" her words stopped as she started screaming.

Warmth spread through his guts as he watched the scene below him unfold.

The rubber stopper was spat out of the water and ricocheted off the ceiling before hitting the floor and sliding under the toilet.

"My foot!" she screamed. The water bubbled and frothed red around her.

Mm, look at them titties jiggle! Kenneth sneered. His hardness was almost too much to bear, but he managed to ignore it, as he watched the youngster squirm, yell and bleed.

"Uh-ugh! Help..." she panted as the life and strength drained from her. Her arms grabbed for anything to keep her steady but, of course, there was nothing. Kenneth had planned it that way. More and more of the water turned red, as it continued to swish over the side and drench the floor – the mat was now a sodden mass of crimson material.

"Bye-bye, Lucy!" he whispered as he watched her body get pulled through the plughole. Blood jettisoned up the walls and splashed the ceiling. Kenneth could hear the girl's bones snap, break and bust, as she was dragged through the minuscule hole.

"I guess I can put her room up for rent in the morning," he said, getting to his feet. "There's quite a nice bit of profit in this!" He loved that side of it; constantly stealing bonds from students who couldn't afford it was a delight in his eyes though he loathed the constant cleaning of the season. Sniggering, he moved on to the next hole in the roof.

Below, the bathroom was empty.

Not wasting any time, Kenneth kept shuffling along the attic, until he was directly above the next one. Finding that one unoccupied, too, he moved to the last house in his collection.

To his amazement, he found the shower to be in use.

"Oh, I absolutely *love* it when they're in the shower!" he squealed like an excited child in that proverbial shop, then clamped his hand over his mouth. He sucked in a deep breath and continued to stare, but he hadn't been heard. He never was. Exhaling slowly, he relaxed against the boards and prepared for the show.

Matthew, who had been renting the longest, was also a student. Kenneth never really took any other kind of person on, as students were easy to handle; most of them were young, naïve and had travelled a great distance from home.

The less people around to ask about someone, the better.

Matthew, or Matt as he liked to be called, was currently soaping his body and singing away to music he had playing. It wasn't possible for him to hear the banging pipes – not with all the noise he was making.

Settling into a comfortable position, Kenneth lay and waited. Watching Matthew wasn't the same as watching the girls, but he knew he would enjoy it all the same.

"Poor, poor, Matt," he tutted quietly. "Soon to be eaten and forgotten about." Kenneth giggled. More dust was disturbed by his breath.

The rattling began and his stomach grumbled in anticipation. As if on cue, tentacles burst from the plughole and wrapped around both of Matt's legs – the rubbery-looking feelers were a sickly green colour, with a multitude of different coloured spots and freckles. They came complete with suckers and barbs, which helped it latch onto things.

Matt screamed as flesh was torn from his left leg. When he looked down, his screaming turned into a high-pitched tantrum; blood, bone and vein popped, broke and ruptured, as the tentacles squeezed and crushed, much like a Boa does with its meal.

"Help!" Matt yelled. "For the love of God!" Managing to get one leg free, he got half of his body out of the shower. Kenneth gasped. Nobody had ever put up much of a fight.

"No!" he muttered, but felt relieved when he saw more of its tentacles burst through the hole in the sink and rise out of the toilet.

All Matt could do was scream as the slimy strands of hair wrapped around his limbs and with a sickening squelch, his body was pulled in three different directions.

*

Tina stopped and craned her neck. She thought she heard something. *Never mind.* It had been a long day already, and she knew she must be hearing things. Lectures had been long and boring, and they talked about a lot of political stuff. Things she didn't really understand, but pretended to, so she didn't look stupid in front of her classmates. She thought she might have pulled it off. Maybe.

Moving to the bathroom, she opened the hot tap on full. Time to unwind. Sometimes she wished she had a shower for quickness, but on days like this when the weather was chilly and she needed to de-stress, a bath was perfect.

She stoppered the plughole and watched as the water began to form a puddle in the tub. It soon became a pool, which kept on growing. Sitting on the side of the bath, she poured in a generous helping of bubbles and smiled. At least she could enjoy this time to herself.

Unbuttoning her jeans, she yanked them down her legs and kicked them off, along with her socks. Pulling her top over her head she felt the heat in the room blast her torso. Next came her panties and bra. She shivered as her nipples hit the cold air, and reflexively wrapped her arms around her chest. She couldn't help but feel as if she was being watched, once again. She always felt like that when she was in the bathroom. Most of the time she could ignore it, but something in her gut told her otherwise tonight. Still, she knew it was stupid. Her own flat was attached to four others and none of them had access to hers. She was completely alone. Nobody was watching.

Perching on the edge of the bath once more, she swung her legs over the side, dipping her toes into the water. At first it scalded, the hot water surrounding her supple skin but, as she became used to the heat, she began to immerse herself into the water, bit by bit.

Finally submerged, she lay back against the bath and closed her eyes, which helped push the stress of the day away. She would need it if she planned to study that night.

Tina had been lying submerged for around ten minutes, when a sudden vibration thrummed through her. Her eyes shot open, and as she glanced at the water, she saw it rippling. She frowned. *Weird.* She had no idea what could be causing it. She watched for a while, figuring it would subside in a moment or two. Instead, it kept going, the rippling becoming more of a sloshing. The water in the tub jerked side to side, splashing as it hit the end of the tub and flicked back into the main pool of the bath. It became more violent. Tina pushed herself up, gripping the sides of the bath. There was no way it could be an earthquake, and anything else was out of the question.

She sucked in a deep breath and yelped as the vibration became more intense. Not only was the water shifting side to side as if a storm gathered, but the entire bath shook on its stilts. Something was definitely very wrong. A sudden image of the house being swallowed into the murky depths of the marshland flashed through her mind and her stomach twisted.

Pushing herself up with her arms, Tina made to move, grabbing for the towel hanging on the sink at the same time, but a sudden jolt shook her feet from under her and she hit the bottom of the tub with a dull thud. Water splashed over the side as she cracked her head. Stars spangled in front of her eyes, momentarily dazing her. When they cleared she shook her head and gazed around her. The bathroom light shook, the naked bulb tossing shadows back and forth.

She was about to try again—now convinced that her flat was being devoured by the marshland—when the plug popped from the water. It flew into the air and hit the floor, bouncing once and rolling beside the toilet. Water began to spiral down the drain, suds flowing away and leaving her more naked and vulnerable than she had ever been her whole life.

Tina leaned forward and stared at the drain where the water eddied. Just as she had made her mind up that her bath was done for the night, something shot up from the plughole bringing the whole drainage system with it. Screaming, Tina scooted back, curling her legs up as far as she could while she took in the new thing. It looked like a tentacle. It was long and pointed near the tip where it probed around the bathroom walls. On closer inspection she saw it was a mass of writhing hair. Hair that was matted together in many different shades—too many to count—and all wound together to form this thing.

She squeaked and the tentacle jerked, then slid towards her. She had no idea what it was, but she didn't want to stick around to find out. Scrambling for the side of the bath she hauled herself over and fell to the floor on her back with a dull thud. Her shoulder jarred but she rolled away from the thing in the sink. She grabbed up her towel, wrapped it around her body, and then turned to look at it once more. It was still searching, the slimy, greasy hair tentacle looking for her. She knew it.

She took a step back. She had to get out of there. Out of that house.

Another step.

The door was within reach.

A third step. Her foot landed on the discarded plug and she fell. Her head cracked against the disused radiator on the wall. Confusion wracked her mind as she lay on the floor. Everything was blurry. She couldn't make out anything, didn't understand what was going on. And then something grabbed her ankle. It wound around tight and dragged her back towards the bath.

Screeching, Tina was brought back to her senses. She leaned forward trying to unhook the tentacle. Hair snapped beneath her hands but there was always more to replace it. The grip tightened and slowly it began to trail her along the floor. She was powerless to stop it as the tentacle dragged her towards the bath. With some unimaginable strength, it lifted her body entirely, holding her suspended above the bathtub.

Tina screamed, flailing, looking for purchase on anything she could grab, but there was nothing but tile. Her nails scrabbled at the smooth surface, fingers clawing but they slid down as she was dragged closer and closer to the drain.

Her foot went through first and knives of excruciating pain raced up her leg as her foot was torn to shreds. She clawed at anything as the tentacle kept pulling her down. She grabbed the side of the bath, digging her nails in but the thing kept pulling. She was up to her knee now. Her leg would be amputated. Inch by inch, her limb was disappearing, sucked into the drain. Blood spattered the white tub, pulsing from her leg as her various arteries and veins were burst as her thigh went down. Her left leg hung over the tub and her arse was on the bottom of the bath.

Tears streaked from her face as she heaved herself forward in one last attempt to get free. There was no give. The grip was too strong. In one swift movement, she was sucked under. Her body split in half from the pubis right through to her head leaving a splatter of blood that reached the ceiling. A second tentacle came back for the rest.

*

Kenneth was at the college the very next day putting a 'For rent' sign in the window of the union bar.

A Mirror Never Lies

She caught a glimpse of the body on her bed as she cleaned her face in front of her vanity mirror. It was tangled in the sheets, which had become saturated with blood and small chunks of flesh and guts.

Blood could be seen rolling down the person's arm in the dim light cast by the bedside lamp. It gathered at the wrist and slid down the fingertips. Where the blood had spread out over the forearm, it reminded her of a grizzly roadmap; a roadmap where all roads led to butchery.

She could hear the drips hit the carpet, which kept in sync with her heart; it beat fast with crazy joy, causing a fire to rise from her crotch.

A neat pool was gathered.

They deserved it, Porsche, please remember that.

"Yes, they did," she answered the voice from within, which sounded nothing like her at all. It was passive, weak and pathetic.

It belonged to a person who could bend like straw.

No weight. No conviction, she smiled.

With the blood removed from her face, Porsche smiled at herself – minuscule flecks of blood could be seen on her well-maintained teeth.

"Damn!" she snapped, plucking a tissue from a box close to hand. Delicately, she rubbed and polished them clean. "I'll have to give brush them later."

After running her fingers through her hair, she then grabbed her jar of foundation and applied some of the cream to her fingertips. Content, she started to rub it into her face, giving herself a light coat.

I don't want to end up looking like a hooker; that's not the impression I want to give. I'm sugary and sweet! she thought, again looking at the body on her bed – the haft of the butcher knife caught her attention. Part of it was missing.

Then, she remembered.

The knife had been rammed into her victim so hard that some of the handle had broken off in her hand.

"Delicious," she uttered.

We need to hide the body, Porsche... the voice bleated.

"Quiet!" she insisted, slamming her hand down on the desk in front of her. "First, I want to make myself look pretty. I never had the chance to..." Letting her words trail off, she looked down at her lap. "They made me weak, and took all my confidence! I was never allowed make-up, or pretty dresses."

It's not like that now, Porsche...

"Shut up! Shut up! Shut up!" she screamed once again. Standing up, she turned around and spat on the body, which was relatively close to her. "You won't keep me as a trophy any longer!" Screaming at the body made her feel vindicated for her actions. "Fucking controlling *pig*!"

Porsche...

"I won't tell you again!" She slapped her face once, twice, three times, before collapsing onto her chair heavily.

Looking at herself in the mirror, she could see her eyes glaze with tears.

"No, stop it. We're not *that* kind of person any more. I *won't* cry. Too many tears have been shed in the past..."

You're a strong, sexy and confident woman, Porsche, the voice whispered.

"That's right!" she said, looking at her cheek. The redness was starting to peter out.

Happy, she pushed her foundation to one side and gathered a collection of lipsticks in front of her: pink, red, purple, nude...

"Choices, choices, choices!" Giggling, she whipped the cap off the purple one and eased it up the tube. After lightly coating her lips, she pouted at her reflection, all the while she checked to see how the purple matched her skin tone and eye colour.

"Hmm, it's nice, but a bit too radical."

Plucking another tissue free from its box, she rubbed at the lipstick, causing some of it to smear across her right cheek.

Tutting, she replaced the cap to the purple lipstick and put it back where it belonged. Before moving on to the red, the body caught her attention once again. Her gaze was drawn to a deep, lengthy slash across its stomach.

The sight made her gag, then titter, as she turned away.

Looking back, she could see the intestines had slipped out of the large gash, and currently lay on the floor in a neatly coiled pile.

"*Sausages!*" she cried.

The laugh inside her head was not her own.

Looking up from the mess on the floor, Porsche studied the body. It was her first real look at it. In her frenzy, she hadn't counted the stab and bite marks. Nor had she been cognizant as to where she had stabbed, hacked and slashed.

Starting at the neck, she worked her way down. The face was hidden out of sight – covered by a pillow, which had once been white.

Being a nurse, having opted out of being a full-blown doctor, Porsche could tell that the neck was broken, due to the decolourisation of the skin, bruising and the way in which the neck flopped at an awkward angle.

"The oesophagus is probably crushed, too..." she uttered in a singsong tone. A wry, maniacal smile helped part her thin lips, as she stared into space.

Refocusing, she continued down the body – the chest was pulverised. A rib was found protruding through the flesh close to the heart. "It probably pierced the once-beating organ."

A hacked off nipple lay on the opposite pillow, sending a shiver of delight down her spin.

"How did I manage to cause such devastation?"

Before she could answer her own question, she glanced upon the evidence.

Scattered about the bed was the remains of the second bedside lamp.

It had served as her reading light, before she'd use it as a blunt trauma instrument. She'd beat them around the head with it, which had caused blood to splash up the walls and redecorate the headboard.

The bloody, snail-like trails could be seen on the wall. Through drying, they had turned a brownish colour, which carried with it a hint of sickly yellow in the dim light.

After caving the face in, the body had been battered beyond repair.

She put a hand to her genitals.

Yes! The voice moaned.

This caused her to pull her hand away. "My, you are eager to be pleased!" Grinning, she could see the face that belonged to the voice inside her head, and it was pouting – the bottom lip quivering. "*Aw*, are you going to cry?" she hissed.

The voice remained silent, much like it had done its whole life. Before Porsche had taken over, the previous occupier had been cowed. But not now. Not now the body had its rightful owner in place. It felt good.

She felt empowered.

The old persona knew this moment would come, but it never knew it would come tonight. And in such an explosive fashion.

Continuing her gaze down the body, Porsche found the abdomen to be slashed apart – the privates were mangled. The inner and outer thighs had slices and deep cuts on them.

"I'm sure the subject endured much pain!" A throb of pleasure raced up her insides, and nestled in her stomach. It felt warm, cosy and welcoming. "Mm, yes…much pain. *Great* pain."

The whole scene came across as a hideous diorama.

"Diorama of Death!" she said, finally turning back to her make-up.

After trying, and disliking the red lipstick, Porsche moved on to the pink one, which she found fitting.

Blowing a kiss in the mirror, she then winked at herself.

"Oh, I'm going to look ravishing tonight!" she squealed.

*Oh, yes…*the voice concurred. *You* will *be attending the ball*?

"Yes!" she said, clapping her hands together. Unclasping them, she plucked up the gold envelope that lay on the dresser. Opening it, she took the card out.

As a thank you for joining our online community, you are invited to partake in the fun, games and pleasure at Kinks – the <u>only</u> club to offer such a variety of sexual bliss.

Flipping it over, she found a note inscribed there.

Note: For a good time, ask for Simone

She didn't know if that was a man or a woman, but the gesture produced a wave of fresh pleasure.

She ran her fingers over the grooves caused by the lettering – they had a sexy red hue to them, which brought to mind the word danger.

"Yes, danger. Such a rousing word. Oh, I will enjoy myself – a party to celebrate my rebirth."

The honour is all mine.

"You've had your time. Now it's my time to shine. To glow. To be the person we *both* know we should be!"

Agreed. And I'll be here to help guide and assist you as much as possible.

Porsche smiled her pink-lipped smile.

"This *bitch* has attitude! Not like the old me. What word would you say best described the way you were?"

Stifled.

No, more oppressed.

"Yes, *oppressed*. That's a good word. You weren't allowed to express yourself. Not like I can. It's a good thing for both of us, as I will be able to look after us now."

Porsche could see the face inside her again. This time it was smiling along with her. "That's what I like to see!" she told her reflection.

Finished with the lipstick, she put it away, along with the red and nude colours. Picking up her eye shadow, she proceeded to paint them a light pink, which matched her lipstick and painted fingernails.

"Now for a bit of mascara..." she said, grabbing the mascara wand and applying it to her eyelashes.

Sexy! This is how we should have looked years ago, but no.

"No. Because you held us back!"

They held us back!

"Don't you argue with me, or I'll put you into a dark and dusty corner of my brain, and never speak to you again!"

The inner voice stayed silent.

Blissfully silent.

For now, anyway.

Happy that her make-up was perfect, Porsche stood up and eyed her wigs. It's time for a colour change, she thought. Taking the red one off, she put it in her drawer and took out a brunette, black, blonde and silver wig.

They varied in length and style, and not just colour.

"A girl is so, so spoilt for choice!"

She firstly tried the silver one, followed by the blonde and then brunette.

Unhappy, she lastly tried the black one.

Looking at herself in the mirror, she gasped. "*Perfect!*"

Yes, perfect, the voice chirped.

Taking a hold of her paddle brush, she raked it through her hair, before adding pink ribbons to it, which she tied in big, looping bows.

She then took a new packet of stockings out of her drawer. After ripping them out of the box, she rubbed them against her face – she loved the smell of new, fresh nylon. It excited her.

Setting them to one side, she then crossed her left leg over her right in readiness. Wrapping her hands around her ankle, she drew them up her leg.

"So, smooth!" she uttered.

Picking one of the sheer black stockings up, she bunched the material together, much like a sock, and then slipped her toes into it. Pulling it up slowly, she looked at herself in the mirror.

With the one hold-up on, she looked at her long, curvy leg.

Amazing, she mouthed. "Never was, or would I have been allowed such luxuries with them around! We certainly were oppressed."

Yes. It was always, 'You can't be seen like that!' Or, 'What would the neighbours think'. The thought of us wearing skirts above the knee or stockings - Dam, they would have gone berserk!

"Oh, I agree. They even tried to tell us what the people we work with would think?!"

A slut whore! That's what they would have called us.

Porsche smiled. "Well, there's nobody around to tell us what to do any longer."

With the second stocking in place, she then put her suspenders on, followed by a frilly maid's skirt and apron, which barely covered her privates. Turning, she lifted the back of her skirt, and flashed her arse.

This caused her to giggle coyly.

Plucking a pair of pretty pink panties out of her drawer, followed by a matching bra, Porsche set them on top of the dresser.

"Now, what am I forgetting?"

The body? The voice said, trying not to sound sarcastic.

"Oh, I've not forgotten *that*!"

And that?

Porsche knew what the voice was talking about. How could she not? The *thing* had been in her view all evening. Not only that, it had been on her person for the best part of fifteen years.

She looked at it now.

A 'Circle of Trust'.

That's the name they liked to bandy around.

Lifting her hand to her face, she looked at the little gold ring. Her wedding band.

"Circle of Trust my arse!" Grabbing it, she tore it off her ring finger and tossed it over her shoulder. In the mirror, she watched it bounce off the headboard and land in among the mangled privates, were it sank into the pulpy mess. "*Quicksand*!" she blurted.

She, and the voice within, both laughed.

They laughed together like best friends.

Like lovers.

Like childish schoolchildren.

Like the free birds they now were.

Free and ready to start living life.

They were indeed reborn, and ready to lose their virginity.

"Look out world, Porsche's coming to tear a hole through your fucking heart!"

Behind her, the clock on the wall struck midnight. The taxi was booked for quarter-past.

We should think about…

"*Quiet*! It's a lady's prerogative to be late, you know! Had they not come home and caught us in the act, none of this would be happening. They'd probably still be breathing, too."

They'd been so mad…

"I know. All that rage and anger because I want to be pretty and playful."

Getting up from her chair, she walked over to the body and accidentally stood in the pool of blood, which had coagulated.

"*Ugh!*" she gasped. But, unperturbed, she bent over and plucked the pillow off the body's face.

Not a drop of remorse coursed through her.

"This is what all your efforts led to, you dumb fuck. Your death. Had you listened to me, had you believed in the voice. The inner me. The Porsche..." Her words trailed off.

Shaking her head, she started to laugh at the sight of the smashed face before her.

"Well, now I'm free of you, *Gloria*! My pathetic, dead fucking wife. I can now be Porsche without you trying to keep me at bay. Your fucking husband was as pathetic as you, for taking all the shit he did for all those years!"

*I...*the voice tried, but Porsche was in full swing.

"*Wife*?! That's a fucking joke. Captor, more like." Throwing the pillow back down on top of her wife's face, Porsche turned and plucked the tablets up off the nightstand. "If you knew I was taking these, why didn't you question it sooner? Didn't you think something was up, when I couldn't get my dick hard? When I couldn't fuck you? When my hair stopped growing? Fuck, woman! I was starting to look like a little boy. A pre-teen!"

Turning, Porsche looked at her semi-naked body in the mirror – she'd always had a slim, athletic build. Many people had told her in the past that she looked 'Girly'.

"I'll be back for my knife, sugar!" she said, walking over to the mirror.

Snatching the panties off the dressing table, she slipped them up her legs, which shone in the hold-ups.

Before covering her sissy dick with her knickers, she again opened a drawer to her dresser.

Putting her hand inside, she pulled out her male chastity device, which was made up of rings, cords and padlock. Gently, she grabbed her shrivelled dick and put it into the hardened plastic chamber. She then slipped the rings down the shaft and over her balls – this helped keep the package in place.

Padlocking the last of *his* manhood away, she snapped the key in the lock and smiled.

The voice inside, even though loving every degraded second of the situation, crumbled to the power of the person he had finally become.

"With that whore Gloria dead, I can finally get my tits done!" she said, putting her bra on, which she then padded with socks. "If *you'd* remained in control, we would have turned into a sissy slave! We'd have become a 'Come Dumpster' for *real* men. You wouldn't have wanted to be a cock-swallowing nancy-boy, would you? A drinker of jism and piss?"

No, the voice pouted.

"This way, we get to be a ballsy, dominatrix bitch from hell." She could almost hear the crack of her imaginary whip. "When I do have one, it will flay the flesh from their depraved buttocks!"

With the bra in place, Porsche put the top-half of her maid's outfit on.

"Good enough to eat!" Winking at her reflection, she again giggled. "A mirror never lies!"

Going to her side of the bed, she opened the drawer to the cupboard there, and produced a small handbag; it wasn't quite a clutch, but close.

"Don't wait up!" she told Gloria, as she tore the knife out of the body. It made a squirty-squashy sound as it came free. "God, that sounded like a spent, soggy dick being sucked free of a sticky, over-pleasured pussy."

The simile brought a fresh smile.

Filing the knife away in her purse, Porsche took her leather jacket off the back of the bedroom door and slipped it on. She then put her 'fuck me' boots on, which were hidden at the back of her wardrobe.

"Now that you're dead, I won't have to fucking hide everything!"

With her boots on, she blew Gloria a kiss. "I'll be home with the milkman!" Outside, she heard a horn blast. "Looks like my ride is here."

Before heading out the door, she took one last look at herself in the mirror. "Mrs Bates. Eat. Your. Fucking. Heart. Out!"

You're a Goddess, the voice said.

Porsche smiled. "Oh, I know that. Just look at how gorgeous I am! It's true, you know...

...A mirror never lies"

Caution: Slippery When Wet

Thirty goddamn-fucking-bucket-sliding years I've been sweeping, mopping and polishing this floor. And do they appreciate it? Do they fuck! Richard thought. *They just call me names like Dickie-Slip or Slips for short!*

As the voice inside his head droned on, Slips continued to pull chairs and tables away from the fixed benches inside the restaurant. Once satisfied, he swept the cleared area of debris – stale food, napkins, straws, crayons, cutlery and other bits of shrapnel – into a neat pile before brushing it all into a dustpan and then disposing of it into a black bag.

Before putting all the tables and chairs back, he inspected that area – this section of *his*, not *theirs*, was clean. Squinting, he bent over and took a better look. *Got to make sure she's all clean today, what with it being the last day on the job. Not that they are sacking me...*he thought, a smile creeping onto his face as he looked over at the manager's coffee pot next to the bar.

Oh, they're going to pay!

Standing up straight, happy that his '*girl's*' grooves and lines were spotless, he replaced all the chairs and tables to their correct positions, mindful not to scratch his baby. In all the years he'd worked for the restaurant – Big John's Big Sloppies — he'd not once inflicted a scratch, gouge or dent in his woman.

He took care of her, just like any man would take care of his woman.

Respect cost nothing. Zippo. Zilch. Zero. Nada.

Do they respect you? he asked, looking down at the mottled brown flooring. *Do they bollocks! Damn children, the lot of them. Back in the day, when I first started tending you, the managers had reverence for the both of us. They wouldn't come in early and track muddy boot prints right through the place. If they ever did, they had the utmost admiration, as they apologised. Not this new-aged lot, with their texting, Internet on the go and Mochas!*

Looking at the clock mounted on the wall behind the bar, Slips saw that it was almost ten to six. At seven o'clock, the managers would be at the restaurant to open up. Back in the day, it used to be eight o'clock, giving him plenty of time to sweep and mop – that meant the floor would be bone dry before anyone got there.

That way of working had been perfect for Slips, as by the time they used to come in, he was in the toilets cleaning out – dusting, polishing the mirrors, disinfecting the pans, etc…At that hour of the morning, the restaurant side of his cleaning job was finished, and so he was out from under everyone's feet.

Eight o'clock.

A perfect time for the others to start.

There was no need for anyone else to be there that early, considering the place didn't open until nine o'clock.

The fuckers do it to annoy! I'm positive of that.

He could hear them mocking him now: '*It's only wood, Slips! Don't be so sensitive!*' Danny, the top manager, would say. '*Yeah, Slips – why have you got such a stiff cock for it? You take your job too seriously. You're just a cleaner!*' Trevor, the deputy manager, would chime. '*You need to get yourself a piece of arse!*' Carl, who was training to be an area manager, would constantly rib.

"Fucking dildos! The bag of dicks wouldn't know a hard day's work, even if it bit them on the nose," he said with vitriol. Every word unleashed sounded as though it was fired from the bottom of his guts with a great deal of firepower – like a shell being blasted from a tank's turret.

He took another glance at the coffee pot. *That stuff will kill ya!* A harsh laugh burst from him as he continued to move chairs, stools and tables. He got his brush into every nook and cranny – no section was left untouched, checked and taken care of.

It was a she, and she was his lady.

I mean, you wouldn't fuck with another man's wet woman, would you?!

His thoughts had never been this dark. Hell, they'd *never* been dark. Richard Gregory Sullivan had always lived by the book in a sturdy way. He was a straight-laced, ex-military reserve. When he wasn't cleaning at John's, a job he cared for deeply, he spent his time at the beach walking his dogs, doing crosswords or pottering at his allotment.

When Joan, his wife of thirty-five years, had been taken from him by cancer, something broke inside him.

All hope, reason and care faded by the day.

And, with the world changing around him, it all helped shape a different Richard. A meaner, darker one.

Where he'd once been a willing giver and helper, now he was an expert taker; he'd never been one for being pushed around, but now he made his feelings known.

He found it hard to give respect to those in power who didn't deserve it, didn't earn it – who treated him and his work like shit. Before the 'teens' started running the show, Richard had got on well with his managers.

But not now.

For the last year, he'd been subject to borderline bullying.

They may think I've been taking it on the chin, but no—I've just been biding my time, waiting for the right moment to strike. Isn't that right, Floorence? he thought, looking down at her.

When the floor was completely swept, he took ten minutes to walk around the restaurant. Slips strolled up the aisle that contained the booths and checked under the tables – all the corners were clean.

"Excellent!" He then checked under all the other tables and chairs before finally inspecting the bar area.

The coffee pot caught his sight once again.

Bleach! His mind raced as he looked at it. *I don't think I have much left. Not that I'm going to need it. Last day today, remember?!*

Sighing, he checked the wall clock. It was almost eight.

Nodding, he grabbed his brush and made his way to the backroom. Once there, he went to his cleaning cupboard. He removed two large plastic buckets – one red, for the toilets, and one blue, for the restaurant floor.

He filled them both with water and the correct liquid. Satisfied, he grabbed the mop and took it, along with the full buckets, out to the restaurant.

The clock ticked over to eight.

Any minute now…

Plonking the buckets down, he put his mop to one side. *I won't need that just yet.* Going to the coffee pot, he lifted the lid and whiffed the contents inside. *Mmm!* he thought, replacing the lid. *It's going to be delicious!* He laughed again.

"I'm going to miss you, old girl!" he said, looking at the floor. "I hope the next person treats you as well as I have."

The spot he was looking at glinted in the light.

"No need to wink at me. I've enjoyed every minute we've spent together."

From where he stood, he traced the floor – not a dirty mark could be seen. Yesterday, he'd taken his time in giving it a second mop, after the managers had once again carelessly walked all over her wetness. Once she'd dried, Richard had polished her.

"The fuckers won't muddy or hurt your feelings again, baby!"

At five past eight, Danny, Trevor and Carl turned up at the door – the locks disengaged. Danny, who led them in, was a tall, fat lad for his twenty years. He constantly looked grubby with his food-stained shirt hanging out at the back of his trousers – this crude fashion statement of his usually ended up displaying his sweaty arse-crack every time he bent over.

If you got too close, you could smell his body odour and see the damp patches under his armpits.

He was a chunky, useless slob who found everything funny. The waitresses, who he treated like something he'd scraped off his boot heel, had named him Chuckles.

More like Wally! Slips thought, watching Danny enter John's.

"Morning, *Dick!*" he said with a smile, which exposed his grotty teeth – bits of food could be seen stuck in the slender culverts between them.

Slips turned his head to one side and didn't bother replying.

"Fine, be like that!" Danny said, then muttered "miserable cunt" under his breath.

"Excuse me?!" Slips bit back.

But Danny ignored him, as he made his way to the coffee pot.

"Morning, Slippy!" Trevor said. "No wet floor signs today? If anyone falls and breaks their neck, it'll be on your head!"

Again, Slips ignored the greeting. *It shows how much notice they take! I haven't used the 'Caution: Slippery When Wet' signs in months. What's the point? They are going to walk all over my baby, anyway.*

"Haven't you started mopping yet? You lazy shit!" Carl said. "We're going to be open in an hour, old man. Chop-fucking-chop!"

"Sorry, I'm just a bit behind this morning. My back, it's playing up," Slips said, giving it a rub. "I've normally started by now, as you well know. Disappointed you can't track through my wet floor?"

"Pardon?!" said Carl, who had started walking away.

"Nothing. Sorry, Carl," Slips said, bowing his head and looking at his feet.

Carl, who was only nineteen, was the smallest man in the restaurant. The rest of the staff, apart from Danny and Trevor, thought Carl suffered from SMS – Short Man Syndrome. His face looked like a badly topped pizza.

"I should think so, too!" Carl said. "Now get mopping."

"Can you believe the mouth on him?!" Trevor said.

As all three men congregated around the coffee pot, Slips moved to the main door and engaged the locks. "I wouldn't want anyone disturbing me, now would I?" he muttered.

"I wish we could just sack the motherfucker!" he heard Danny say.

"Agreed," Trevor said. "He's been here that long, that I'm sure they built the place around the old fuck."

Carl laughed.

In the background, the coffee pot bubbled.

Cups and spoons could be heard rattling.

With the outer door locked and bolted, Slips backed through the inner door and did the same.

Nobody was going anywhere.

"Did you just lock the doors, Slips?!" Danny asked.

"Yeah, I'll unlock them once I've mopped this area. I don't want people walking all over my floor," he said, and then muttered, "Especially you pricks!"

"Him and his fucking floor!" Carl exclaimed.

"He probably wanks his tits off to the sight of it when we're not here in the morning!" Danny chortled.

"Sick old fuck!" Trevor grimaced.

Where's the harm in a man loving his work...?

When he saw them filling their mugs with coffee, he smiled, grabbed his bucket and mop, and moved closer. He wouldn't want to miss the show.

"Before you start drinking, fellas, there's something I need to show you," he started.

"What now?" Danny snapped.

"Wait here, I'll go and get it. It's pretty damn important."

"Hurry up, then!" Carl snarled.

Without another word, Slips disappeared into the back again.

A few moments later, he reappeared in a heavy-duty apron, which covered most of his body. He also wore thick gloves that extended beyond his elbows. On his face, he wore something that resembled a welder's mask.

As he walked over to the three men, they burst out laughing.

"What the fucking hell, Slips?!" Danny said.

"It's the Rubbernator!" Carl hooted, trying to take a mouthful of coffee.

Trevor bent over with laughter.

Stopping by his bucket, Richard flipped the lid of his mask up to reveal a big, cheesy grin. "At least you arseholes are going to die smiling!"

Trevor stopped giggling and stood bolt upright. "What?!" he asked, as if he couldn't believe what he'd just heard.

"Oh. Nothing!" Flipping the mask back down, he grabbed his bucket and raised it off the floor. "You should have brought umbrellas!" he said, which came out muffled.

"Huh?!" Danny gasped.

"What's in the—" Carl said, but Slips cut in.

"Hydrofluoric acid, son – this shit will cut through ceramic. Enjoy!" He then threw the contents of his bucket over the three of them.

The majority of the acidic tidal wave washed over Danny and Trevor, with mere splashes finding Carl.

"*Argh*! My fucking eyes!" Danny screamed a high-pitched scream. He sounded like a little girl as the acid melted through his epidermis, then dermis, before finally stripping him down to the hypodermis – his blood vessels popped and burst like water balloons. The crimson liquid, which sizzled and spat, mixed in with the yellowy fluids. They ran off his face and gathered on the floor below him.

As Danny stumbled around, he crashed against the jukebox, which brought it to life. "Disco Inferno" boomed out of the speakers, which brought a smirk to Slips' face.

Danny rebounded off the music box and collapsed against the bar. His head resembled a melting ice cream cone. He'd stopped screaming and moving. Acid continued to trickle down his body, eating through his clothes and flesh.

Trevor, who was in an equally messy way, was crashing into tables and chairs. Cutlery clattered onto the floor. Where he'd used his hands and forearms to try and wipe the Hydrofluoric off his face, it had chewed through his limbs – the bones beneath were glistening under the ceiling lights.

His screams were wet. Soggy.

After pin-balling into another table, he fell on top of it. His shell was a sizzling, smoking wreck. Sludge, which had once been his face and arms, pooled under him.

Slips didn't have time to watch Trevor die, as Carl, who seemed like he was making a run for the door, distracted him.

"Get it off me!" he yelled. Only a portion of the right side of his face had been hit – his ear was nothing but a running mess. "It's scalding!" he cried. Grabbing the second bucket Slips had brought in, Carl dumped the contents over him, thinking it was filled with water.

But no.

Slips had also filled that one with acid, just in case he needed more…

Carl's end was brutal. His whole body was drenched in the searing acid.

Slips didn't bother standing to watch the youngster run around flaying his arms and slipping in his friends' goo.

Instead, he went out back, grabbed his 'Caution: Slippery When Wet' signs, and placed them about the restaurant.

Scrapbook

His stiff cock caused him to open his eyes. The room was dark.

Light traffic could be heard passing by outside. *Midnight*, he mouthed.

Seconds later, his alarm clock rang. More often than not, a raging hard-on woke him first. Hearing her soft snores to his side, with a cold elbow and shoulder pressed into his back, he shimmied over.

Fucking whore.

Flicking his laden eyes up, he looked at his clock on his bedside table. The big red numbers read *00:03*.

"*Ugh!*"

Rolling onto his back, he thought about the only good thing he had to look forward to: his daily tug in the shower. The thought of how good the warm water would feel against his exposed bell-end, combined with that of the slippery, lathery texture of soap...He groaned and turned over.

He was now facing her back.

A cold, hard slab.

A fucking tombstone.

Imp-like, he pressed his hardness against her arse. *Maybe she'll surprise me*, he thought, rubbing the sticky end of his dick against her anus. The sensation caused his nuts to tighten – he could feel his love muck glide up his tubes.

"*Frank!*" she snapped, swatting at his cock and hand. "You know I need my rest, damn it. I have a hard job and a busy life to get up to in the morning, and I could do without your fun, games and harassment at midnight. Now, put your *nub* away, and leave me alone!"

Sighing, he retreated, just like little Frank.

Nub. She always called it that – '*No bigger than an eraser!*' she'd said after seeing it for the first time.

Is this as good as it gets? he thought. *A lousy child-and-sexless marriage, copious amounts of bills, a lack of respect and a constant barrage of arguments between her and me. It's a joke. No, it's worse. It's a fucking bleak, shitty façade.*

Where had it all gone wrong?

Marriage, that's where.

Throwing the covers off, he sat on the edge of the bed. Rolling his neck, he heard it crick, bringing a satisfying smile to his face. Had she been awake and not snoring her fat fucking arse off, it would have annoyed her.

How she loathed him cracking his joints.

Just then a loud snore seemed to rock the bed.

One of these days, I'm going to shove our toothbrushes up her fucking nostrils!

Avoiding the temptation, he got up and walked downstairs to the kitchen. He filled the kettle, put it to boil, rinsed a mug, set a teabag in it, and then left for the toilet.

Life hadn't always been like this.

It had been good.

Grand, in fact.

Lifting the toilet seat, he took his cock out and started pissing. It came out in a hot, angry stream. Finishing, he looked down at it before putting it away.

Nub. The word haunted him. Had for the past three years they'd been together.

Why did I marry her?

You know why...

Before she'd come along and pushed him to thinking about swinging from a rope by his neck, he'd had it all: a positive frame of mind, an eagerness to get on in life and be spectacular at his job, and, best of all, the respect and attention he'd deserved.

She'd turned him into a pathetic fucking joke.

He'd lost his heart, will and drive.

And through this impotence, he'd lost the admiration of his peers and others around him. He'd become a ghost. A shadow. A name and number on a fistful of plastic fit for a fire.

A victim of the mundane.

No matter how hard he seemed to try, he couldn't get it back, either.

Slipping his dick back into his pants, he washed his hands, knocked the bathroom light out, and went back to the kitchen where he poured himself a cup of tea.

Looking up at the clock he noted it was twelve-thirty.

Plenty of time. It's not like I've ever been late! Besides, when you're at the top of the chain, you can do as you please. I'm my own boss, he thought, blowing on his tea.

There were worse things in the world than working nights, such as nine-to-fives, afternoons, evenings, taking orders from younger men or having a woman for a boss.

Luckily, I have none of that shit to deal with.

I'm Mr. Nightshift.
I am, the night!
The thought made him smile.

Looking out the kitchen window, he saw the trees and bushes move violently. The wind howled and blasted against the glass. Spits of rain followed. Outdoor jobs may have had their downsides, but so did pushing a pencil in an office.

If it had been up to his father, he would have been a railroad worker. Lifting sleepers and banging bolts into position had never appealed to him, though. Instead, he'd opted for work on the roads.

'*You're not actually built like a navvy, are you?*' she'd said to him on their first date. The *banter* had carried on from that point.

She'd worn him down.

Before her, he'd been a confident, sexual man.

Huffing, he swallowed the rest of his tea, banged his empty cup down, and then made his way to the bathroom once again. On passing the bedroom, he could still hear her snoring, which had increased in volume.

She'll take the fucking floorboards if she's not careful!

Closing and locking the bathroom door at his back, he then opened the window ready for the steam to escape, before turning the shower on.

"Damn, that feels good!" he said, putting his hand beneath the warm water.

Stepping out of his vest and pants, he dove beneath the spray. It pelted his body as he rubbed soap into his prickled flesh.

His cock started to stiffen.

Lowering his hand, he began stroking it to its potential.

His mind started to swirl.

That's it, take it up the shitter, slut!

He started jerking his cock furiously.

"You know you want it," he sneered. Gasping, he clubbed his fist against the wall.

Thunderous knocks on the bathroom door brought him out of his spank-trance.

"*Frank*! What are you doing in there? You've been ages. I need a pee!"

Fuck, fuck, fuck! What the fuck is she doing awake! Trust her to ruin my only bit of fun.

He wanted to beat his head against the wall, but refrained.

"*Frank*!" she bellowed, welting the door some more. He envisioned the wood shaking in the jamb as her fat fist collided with it time and again. "*Frank*!"

Dropping his cock, he felt his hardness shrivel.

"*What*?!" he shot back.

"I need a wee! Let me in."

"Hang on, I won't be long!" he yelled back, wishing he'd been *that* man. Had he been, he would have told her to fuck off.

"Shy? Worried I might see it?" she taunted.

He could hear her hateful laughter over the sound of running water.

Bitch.

Leaning over, he unlocked the door, causing her to spill forth like a tidal wave of hate and rage.

Going back behind the curtain, he finished washing, but didn't get out until he heard the toilet flush. After towelling off, he went to the bedroom and removed his uniform from the cupboard. He took it into the living room, where he preferred to get ready.

Had he knocked the bedroom light on, she would have woke up and gone apeshit. It was easier to dress in another room than go toe-to-toe with her.

I don't need the hassle, what with a fresh week ahead of me. I'm determined to get back to the man I once was.

It was a promise he'd made to himself at the end of last week.

Time to remove my balls from her teabag tin and reattach 'em!

Once dressed, he picked his keys up off the kitchen counter, knocked the lights off, and headed into the hallway. There, he slipped into his steel toe capped boots and took one final look in the hallway mirror.

His uniform was immaculate.

Unlocking the front door, he stepped outside and switched the hallway light off.

Frank made sure to close the door as hard as he could, bringing a satisfying smile to his grizzled chops.

His work van was parked on his drive, which had *British Roads: Highway Maintenance* written across the bodywork. Jumping in, he kicked the engine to life and pulled away.

He felt miserable, even though he'd taken himself to one side over the weekend and tried to get his head back in the game.

I shouldn't be bothering tonight. My heart just isn't in it. Maybe I should just pack it all in? I don't even need to work, what with all the money I've managed to save. Not only that, the house is mine. It's all paid for, thanks to mum and dad.

He looked at himself in the rear-view. He hated what he saw.

She's right, isn't she? I am fucking pathetic. I'm not a man – I'm a bed-wetting pussy boy. Any man would have put her in her place a long time ago. Would have fed her the strap and kept her close to the oven.

But no, not me.

She's bulldozed me into submission.

Thumping the steering wheel, Frank cursed himself into a heap.

Broken by a woman. *My dad would be ashamed of me.* Tears threatened. *My spirit has been broken. I honest-to-God thought I could have put up with being a cash cow for her spoilt ways, because I thought I would have moulded her into my perfect woman. A little puppet. But no. And once she had me where she wanted me, she crushed me beneath her boot heel and gained a ton of weight.*

I'm trapped, and the walls are closing in. My air supply is running on empty.

She'd caused a mental block. Had got inside his head.

Once achieved, the cheating had begun.

He found himself powerless to her ways. To be able to react.

Fuck, she didn't even try to hide it.

I wonder if that dozy prick will bring the wrong mail again today? They must think I'm thick, if they believe I swallow their lies. Fucking retards. There was only one reason he dropped the wrong mail off at ours, and that was so he could return at a later date and screw her fucking brains out.

The best of luck to him!

When did I stop caring?

A handful of red letters ago, that's when. She's made it quite clear in the past, present, and more than fucking likely, the future, that me and my equipment fail her.

Fuck her, him and whoever else she's screwing.

A tick developed at the side of his head. Slowly, a small fire kindled in his guts. Frank could almost taste the smoke at the back of his throat and in his nostrils.

It wasn't just the postman she was screwing, but the milkman, the fireman who lived next door, her yoga instructor and probably half the sixth formers she was teaching.

It's not just their minds she's moulding!

He was a laughingstock, and he knew it. Even his friends knew he was under the thumb. How controlled and abused he was.

'*He'll snap one day...*' he'd heard a neighbour once say.

Stopping at a set of lights, he again looked at himself in the mirror.

I have no idea who I am, anymore. It's as if I'm on the outside looking in, and I don't like what I see.

The traffic lights changed from red to green and he put his van into first gear. As usual, the roads were empty at this hour. It was peaceful, just the way he liked it. It allowed him time to mull things over.

Push for a divorce?

Divorce? Fuck, she'd take me for everything...

Driving on, Frank felt his mood and temper worsen. He was at an all-time low. Sure, he'd had thoughts of ending it before now, but the misery he felt at this point in time was crushing.

Taking a left onto a back road, Frank continued to let his mind wander – he'd travelled this route for years and could pretty much do it blindfolded.

It wouldn't be so bad if I ploughed into something. At least it would be over. All of it.

And let her win? said the small voice at the back of his mind; the voice of yesteryear, the voice that had not spoken to him in almost four years.

"Where have you been?" he uttered.

Had the stir of rage sought it out?

By taking the next right, then left, he was close to work – a freight train thundered by on the lines opposite.

Stopping at the next junction, he stayed there. His full-beam lit the building the opposite side of the road.

British Roads: Highway Maintenance was written across the huge metal gates. Beyond the locked entrance was the employee car park.

All the lights were off inside and around the building.

"I wonder what they actually do in there? After all these years, I still wonder the same thing."

His van idled.

When people had first asked him what he did for a living, this place had sprung to mind. In his head, the people who worked for the *British Roads: Highway Maintenance* firm were men and women who maintained motorways and such.

But as he looked at the building now, he realised for the first time in years that he didn't have a fucking clue what they did there. For all he knew, they built carriages for trains.

Maybe it's a chop shop? Or, maybe they ship AK-47's out the backdoor to gangbangers?

Looking in his driver-side mirror, he could see the area behind him was aglow, much like it was every night. His *true* place of work: the city's park, where the bushes acted as his office and the surrounding buildings were his filing cabinets.

"After all these years of being married, you'd think she would have questioned me about my job, or rang the place looking for me, or sprung a surprise visit…I guess that's the best thing about being married to someone who doesn't give a shit."

Taking his foot off the brake, he eased his foot down on the accelerator and parked in front of the *British Roads: Highway Maintenance* building. The place had acted as his work cover for almost fifteen years.

Switching the lights, radio and engine off, Frank sighed. His shoulders sagged.

"Well, look at that – they've changed the colours of their vans," he whispered, looking at the fleet of maintenance vans parked beyond the padlocked gates. "They used to be yellow, back in the day. Best I get this heap of mine spray-painted red next week. I wonder when the change occurred?"

Sitting in the darkness, he wondered if he could finally lift the cloud and get back in the saddle – to step away from the brink of self-destruction.

The edge of darkness.

Deep breath, Frank. One, two, three... breathe.

He bowed his head. His forehead touched the cool steering wheel.

I can't.

Tears welled in his eyes. His body and hands trembled. He was a wreck.

If she doesn't divorce me, I'll...I'll...I'll...

Frank completely lost it, and started blubbering like an infant. Tears rolled down his cheeks in fat droplets. Never had he lost his shit quite like this. All the emotion, hatred, frustration and anger bubbled to the surface and came out in a way he'd never expected.

Come on, get a grip.

Straightening, he pressed his back against the seat as hard as he could. His fists gripped the wheel fiercely.

"That nub of yours can't please a real woman, Frank!" he could hear her say.

She was his Kryptonite.

"Fucking bitch! I should have killed her when I had the chance. Back when I had the whole town in my palm. What was it the papers called me?"

The Black Veil.

The remembrance of his tag made him smile. A titter escaped him. The tears dried up.

"My peers – the other nutters who stalked the night – were in awe of me. But when that, that—*whore!*—came along, she killed my mojo. Repressed me."

"The Black Veil has not struck in many years, causing the police to believe that either he or she has died or moved away..."

"I'll never forget that police statement. I only married her in hope that she could change me. To help me out of the double-life I'd been leading."

Before the humdrum lifestyle, Frank had been someone. He'd been a god in the shape of a night slayer.

The van, the job. All lies. A façade. A mask worn to protect his true identity from his wife, family and friends.

Who needs work, when you can kill and rob people? It worked for me. I managed to save a pretty penny, which is a good thing. My murder drought has caused me to eat away at my 'rainy day' money. Still, that's what it's there for.

As 'The Black Veil', he'd been a body of mass power, pride and destruction.

But now he was a withdrawn and intimidated schlub. Huffing, he put his hand to the door handle and pulled. Getting out, he slammed it shut behind him and walked to the van's side door. Opening it, his eyes fell on the rope he had there. It was six- feet in length.

Tonight was the night, Frankie boy...

No. I'm not doing myself in unless I'm entirely sure...

His eyes fell on something else he hadn't seen in a long time.

"Is that my old garrotte?" he whispered, pushing a few things aside. Picking up the instrument used for throttling, he noticed small chunks of flesh still clinging to the red-stained wire between the wooden grips, which were still tacky themselves.

"Jesus, I killed and robbed six women throughout two-thousand-and-one with this bad boy. What was the first one's name? The last was Suzanne Small. I remember finding leaked pictures of her dead body on the Internet."

But who was the first...

"Of course, Brenda Sims," he recalled.

The attack had been sloppy. He'd burst from the bushes, wrapped the garrotte around her throat in a haphazard way, allowing her to break his hold. However, once he'd finished playing hide-and-go-peep with her in the darkness of the park, he'd run a double-edged blade up her back.

Putting the instrument down, he noticed more memories: a sickle he'd used on a businessman. An axe he'd used to cleave open two teenage girls. A hatchet used on lovers down lovers' lane. A hammer used to smash the skulls of the homeless. The list was endless, their faces clear.

His van was the scrapbook to his soul.

Then he spotted something else among his life's work.

"What *the*...?"

Moving a box, he saw a hat. Picking it up, he noticed it belonged to a postman. Turning it over, he found a pair of her panties crumpled inside it – they were welded to the hat's rim by stale jism.

He could smell it.

The disrespectful bitch! Fucking the postman as I sleep off a nightshift. I knew she was drilling him. Knew it! But this...this is...

"This is something fucking different altogether!"

The fire that had been stirring in his guts burst into a blaze.

As though a switch had been flicked inside his head, he felt the Veil wash over him. It was dark, cosy, and had a feeling of utter mercilessness.

"Make a fucking cunt out of me, will she?"

All the neighbours are laughing at you...

"We'll see who's fucking laughing!" he bellowed. Curling a fist, he repeatedly punched the flooring of the van until he heard a knuckle pop.

Going to his workbag, he rifled through it and found his blood-stained balaclava and hammer.

They hadn't been used in almost four years.

Removing them, he closed the van's side door and got behind the wheel.

Kicking the engine to life, he reversed and turned around.

He drove at a breakneck speed, not caring if a stray copper should be watching the roads.

'*What are you doing home?*' he could hear her ask.

"I wasn't feeling too well, so I thought I'd come home!" he muttered, stroking the work tool and face covering by his side.

When he pulled up outside his home, he noticed there was a light on inside.

A car he didn't know was parked in his drive. *His* drive.

Killing the engine, he got out of the van with renewed energy.

Slipping the balaclava on, he grabbed the hammer and headed up the drive to his front door. Taking his keys out of his pocket, he opened up.

He could hear them screwing on *their* bed.

Standing in the darkened hallway, he gripped the hammer so tight, he thought he was going to snap the thick, wooden handle in half.

"Yes. I'm not feeling *myself* at all, honey!" he muttered from behind gritted teeth. "Not one damn bit," he finished, slamming the door closed behind him.

Dark Woods

When she opened her eyes, her mind instantly flooded with a series of questions. But one question above all the others stood out, and triggered her fear and set her heart to racing.

What's my name?

Her proceeding enquiries did little to soothe her rampaging anxiety, either.

Where am I?

Why can't I see?

Why are my arms suspended above and my feet tied?

What's that smell?

Where are my friends?

Her mind unravelled. It folded like a house of cards, causing her rushing thoughts to derail like a runaway freight train

I want to go home...

Over her quick gasps, which sounded like staggered stun-gun fire, she could hear the squeak and scurry of rodents about her feet. This caused her mind to empty, and she broke down sobbing.

Her shoulders jerked as she wept, making her joints ache.

"*Please...!*" she begged and gasped. "Untie my hands...they hurt!"

As soon as she started wriggling her hands, she regretted it – the rope tightened, making it bite into her flesh. A fresh sting of pain tore through her. Skin ripped. Blood squirted.

"*Argh*! Please..." But there was no use in trying to speak or yell any further, as her throat was Sahara-dry.

When her tears finally found their way out from underneath her blindfold and rolled down to her lips, she licked them dry. The salty water felt good, even though there was only a small amount of it.

After a while, even her tears dried up. Her body was so tired; it had nothing left to give.

Limply, she hung there and dry-sobbed.

"I want to go home," she bleated. "*Mum...*"

Slowly, she rotated, causing the rope to creak as she turned.

Who's doing this to me, and why?

Giving up on anyone coming to her rescue, she hung there in silence. Even her thoughts had now opted out, allowing the sound of the rats and the groaning of the rope to get inside her head.

Then she heard something.

Something that gave her hope.

A groan.

"Hello?!" she rasped. Her voice cracked.

Nothing.

Her head lowered once again.

Why would someone do this...?

Stretching her legs out as far as they would go, she noted that her toes barely touched the floor, which felt soft. Pushy, almost. Kicking her feet back and forth, she could hear the floor being disturbed.

Dust?

No, it sounds more like grit.

Am I on a beach...?

Why would there be rats on a beach? And that smell...

From above, floorboards creaked, disturbing dust, which cascaded down onto her hair and face. Some of it made its way into her mouth, causing her to cough, gag and splutter.

Ugh! She gasped, trying to fill her lungs with clean air.

Fresh tears rolled down her cheeks.

A cellar...I'm possibly in a cellar!

The footfalls were followed by muffled sounds of conversation and raspy, harsh laughter.

Motherfuckers!

"The *beach!*" she blurted. "That's right. We were by water. Not a beach but... a river? No, *yes*...We'd made a dam...Had planned to go back. Get drunk. Get high..."

'*Fuck, drink and have wild times...*' she heard Jonathan say inside her head.

"Jonathan," she muttered. His name seemed to hang there. "Where are my friends?!" she managed to bellow. A fire started to kindle in her belly.

The voices and creaking stopped.

More harsh laughter.

They're fucking taunting me!

Silence engulfed her once again.

What the fuck *is my name?*

Her small flames of rage combusted into a blaze as she pulled and yanked at the rope that bound her hands.

Something from above started to give way. Wood splintered.

Come on! She screamed on the inside. *Fucking pull!*

More sounds of cracking.

Debbie, Debbie, Debbie. What a pickle you've found yourself in once again. Didn't I tell you that your friends would lead you astray?!

"The last thing I need to do right now is to think about my mother!" She grunted as she continued to pull down on the rope, which tore, bit and ripped at her wrists.

"*Debbie*. That's it. My name's *Debbie*. And I'm not going to take this fucking shit!"

Taking a few deep breaths to calm herself, she then wrapped the rope around her wrists as tight as she could.

Remember your training…

Yes! Of course. I'm a black belt…

The sound of someone groaning close to her rang out again.

"Who the hell's there?!"

Silence.

"Answer me, damn it!"

"Deb…" the new voice moaned. "I'm hurt, *real* bad."

"Lori! Is that *you*?!"

"Yeah, hon," Lori said, coughing. It sounded wet.

"What the hell's going on? Where are rest of our friends?"

"I–" Lori started to talk, but again coughed violently. Gasping for air, she continued. "I'm not sure… Before I had my glasses knocked off I saw them take Dani and Natalie upstairs. The crotch of her trousers was covered in blood…"

"On, no," Debbie muttered.

"She was screaming and crying… There was nothing I could do."

"Not the baby…!"

"I think she may have lost it," Lori said, starting to sob in a hysterical fashion. Debbie didn't know how to respond. A bow developed in her throat. *I need to get the fuck out of here. Lori, too.*

With that thought, she raised her legs until the soles of her feet were pressed against her buttocks. She then pulled downwards with all her might. Fillings of wood sprinkled her hair as Debbie heaved, muttered and groaned.

"Come on, come on…"

"What are you trying to do?"

"I'm. Almost. Free!"

"*Argh!*" Lori suddenly screamed. "Get them off me. Argh, they are chewing on my–please! Debbie! Help!"

"Shit, shit, shit! What's going on?!"

"It's okay, I've managed to dislodge them. *Ugh*, the little fuckers were chewing on a bit of exposed bone. It's jutting through the side of my knee, I think."

"Did they do that to you?"

"No, I fell, when I was trying to run away from them back at the dam."

"Who are they? Do we know them?"

"I don't know," Lori said. Her words came out in a quiver. "I didn't get a look at them, really. I was blindsided, and hit over the head with something hard and heavy."

"All I remember is screaming, then nothing. When I first woke up, I couldn't even remember my name."

"Are you okay, apart from the head?"

"I think so. Nothing seems to be broken or cut. Although, I think my head my have been bleeding at one point – my hair is matted to the back of my skull."

"What are we going to do?"

"I have no idea."

"Didn't you say you were almost free?"

"Yes." Debbie grunted. "I can't see jack shit, though. I have a blindfold on."

"Me, too. My hands are tied and handcuffed to something metallic."

"That doesn't sound good!"

"I want to go home!" Lori sobbed.

"Hey, we're going to be fine. If I can just get out of this…"

A door slamming shut caused Debbie to stop moving. Her heart hitched before continuing to beat at a high a pace.

"What was that?!" Lori said.

"I don't…"

Heavy footfalls, which sounded as though they were descending, filled Debbie's ears.

"Oh, shit!" she whispered.

Suddenly, things seemed to get much brighter, as a light flooded. The blindfold she wore was fairly transparent, and now, for the first time, she could see Lori. Her friend was sat on the floor with a Hessian sack over her head, her hands bound and cuffed to an old radiator.

Debbie hung less than twenty feet away from her friend.

"What's going on?!" Lori screamed.

"Try and keep calm!" Debbie said. "It's scare tactics." Looking down, she could see the floor moving. "What the…?" On closer inspection, she could see the ground was covered with rats, worms, beetles, maggots and all other sorts of beasties.

She threw up in her mouth, but managed to keep it in.

Swallowing the lumpy liquid, she closed her eyes as tight as she could. Her body quivered.

Ugh!

The footsteps grew louder, until she felt as though the person was right on top of her. Looking left and right, Debbie tried to see her captor, but couldn't.

However, she did take in her surroundings. There appeared to be a window at the farther end of the room, which was covered by a sheet. In the centre, there was a large object, possibly a table. It held many objects, but she couldn't make out what.

To her right, she could see the staircase.

A lone, hunched figure shuffled down it.

"I see you!" Debbie whispered.

When the person reached the bottom, its feet could be heard crushing the bugs that scurried along the floor.

"*Hmmm!*" the person groaned.

"Please, untie us!" Lori said. "We didn't see anything. We don't know who you... just let us go! We won't tell."

Debbie watched as the person ambled over to the table and picked something up. It sounded heavy.

"Tell them, Debbie!" Lori pleaded.

But Debbie knew this person was not going to be bartered with.

It walked over to Lori, the implement from off the table hanging by its side.

By tilting her head back, Debbie could see underneath the blindfold. The person had its back to her, looking down on Lori.

"Oh, no," she uttered, and then pulled on her restraints once more.

She kept her gaze trained on their captor as she did, and witnessed it yank and play with the exposed bone jutting from Lori's knee. This caused her to howl, kick and spit.

The person's laugh didn't sound human or beast-like. It had more of a mechanical lilt to it.

That's not possible. I'm hearing things, surely. The blow to the head...

A fresh scream from Lori tore through Debbie's skull, as she fiercely fought with her ropes.

I have to help her.

"Get off me!" Lori shrieked, and then screamed when the person took to her leg with the object it had in its hand. The sound of sawing cut through her and set her nerves on edge – the hairs at the back of her neck stood on end.

"Oh, my God!" her friend bellowed. "My leg!"

The sawing intensified.

Bones snapped.

Blood spewed across the floor and up the radiator.

"*Lori!*"

With her legs once again tucked under her arse, Debbie gave it everything, causing blood to rush to her head.

The beam above her cracked for the final time, and gave way.

Before she knew it, Debbie was on the floor with the bugs and rodents.

The person carving Lori up like a Christmas turkey hadn't even noticed that she'd worked herself free.

Shaking her head, trying to clear the dizzy sensation, Debbie got to her knees and pulled the blindfold off her face. The true vileness of her situation collapsed in on her.

"Holy shit!" she blurted, but this didn't distract the thing from working on Lori's leg. It did, indeed, have a saw in its hand, and it was using it to cut her friend's leg off above the knee.

Lori had passed out. Her face had turned an ashen colour, which had minuscule flecks of blood blended in with it.

Not stopping to drink in her surroundings, now that she could see, Debbie ran over to the person attacking her friend and shoved it off balance. This caused them to crash head first into the radiator, and rebound. When they hit the deck, Debbie got the chance to look the person in its face, if that's what you could call it.

It snapped its head in her direction and snorted with rage.

One half of its face was comprised of a mouth like that of a wolf, complete with canine teeth, whiskers and patchy brown and black hair. The eye on that side was pure black. The pupil couldn't be seen. It looked as though it had a black pearl for a left eye.

On the other side of its face however, it had human features. Strangely though, its right eye was ruby red, as though it was in an exaggerated bloodshot state. Its nose was flat against its face, and mingled in a hideous fashion with the doggy one; it had a lopsided bullring through it. The teeth on that side of its face were like hers, but most of them were either broken, chipped, discoloured or missing completely.

"What the *fuck* are you?!"

Snorting some more, it placed its hands behind its back and pushed at the flooring. Bugs squished between its gnarled fingers as it got to its feet.

Getting into a stance, she braced herself – this would be the first time she would have to use her training, even after all the years she had been practicing the ancient art form.

"Stay the fuck back!"

It lunged at her, but her whirlwind kick was too fast for it. Her booted heel connected with its robust jaw. Broken teeth ricocheted off the wall and radiator as the thing was sent back to the floor. It hit the dirt with a hard, rib-cracking thud and howled in agony.

"I won't tell you twice!" Debbie said, landing a well-placed heel in its crotch.

The man-beast rolled onto its side and curled into a ball. When it started vomiting, Debbie turned to Lori.

Her friend's leg hung by a few threads of flesh and sinew – a pool of blood had gathered around them.

Putting her fingers to Lori's neck, she felt a weak pulse.

"Oh, shit...I need to get you–"

"*Argh*!" the beast-man raged, as it rugby-tackled Debbie and took her to ground.

As they rolled about the floor, she again managed to catch the thing in its balls by kneeing the area as hard as she could.

The thing fell off her.

"*Bastard*!" Making her hand claw-like, she swiped the tips of her fingers across the thing's vision, managing to rip the ruby red eye free of its socket.

It shrieked and howled as it put its hands to the rupture and covered it. Blood spurted and flowed between the thing's hideous fingers.

"Lori, come on! We have to go," she told her friend, trying to put her arm over her shoulder. "You have to help me!"

"I...I..." Lori panted.

"I can't hear you," Debbie said, putting her ear close to Lori's mouth.

"Leave me. I'm done. I can't walk, and I've lost too much blood."

"No, I'm not– "

"Look out!" Lori said, causing Debbie to turn around. She had enough time to see the beast fly at her, and to dive out of its way and crash into the table. This caused many implements to fall off the table in a shower and clatter against her and the floor.

Among the assortment, Debbie saw a scalpel.

The beast had landed on Lori, who screamed as it tore its fingers and teeth through her clothes and stomach and ripped her innards out. It stuffed her entrails into its greedy, drooping maw and smacked its lips with glutinous excitement.

Grabbing the surgical tool, Debbie rushed up behind the thing, pulled its head back by a tuft of hair, and savagely ripped the scalpel across the exposed throat. Blood gushed out of the wound and splashed Lori's face.

Even though she knew she'd dealt it a mortal wound, Debbie didn't stop. She continued to run the surgical knife back and forth, back and forth, until the beast's head came off in her hand.

Screaming, she dropped the head and stamped on it, repeatedly. She witnessed the other eyeball squish under the might of her stomps.

Going to Lori, she sat by her side and put her head in her lap.

"I'm so sorry!"

"*Ugh...uch!*" Lori gargled, and then vomited blood. It was mixed with another liquid, which had an ungodly colour to it.

As Lori struggled to cling to life, Debbie tried to soothe her by stroking her hair. All the while, she sobbed and told Lori everything would be okay.

Within minutes, she was dead.

"*No!*" Debbie bellowed as she beat her fist against the wall behind her. "You son-of-a-bitch!"

Lifting Lori's head off her lap and gently putting it on the floor, Debbie got up. Walking over to the man-beast, she spotted something large on the table, which was covered by a bloody sheet. She hadn't noticed the mound at first glance.

"What the hell?"

She went over to the sheet, grabbed the corners nearest her, and whipped it off the covered article, much like a magician whips a tablecloth off a dressed table.

Abracadabra!

"*Jonathan*!" she screamed on seeing her friend, who had been bound to the table with thick cord. Eight-inch nails had also been driven through his ankles and wrists to help keep him in place.

Putting a hand to his neck, she couldn't feel a pulse.

All his fingers, along with his toes, were missing. They swam in jars by the side of his head, along with his eyeballs and testicles.

Turning, she emptied the contents of her guts onto the floor. Some of her spew splashed onto a rat, turning it into a psychedelic rodent.

Raising back up, she looked down at her friend. A friend, much like Lori, she cared for very deeply. Stroking his bearded face, she gave him a kiss on the forehead and moved to the stairs on the other side of the room.

Before climbing them, she took one last look around the basement. On the wall to the side of Lori's body was an arsenal of bludgeoning, stabbing, chopping, hacking and slashing weapons: axes, knives, scythes, cleavers, hammers, shears, clippers, snips, loppers – the collection seemed inexhaustible.

Running over to the wall, she took down a pair of long-handled shears, and opened and closed them a few times. This helped work the stiffness out of them, as rust rained from the blades to the floor.

"Payback is a fucking bitch!"

Going back to the stairs, she started to climb them, slowly. They groaned in protest as she placed her weight on them.

"How fucking clichéd!" she uttered.

When she got to the top of the staircase, she was greeted by a wooden door. A strip of light infiltrated the crack between the bottom of it and the floor. Beyond the exit, she could hear something. Possibly a radio or a TV was playing. The sound was down fairly low.

Taking a deep breath, she put her hand to the doorknob and gradually turned it. The thing didn't squeak as she'd expected it to. Exhaling, she pushed the door open an inch at a time. Once enough of a gap had been created, she stopped the door's progression, and spied through the sliver.

She couldn't see much to her left or right, but straight in front of her was a shoddy-looking sofa, complete with matching armchairs. A woodlice-infested coffee table stood between the furniture; a TV stood on an equally degraded wooden unit in the corner of the medium-sized living room.

From what she could see, the walls were made from logs, suggesting she was in the woods somewhere.

Probably the backwater of Hell!

Nudging the door open some more, Debbie could now see the far end of the sofa. Her breath hitched in her throat.

There was someone sitting there.

Another one of my captors to torment me?

Her hands tightened around the gardening implement. Pricking her ears, she could hear the soft sound of snoring over the show playing on the TV.

"Oh, your time is coming, you cunt!" she muttered quietly. "You should have killed me when you had the chance!"

She pushed the door completely open and walked into the living room. She ducked her head around a door to her immediate right. The kitchen lay beyond the entranceway.

Turning her back to the kitchen, she walked slowly and carefully over to where the person on the sofa sat and slept.

To her surprise, it wasn't another man-beast.

It was a young woman. A woman who wasn't much older than Debbie's twenty years. She wore a Hooters tee, but had no tits to speak of. Unlike Debbie, she was bone thin, and reeked of piss and stale meat. Her black hair hung unkempt and unwashed.

Rats' tails!

Raising the shears above her head like a knife, she was about to bring it down when she heard a door bang open, and then slam shut.

Startled, Debbie dashed behind the armchair opposite the sofa. There, she hunched down and peeked from behind the chair's padded arm.

Into the room walked a giant of a man.

Shit, he must be close to seven feet tall! thought Debbie incredulously.

Just like the man-beast downstairs, this one was almost identical, apart from the height and weight. He was shirtless, which in turn, exposed tufts of hair and odd tribal markings. It didn't so much speak, as growl.

"*Woman!*" It kicked the side of the sofa with such force that Debbie thought it was going to punt the whole thing through the living room wall.

"Wha', pa?!"

That's her fucking father?!

"Talk to me like that again, gal, and you'll get the rough side of my hand!"

"I was sleepin'!"

"I got somethin' for *you* and somethin' for *me* outside…"

Her eyes seemed to light up. She got to her knees on the sofa and clapped her hands like an over-excited child in the proverbial sweetshop. "Wha's in the bag, pa?" she squealed.

"Somethin' for the *family!*" he said, and then bellowed with laughter as he lifted the sack into the air in front of him.

Blood seeped through the rough sack and dripped along the floor as he walked over to the girl.

"Wha' is it?!"

"We have unborn baby for dinner!" he laughed.

"You cut it out of her, pa?"

He said nothing, just nodded.

Debbie clapped a hand over her mouth, which stopped her from gasping. Tears rolled down her cheeks as she quivered on her haunches.

"Where's the rest of the bitch?!"

"Outside, gal."

"Let's get her!"

"Wait! I want to put this out there," he said, walking towards the kitchen.

When he returned, he took her hand in his, and led her outside.

"*Motherfuckers*!" Debbie whispered.

The cabin became animated once more, as it was filled with screams, laughter, and the sound of dragging.

"Let. Me. Fucking. Go! Cunts!"

Dani!

"Bring them in here, pa! I'll cut this dead pig up for dinner. I'm sure she'll go well as a side dish to her baby!"

The father howled with laughter.

When the young girl entered the room once again, Debbie could see blood on her t-shirt, face and bare legs.

"Drop that one here! I'll take her out to the kitchen and start chopping her up!"

When the hulking mass walked into the room, he offloaded the body draped over his left shoulder. It hit the floor of the cabin with a dull, mushy thud.

Natalie! *Oh, God...Nat. What have they done to you*? Debbie bit into her fist to keep from gasping out loud.

Her friend's chest and stomach had been torn open, the innards scooped out. Her eyes stared at the ceiling, unblinking. The warm colour she normally possessed in her cheeks had gone.

'*Adam and I are so excited about the baby*!' That had been the last thing she'd said to Debbie at the dam.

The day was supposed to have been a fun one. The location had been perfect—or so they had thought. A secluded lake in the middle of the woods close to where they all lived; after discovering it, they'd planned to spend their graduation day there. Away from the noise and bulk of happy-clappy students who had just passed their chosen University degree.

Drink, fun and games.

Not death, torture and misery.

"You gonna play with tha' one, pa? You and Stan Jr.?"

"You mind your business, gal!"

"Take your fucking hands off me!" Dani screamed, who was being lugged over the thing's right shoulder.

The man-beast turned his torso swiftly to the left, causing Dani's body to swing violently. Her head connected with the door jamb. A cracking sound ensued, followed by Dani going limp.

Pa smiled.

"*Ugh!*" the girl said, grabbing Natalie by the hair. She then proceeded to drag the carcass behind her without effort, heading towards the kitchen. A thick, slimy blood trail was the aftermath of the young girl's endeavour.

"Do everythin' ya bloody self 'round here!" Debbie heard the girl mutter, still looking in her direction.

Turning her head back to face the man-beast, she noticed he'd gone. She could hear his heavy footfalls pound the wooden stairs to the third floor.

I never knew wood cabins had so many floors!

With the father gone, Debbie turned her attention to the daughter. Grabbing the shears by both handles, she opened the fierce blade and snapped it shut again. *You're going fucking down. All of you!*

Standing, she crept as slowly and as quietly as she could into the kitchen, where she found the young girl with her back to her. She was muttering something about the cleaver she held in her hand – its steel was covered in stale blood, mucus, particles of flesh, and fine strands of hair.

The sight caused Debbie to look away, but it didn't stop her in her tracks.

"Fucking cunting thing is blunter than a butter knife!" she bellowed, bashing the butcher tool against the sink. "Couldn' cut hot shit with it."

Debbie watched as the young girl hoisted the meat cleaver above her head and brought it down on Natalie's face with all her might. The impact drove the steel deep into the face and split it in two.

Dislodging it with a slurpy tug, the girl wiped the cleaver's blade on her bare leg. "Guess it will do 'en."

Little fucking bitch!

Drawing the shears back, Debbie got ready to charge at the girl and stab her through her back.

But the girl's next action stopped her.

Opening a cupboard door to her right, she got on her tiptoes, and reached inside with both arms.

"Gotcha, sucker!" she said, pulling forth a soiled blender; it was caked in filth, blood and skin. Plugging it in, the girl tried it. At first, the blades sounded as though they were having difficulty in turning, due to old chunks of meat or God knows what else was trapped between them. They whined. Thick strands of black smoke started to lift from it.

"Goddamn it!" she yelled, giving the thing a whack with the cleaver.

The violent action must have dislodged something, because now the rotary blades were running smooth.

"Yippee!" But her victory was short-lived. "*Ugh!*" she grunted as Debbie drove the shears into the girl's back with immense force. The tip of the blade broke through her breastbone.

Ribs cracked.

Blood burst.

Her knees buckled.

"That's for my friends, you fucking whore!" Debbie whispered into the girl's ear. "If I had more time, I'd chop you into small pieces and feed you to wild dogs. *Cunt!*"

"Ugh…uch…!" the girl bleated as the shears were wiggled and twisted in her back. Gore exploded from her mouth as she coughed.

"You fucked with the wrong one this time…Reap what you sow!"

The younger girl wheezed and spluttered, as she tried desperately to cling to life.

With a smile, Debbie forced the handles apart, causing flesh to tear.

Bone popped. When the girl's body started to flop, it reminded Debbie of a bait worm trapped on a hook.

Closing the blades, she ripped the blade out with force, but the girl didn't collapse as expected. Putting a hand to the back of the girl's head, Debbie pushed it down, hard. It smashed through the glass of the blender and tangled with the thing's blades. Now they truly were whining as Debbie held her head down. Blood spattered the kitchen walls and floor.

Her neck snapped. Bones punched through the soft skin around her throat.

The blender sparked and fused, causing it to come to a halt. Removing her hand, Debbie let the bitch fall to the floor. Looking down at her, she could see most of the letters in Hooter's were covered in blood. All that remained were the OO's, which were shaped like a pair of tits.

"Two down…" Her words trailed off when she heard Dani screaming from upstairs. "The sick fucks!"

Going to the bottom of the stairs, Debbie looked up and listened. She could hear the man-beast moving around up there, which was slightly silenced by the sound of fabric tearing.

"No, please!" Dani begged.

"Shut up!" her tormentor said. This was followed by the sound of flesh connecting with flesh. Dani bleated in pain. Debbie could hear the thing sneering back at Dani's pleas.

Putting her foot to the first step, Debbie tested its reliability with her weight. It didn't groan. Neither did the next one, or the one after that. With her back pressed against the wall, she kept her eyes trained on the space above her.

As she continued to climb a banister came in to view, followed by wooden spindles. Levelling her eyes, she looked through the spindles partings, and saw an empty room beyond them.

The sound must be coming from elsewhere.

Beads of sweat rolled down her face and stung her eyes. With her forearm, she wiped her face dry, and licked her lips. The shears dangled at her side.

Dani continued to yelp.

When she got within a few steps from the top, another room came into view. There was someone or something in that room for sure, as Debbie could see shadows dancing on the walls.

"Please…" she heard Dani say once more. More sounds of cloth shredding. Dani's pleas turned to that of wet sobs, gaining her more slaps and shouts from the beast.

Getting to the top step, Debbie dared a peek around the corner. Her jaw sagged when she saw Dani tied to a bed, her body devoid of clothing, which lay in a shredded heap at her side.

"Oh, Jesus!" she whispered.

The thing stood over her, running its sharp talons up and down her body, leaving deep and lengthy scratch marks in their wake.

Without warning, it opened its huge maw and latched on to one of Dani's exposed nipples.

She screamed as it chewed and then ripped the appendage free.

Debbie felt a large tremor roll down her body as she watched the thing swallow the nipple and lick its lips.

Dani's eyes fluttered as the beast took to her other breast and mutilated that one in the same way before clawing at her face and chest. It drove its knee into her crotch, then flopped all its weight onto her.

"*Ugh!*" Dani exhaled, the air rushing from her lungs.

It grunted as it gyrated on top of her, causing Debbie to put a hand over her mouth.

Then, her eyes locked with Dani's.

Tears rolled down her cheeks, as she mouthed '*Help me...*'

Pushing herself off the wall, Debbie screamed a warrior's scream and charged into the bedroom with the shears held high above her head. As she brought the gardening implement down, she saw the beast spring off Dani with cat-like speed.

But it was too late to stop her plunging motion. The blades punched through Dani's midriff and pinned her to the decayed mattress. A fountain of blood splashed up and entered Debbie's mouth.

"*Fuck!*" she yelled, but had little time to react to what she had just done, as the beast-man backhanded her off the bed with brute force. Her body smashed against something that resembled a chest-of-drawers, but one that had seen better days.

Wood cracked and splintered under her weight.

When she hit the floor, Debbie felt a rib pop, but again, she had no time to react, as the man-beast ripped her off the floor by her hair.

Throughout the melee, Dani could be heard choking and dying on her own blood.

"*Argh*! Get the fuck off me!"

The beast lifted her high into the air, causing her to thrash her legs.

Where the fuck is the floor?!

It pulled her face closer to its open maw-mouth. A stink unlike anything she had ever smelt before blasted her face, causing her to gag.

I'm not going to be used as dog food! she thought, kicking her leg out as hard as she could. Her foot slammed against the beast's crotch, causing it do drop her and double over in howling agony.

Once flat on the floor, she crawled over to the bed and put her hands on the handles to the shears. As she tried to pull them out of Dani, her hands slid up the wet, sticky handles.

Before she could get the weapon free, it was on her again, punching her repeatedly in the small of her back.

"*Bastard*!" she yelled, swinging her arm back towards its face, but it stopped it mid-swipe. Smiling, it shoved her headlong into a wardrobe. Her face connected with one of the hard wooden doors.

Rebounding, she hit the deck with a hard thud.

The man-beast laughed.

As she staggered around on all fours, trying to shake the daze from her head and vision, she heard someone scream. Flopping onto her back, she saw a battered and bloody Kevin emerge from the wardrobe she'd been hurled against.

"*Kev!*" she blurted, trying to stay awake. He was the only one of her friends left standing. "Get him!"

She watched as Kevin lay into the beast with a large piece of timber. He clubbed the thing about its head, but it didn't seem to cause much effect.

"Die!" Kev said, belting the thing around its chops once, twice, three times, causing the wood to splinter and break in half. "*Shit!*"

Before he could lash out again, the wood was snatched from his hand and stabbed through his eyeball in one fast, smooth movement. His legs buckled. His body crashed against the floor, where it flopped and jigged until he died. A pool of blood spread out beneath his body.

With one last effort, Debbie threw herself onto Dani and gripped the shears again.

As it rushed to try and stop her, the man-beast slipped on Kev's blood and flew into the air. Whilst it was down and disorientated, Debbie managed to force the clippers free and lunge at the beast.

Without giving it an inch, she poked the blades into its eyes, which burst like water balloons, and drove downward.

It writhed, kicked and slammed its fists against the floor as blood pumped out of the ruptured eye sockets.

When it finally stopped bucking, she got up and staggered over to the door.

She'd won.

They were dead, and she was alive.

"I did it..." she gasped.

"Pa?! You up there?"

Startled, Debbie moved to the landing.

"Pa?!" the voice came again.

She detected it was coming from outside. Looking around her, she saw a sickle leaning against a wall. Picking it up, she hobbled down the stairs.

"Where the hell are ya, pa?!"

When she got to the front door, she heard footsteps moving in her direction. Before she could put her hand on the doorknob, she saw it turn.

Shit! With a clutched breath, she hid behind the door. *I'll take it by surprise.*

Her hold tightened on the sickle.

The door slowly creaked open.

A breath caught in her throat when she saw the curved edge of a machete.

She raised her own weapon...

....and prayed.

Dacchas

The thick, cloying stench of fuel, smoke and burning wood assaulted her nostrils and stung her eyes, but she didn't care, nor did she avert her gaze. No. She felt like stripping, applying war paint, and dancing naked around the burning chalets with ferocious delight as the flames flickered in her eyes.

She felt squaw-like.

She was ready for battle.

The starting of the fire was a warning shot across their bow.

There would be no running this time, only attacking.

Killing.

When Vickie Halsey decided to go back on her word of never, *ever* returning to the hamlet of Invercurie or the hills of Blair Long, she never would have guessed the chalets would still be standing. It had been close to twenty years.

Even the shells of the Morris 1000, Daf and VW Dormobile still lay here; their bodies rusted and eroded by the harsh highland winds and rain over the past two decades. Their owners, like Vickie's brother, were long dead – their ghosts still roamed the hills, along with the white, cave-dwelling creatures known as Dacchas.

She could sense them.

Feel them, almost.

She looked over her shoulder, up at Blair Long. '*The hills have eyes... they're there and they're watching; watching me, my companions and the blaze. Well, let them. Tonight, they die!*' she thought. A shiver slid down her back.

After arriving at Invercurie, the first thing Vickie had checked before heading towards the chalets was the town itself. She didn't want to cause harm to anyone who may have still been living in the hamlet, but she needn't have worried, as the place had been sacked by the Dacchas long ago.

Nothing moved.

All the buildings had been hollowed out by fires. Those fires had gone cold many years ago. Their windows were smashed, resembling awful, yawing mouths filled with needle-sharp teeth. Doors hung from single hinges; roof slate lay smashed and scattered in the debris-filled streets.

Invercurie was nothing more than a ghost town.

A place time had long forgotten, along with its dark, Dacchas secret.

But Vickie had not forgotten. Neither had Phil Drake; the police officer who had helped her and her family out of their living nightmare all those years ago.

Where has the time gone...?

Phil, who had stayed in constant contact with her father, Frank Halsey, via phone calls, had also sworn never to return to this burnt, cursed ground. But it had eaten away at him, or so he had told Frank.

Vickie had been at the house the day Phil had called in to see her father.

"They've given up searching, Frank. The police and army..."

"It has been five years, Phil. They probably all died in that fire you set."

"No, there were only a handful of charred corpses discovered. They've found a new home. A home beyond Blair Long. I plan to go back and finish them off!"

"That would be suicide, Phil!"

"I need to know, Frank. I have to!"

The conversation was still clear in her head. In the years that followed, Phil and her father kept in touch, with Phil staying clear of Invercurie. He couldn't find the nerve to go back, even though he wanted to. Badly.

In the later summer of eighty-seven, Vickie lost her father to a massive heart attack. He never did manage to fulfil his wife's dream of becoming a bank manager, much to her disappointment. Two years after her father's passing, her mother was also taken. Cancer.

After her father's death, Phil had started corresponding with Vickie. They'd grown close and he had told her in several letters how he still had nightmares. How they pervaded his every waking thought. Realising he wasn't getting any younger, he had finally decided to return to the place where he had almost lost his life to the things with webbed hands and feet; to the powder-white beasts who had a taste for warm, human flesh.

The Dacchas – cannibalism born out of inter-breeding.

In his final letter to Vickie, Phil had told her he was heading back to Invercurie. That he was packing his car with dynamite and guns. *I won't be coming back until I've removed every last one of those sons-of-bitches from the face of Earth, Vickie. If you haven't heard off me in a few weeks, you will know that I've succumbed to them...'*

His words had chilled her.

Scared her.

Vickie had spilt tears for him.

Even though they had escaped that day, the nightmare had never truly ended. It plagued Phil, her and her parents. Her mother had sought counselling, and had been placed on strong medication. The death of Jamie, her brother, had affected her mother in horrendous ways – nightmares, daydreams, visions, voices in her head, mirages of her dead son...

Vickie had caught her mother trying to take her own life on many occasions.

Her dad, who had managed to remain a little stronger of mind, had taken to drinking. He'd never been a drinker. "It helps soothe the demons," he had once told her. The excessive intake of whisky had been the final nail in his coffin, causing the massive heart attack he'd suffered.

Those fucking cunts in the hills tore my family apart! They may not have ripped them limb from limb and drunk their blood like they did with Jamie, but they did enough, she thought, spitting at the collapsing chalets.

Her cheeks were starting to burn, but she refused to move until she saw every last rotting, woodworm-infested piece of timber reduced to a pile of smouldering ash. There was nothing to gain from burning the skeletal structures except satisfaction in her quest for retribution.

Once a calendar month had passed without a single word from Phil Drake, Vickie had feared the worst. Within a week, she had made her mind up – she was going to return to Invercurie and finish what Phil had probably started.

Evidence of his return had been clear. For one, his car had been left the other side of the drowned causeway – it had been only a matter of time before the sea claimed that piece of road. Also, a small number of their shared enemy lay scattered about the land. Some had slashed throats and bodies; others had multiple bullet wounds. A few had been blown to pieces, with gobs of flesh flung far and wide.

Vickie had even found a decapitated head. Its third eye had been ripped or dug free by a knife or robust fingers.

On searching Phil's car, Vickie and her two male companions had discovered dynamite, two rifles and a dozen boxes of ammunition.

He really did mean business! she'd thought, removing the dynamite and rifles. She'd then loaded the explosives into a waterproof holdall, along with the ammo. Vickie, along with her fiancé Tom and his best friend, Mike, had then crossed the causeway by swimming it in wetsuits. When they reached the other side, they had changed into the dry clothes Tom and Mike had packed into other holdalls.

After dumping everything close to the causeway, the three had moved to the chalets, where Vickie had started a fire.

Now, with the chalets nothing but a blackened pile, the three set about preparing for their assault.

"What's the plan here, Vicks?" Tom asked. He'd tried talking her out of this crazy suicide mission but had failed.

"Look, I'm going, with or without your permission," she'd told him at the time. "Those fuckers killed my family. They tore my brother apart. I have to finish this shit, once and for all. I want to try and move on with my life while I still have the chance, Tom."

"Okay," had been his reply with a shrug and his hands up and splayed in surrender.

The three of them had thought out their plan carefully. Tom, after agreeing to accompany Vickie, had suggested a four-week prep. "We'll need to learn how to handle guns and explosives, not to mention getting our hands on some rifles."

She'd agreed.

She snapped back to the present. "We shoot as many of the bastards as we can! I was hoping the fire would have needled them into attack, revealing their new hideout…"

"I don't see it working," Mike said.

"Just keep your eyes open, Mike. They could rush us. Is your safety off? Are you fully loaded?"

Mike nodded.

"What about you, Tom?"

"Yes, I'm ready."

"Good! Once we know where they are hiding, we'll set the explosives and blast the rest of the fuckers to kingdom come!" she exclaimed, cocking the bolt-action hunting rifle she had brought with her. Phil's guns lay on the floor, next to their holdalls.

"We can take up position by the car husks!" Mike said, pointing at the Morris 1000 with his rifle's barrel.

"This isn't Rorke's Drift!" Tom said.

"I think it's a good idea." Vickie moved behind the Daf, kneeled by its wing, and placed the rifle across the bonnet. She peered through the rifle's mounted scope, clearly seeing the mountains of Blair Long. "There's movement!"

"Where?"

"Over there, Tom. Look."

Kneeling by her, he too looked through his scope. "I see it. Mike, drag the rest of the guns and ammo close by."

Mike did as instructed and then took up position behind the Morris 1000. "We could get inside the cars and point our guns out the broken windows."

"Sounds good, but if we get surrounded, then we will have no place to run. At least out in the open like this we have a chance of retreating."

"She's got a point," Tom said. "Plus, we have no idea how many we're up against – there could be hundreds, especially if they've been breeding undisturbed for the last twenty years!"

"Remind me why I let you two talk me into this again?!"

"Because you're a good friend, Mike," Vickie stated. "Not only that, you pair grew up with Jamie. You were his friends. Don't you want revenge for what these sick fucks did?!"

Silence fell among the three. A keen wind picked up. On it, they could hear the faint rustle of the things' footfalls as they made their way down the hills. Behind them, the last of the flames were starting to die out.

"Must be a load of them if we can hear their approach from here!" Tom remarked.

"Agreed. Tom, set some of your charges here, just in case we have to fall back – we can blast their numbers apart in our retreat."

As Tom fumbled with his explosives, Vickie noticed Mike rummaging through her pack. He removed a couple of sticks of TNT they had found in Phil Drake's holdall.

"Got a lighter somewhere..." he muttered, patting his pockets down. "Ah, here it is."

"Get ready, guys!" Vickie put her eye back to her scope. "There's quite a number of them getting close..." A crack rang out. In her peripheral, she noticed Tom's shoulder jerk. Through her scope, she saw a shadowy figure hit the dirt. "Jesus, hold your fire! There could be people like us among their flank, or just people in general."

"Fuck that!" Tom said, cocking his rifle. The spent shell flipped out and ricocheted off the Daf. "I'm not taking any chances."

"Shit! Are those charges set?!"

"Yes. If anyone in work finds out I took them, I'll be in deep shit, Vickie!"

"Nobody's—" Another crack of gunfire. This time from Mike's gun.

"I got one of the fuckers!"

Then Tom's gun.

Mike's.

Tom.

Then, finally, hers called out a report. She noticed them drop in the distance like bowling pins. "They're not stopping!"

"What do you mean?!" Mike asked, loosening off another round.

"Last time they were hesitant when attacking armed individuals..."

"They've got their tails up! Not to mention they have a sheer volume in number – there's more spilling down the mountain behind the first couple of waves," Tom weighed in.

"Oh, fuck. This was a bad idea!" Mike yelled.

"Keep offloading," Vickie cocked her rifle and fired. More shapes fell under the rising sun. "We can always fall back!"

"Think they can swim?" Tom raised his voice over the cracks of gunfire.

"How the hell should I know?!" Vickie bellowed. "I didn't stick around long enough to ask them if they had their one-mile swimming certificate!"

"What are you thinking, Tom?"

"That we could swim across the causeway and douse the water with petrol once we're are on the other side..."

"Good idea!" Vickie said. "*If* they follow us across, we can light the fuckers on fire. Thin their numbers out."

"We need to do something, because we're starting to draw a fucking crowd!" Mike bellowed, loosening off three quick shots. All around them, brass casings glinted as the sun caught them.

When Vickie took another look through her scope, she could make out the faces of the closest Dacchas – they were practically on top of them. Behind, rows and rows had gathered at their comrades' backs.

"Shit, we need to fall back. Now!" she yelled, grabbing two of the three bags.

Tom lowered his gun, shouldered it, and ran after Vickie. "Come on, Mike – we need to get to the other side of the causeway. Now, man!"

"Go on ahead, I'll catch up."

Vickie chanced a look back and saw Mike setting some dynamite by the cars.

He'll never make it...They're on top of him.

When she saw the first of the Dacchas jump on the bonnet of the Daf, Mike was sparking the fuses, which caused the man-eating fuck to stop dead in its tracks.

Fire – it scares them! she thought, watching the thing put its webbed hands up to protect its hideous, three-eyed face. *Fucking freaks of nature...*

She then tripped, falling headfirst into the water that covered the causeway.

"Swim!" Tom yelled, pulling a jerrycan out of one of the backpacks Vickie had dropped in her spill. He emptied the lot into the water before diving in to swim after her.

When Vickie reached the other side, she dragged herself out of the water and gagged at the smell of fuel that was plastered to her saturated clothes. She started to cough before a huge explosion rocked her – clumps of earth and small stones were tossed against her. She fell onto her arse, hard.

She held the tears back and concentrated on Tom, who was halfway across the causeway. Over his shoulder, slightly in the distance, she could see Mike running towards the water. Behind him, bodies lay broken, scattered and burning – one of the Dacchas had been blown into the ashes of the chalets.

On closer inspection, Vickie saw one of the bomb-damaged things crawl along the floor. Its legs were a pulped, mushy red mess.

A robust, nauseating stench of charred flesh permeated to the air.

But the vicious defence tactics didn't stop the swarm of cannibals, as they emerged through the smoke and destruction.

As Vickie snatched glances at them, she aided Tom out of the water.

"Here!" he gasped, putting his lighter in her hand. Before taking a dive into the flooded causeway, he'd had the good sense to wrap the lighter in a small cellophane bag which he'd used to keep his weed in. "Light it up!"

"Hurry up, Mike!" she yelled, as he took to the water. Vickie watched on as the things entered the water behind her friend. They were unafraid of it, which is what she'd hoped for.

When Mike got to Vickie and Tom, they helped him on to dry land.

"Will our guns still fire?!"

"They should do," Tom said, taking aim with his rifle and popping a couple off as Vickie sparked the lighter. When she touched the flame to the water, it erupted into a blaze, which ripped across the water and burned everything in its path.

"Come on, guys – it won't hold them for long!" she said, watching them burn. Some had swum back and were now rolling on the floor, trying in desperation to kill the flames that engulfed their pale bodies.

Their screams, which were more shrieks than anything else, were ear-splittingly sharp. A sound only a wounded animal would make.

"Jesus Christ!"

"Not quite, Mike!" Tom said, unloading round after round on the Dacchas – bodies fell into the hot, fiery, Hell-like pits and caught alight. "Come on, help me. Shoot the fuckers!"

Vickie and Mike joined in, picking off as many as they could.

Then a couple of Dacchas burst from the water. Mike was grabbed by the ankle and ripped off his feet. His finger pulled down his rifle's trigger, which ejected a shell into the air.

"*Argh!*" he screamed. "Get it off—" Before he could finish his sentence, his attacker's head was blown apart like a ripe pumpkin hitting concrete. Bits of bone and flesh were thrown back into the water, along with the defeated man-eater.

"Pull back to the town!" Vickie cried. "They're swimming underneath the flames."

"Let's just get in the car and fuck off!"

"No, Mike – we have to see this through."

"Why, Tom? Because your girlfriend says so?"

"Knock it off!" Vickie said, grabbing her gear and retreating to the town. "You pair can go if you want, but I'm staying!"

"Hey, look…" Tom said, getting close to Vickie. He took her hand in his. "I know how much this means to you, and I told you I would see it through."

The crack of gunfire from Mike's rifle acted as a full stop to Tom's sentence.

"If you two have finished your moment of slush, maybe we can get our fucking arses out of here!"

"Thanks," she told Tom, tightening her grip on his hand. "Let's move on." Looking behind her, Vickie could see a great many of the Dacchas had gathered this side of the causeway. "Maybe we should take cover somewhere – do a bit of defending?"

"Agreed, let's get stepping!" Mike said, rushing off in front of his friends.

After a few minutes of walking, the trio found themselves in the heart of the hamlet – nothing appeared to move from within the ghostly buildings that stood around them.

An old sign groaned.

A window swayed slowly on its hinges.

A can rattled down the deserted road among other debris, which blew wild in the wind. The noise their footsteps made sounded heavy, cumbersome almost.

"Where are we headed?" Mike asked. He turned around and saw they were not being followed. "Looks like we've lost them. For now!"

"What about the shop?" Vickie suggested.

"Where is it, baby?"

"There, Tom," she said, pointing across the street. The men looked in that direction and saw the old building. It appeared to have fared better than the structures around it.

"It doesn't appear to have a broken window, which is good."

"True, Tom. We could board up the lower windows – there must be some wood inside?"

"We could rip the cupboard doors off? Use the tables?"

"Nice thinking, Vickie…" Tom's words trailed off. He heard a noise carried on the wind. It sounded like a voice.

"What is it, Tom?" Vickie asked.

"Shh!" he barked. "Do you hear that?"

They all strained their ears. In the distance, they could hear the approach of the Dacchas – they shuffled their feet, hissed, growled and sniffed out their enemy.

"Fuck, they're getting close!" Mike said. "Quick, inside."

"I didn't mean them… Listen."

"Over here!" came the unknown voice. "*Now!*"

"*Phil*?!" Vickie said, edging closer to the shop.

"Yes! Get over here, now!" the ex-copper said, poking his head out of one of the bottom windows.

"I thought you were…"

"We'll talk when you get in here. Shift your bloody arses!" The cop closed the window as quick and as quietly as possible before disappearing back out of view.

The three friends quickly moved over to the entrance of the shop and went inside. Mike, who was taking up the rearguard, closed the door and fastened it the best he could.

"We're going to need something pressed up against this!" he advised.

"In here!" Phil whispered. "And keep your heads down."

When they walked into the main part of the shop, they saw Phil Drake gathering shelves – he had a hammer and a pot of nails on the counter. "Help me here, lads," he said, taking as many planks over to the windows as he could. "Once these are protected, we can secure the door."

"Best we hurry, because those things are hot on our arses!" Mike said, taking more boards over to Phil. Tom joined in. As the men went about securing the windows, Vickie went back to the door to take a look.

A deadbolt was in place, but it didn't look strong enough – it had rust all over it. "One fierce kick or shove, and that lock's coming off," she muttered. Looking about her, she noticed the boys had left behind one plank of wood, which appeared to be too long for the windows.

Picking it up, she took it over to the door and used it as a prop, with one end of the board placed under the door's handle; the other was rammed against the counter.

"Can you bring the hammer and nails in here?!" she called.

"Here," Tom said, giving her what she wanted.

Taking a few nails from the pot, she hammered them through the 'prop' and into the door. "There, that should hold it," she said, giving it a shake. "Solid as a rock."

"If you say so," Tom said, stepping in to kiss his woman.

"I love you even more for doing this for me, Tom. We could end up dead meat for the Dacchas..."

"Let's not think about that!"

"Right, everybody upstairs," Phil called.

Vickie looked over Tom's shoulder and saw Phil and Mike go through another door. Once they'd disappeared, they could hear footfalls above them.

"Come on," Tom said, taking Vickie's hand. He led her to the back of the shop, where they found a brittle-looking staircase. "Fucking hell, the place looks as though the Munsters own it!"

"In here!" Vickie heard Phil call from one of the rooms to her left at the top of the stairs. Walking in, she saw the old copper reloading the rifle Mike had been using.

"Are your weapons ready to go?" he asked.

"Yes," Tom said. Vickie nodded.

"Good, then get over here with them. This window looks down on the street – we can pick the bastards off from this vantage point."

"Sounds good."

Tom and Vickie took up positions in the windows close to Phil.

"Mike, get the dynamite ready – as we're shooting the bastards, you throw the TNT in amongst their ranks. Help thin them out."

"Phil, what the hell happened to you? I never heard from you. I thought you were—"

"There's no time for explanations now. Look!" he said, pointing out the window. In the near distance, a horde of white-skinned, flesh-eating hill-dwellers poured into the rundown streets.

"Talk about high noon!" Mike muttered.

Phil's rifle broke the silence. "Eat it, you bastards!" he screamed as he violently jerked the bolt back on his gun – a hot piece of brass came flipping out of the chamber. "There's more where that came from."

Vickie and Tom exchanged quick glances before engaging in gunfire.

Even though the Dacchas took an immense amount of casualties in their charge, it didn't stop them. They crashed against the old shop and beat their short arms against the structure, which felt as flimsy as a house of cards.

Glass broke.

Planks from behind the windows downstairs could be heard being pried and pushed.

Some fell to the floor.

"Hit them with the fucking dynamite, Mike!" Phil bellowed, reloading and firing.

When the first stick of TNT was lit, Mike threw it out his open window – it landed towards the back of the pack. Before it detonated, he managed to toss two more sticks of dynamite into their flanks.

"Cut the fuses back, man! They're taking too long to—"

An explosion rocked through the building, followed by a second and third. The sound of splintering wood, breaking glass and obliterating bodies was nothing compared to that of the awful, blood-curdling screams of the Dacchas as they clutched spurting stumps and torn flesh.

"Cease fire!" Phil called.

As the smoke from the dynamite cleared, Vickie poked her head out her window. The street looked like the floor of an overused abattoir – the road ran red. Hunks of Dacchas meat clung to walls, doors, windows and long-abandoned vehicles.

Their numbers had been severely cut.

The able-bodied ones ran back towards the causeway, leaving behind their dead and dying who wailed and screamed in agony. Some of the ones that littered the streets below had shrapnel stuck in their faces and bodies. Others were blown to bits and could quite easily be swept into an empty crisp packet.

"Where the hell are they going?!" she asked, watching the fleeing Dacchas jump into the water.

"I don't think they expected such a loss! Save your bullets. We'll club the wounded to death," Phil said. His face was expressionless.

"No, I couldn't..." she said, trailing off.

"I agree," Mike said. "Although I think bludgeoning is too good for the dirty bastards."

"Tom, are you coming with Mike and me?"

"To finish them off?"

Phil nodded. "Yes."

"No, I'll keep Vickie company."

"But aren't you worried they'll come back?"

"Not at all – they're heading for home. First thing tomorrow, we'll go up the mountain and finish them off!"

Vickie and Tom said nothing, just looked at each other. A deep, choking stench of gun oil and smoke hung in the air between them.

She smiled.

He winked.

"Come on, Mike. We've got a lot of cleaning up to do down there."

"Phil!" Vickie called.

"Yeah?!"

"When you get back, I want to know what happened to you."

He smiled. "Of course. We'll stay here for the night – I don't see any point in moving position," he said. "Whilst we're gone, check our ammo and dynamite situation?"

"Will do," Tom said.

When Mike and Phil were out the door, Tom crawled over to Vickie and held her close to his body. Below them, they could hear the other two crush the skulls of the fallen Dacchas – wet, soggy sounds reverberated off the walls.

"It sounds like raw meat being pulverised with a mallet!" Vickie said, covering her ears and snuggling tighter into Tom's chest.

"Sssh!" Tom said, drawing her closer.

She closed her eyes to try to drown out the sound somehow, but ended up drifting off to sleep – the squelching becoming a hypnotic, snooze-inducing tone as it played out in her darkening background.

Of course, she dreamed of them – the Dacchas, along with her mother, father and brother. Her mind conjured up such terrible images of her and her parents having to watch the flour-coloured monsters as they devoured her brother, along with Mike, Tom and Phil Drake.

The Dacchas danced around massive cauldrons, which bubbled with scalding water. On the surface of the rippling liquid, hunks of meat bobbed and weaved among diced vegetables and bones.

She wanted to run and hide, but there were too many of them pinning her to the floor. When her father tried to wriggle and protest, they slit his throat from ear to ear. Some of his spurting blood found its way into Vickie's screaming mouth.

It tasted of salt and metal.

When they started pulling her father's tongue out through his throat, she awoke, screaming – the room she was in had turned dark. Candlelight kept the shadows at bay.

"Take it easy!" Tom said. He still had his arm around her. "You were just dreaming."

"I can smell the blood..." she whispered, looking down at her hands. "They were ripping them apart. Stuffing their faces with my family..."

"It was just a dream."

"Fuck, Tom. I want to go!"

"Nobody's going anywhere," Phil said. "It's too dangerous out there at night. Besides, those freaks have probably torn your car to shreds by now."

"Phil's right," Tom said. "At first light, we'll get out of here..."

"Yeah, but not before finishing them off once and for all!" Phil interjected. "We've got enough explosives left to cripple their lair – hopefully, with them all inside."

"Maybe we should go sooner than first light?" Mike suggested. "Just to make sure they're all in there."

"First light should be fine," Phil said.

"How do you know where they are?" Vickie wanted to know.

"I stumbled across their new home after I checked all the caves on Blair Long."

"Where?"

"There's another path – it leads around the back of Blair Long, and continues for about a mile. Halfway along, there's another cave, which gets covered by the water when the tide is in."

"You got trapped there?" Tom asked.

Phil nodded. "I did. After going in, I managed to get myself lost in the caves. I was very lucky not to have got myself eaten! By the time I'd made it back to the cave's entrance, the tide was in, cutting off my escape."

"What did you do?!" Vickie asked.

"I kept moving around the cave, which seemed to go on for miles! I found myself a nook, which wasn't too far from the exit, and hid. When the sun rose, I made my way out, but I was detected. In the chase, I lost my gun and bag. Luckily, I managed to lose them and hid here in town."

"You've been here weeks?! How did you survive?"

"I scavenged. Plus, I still had my knife," he said, pointing at the blade on his hip. "I killed game, too."

"Why didn't you just leave at the first opportunity?" Vickie continued with her questioning.

"Because they knew I was here. They kept up patrols – there was no escape. After the explosion you lot caused, that was the first time in weeks I wasn't surrounded."

"You didn't think to take your chance and run after that?"

"No, I decided to stick around – I guessed it may have been people who had caused it. After that, you came here. There's nothing left to do now, except kill every last one of those fuckers!"

After a few more hours of chatting among themselves, the four got their heads down for the night. They knew the day ahead of them would be long, and hard, and they would need all their wits about them if they were to survive the ordeal.

Vickie was the first to wake – the smell of charred bodies still hung heavy in the air, which caused a burning, itchy feel inside her nostrils. Tears formed at the corners of her eyes.

Putting the tip of her thumb and index finger to her eyes, she stemmed the watery flow, sniffed and then rolled onto her side. After she got to her knees, she looked at the others. Mike and Tom were both lightly snoring, but Phil was already awake, keeping vigil at one of the windows.

"Morning," he said, not looking at her. "Sleep okay?" He kept his voice low, measured.

"As well as you'd expect on a hard floor!" she said flippantly. "How long have you been there?"

"Couple of hours. They returned…"

"*What*?!" she gasped, almost choking on her words. "And you never thought to wake…"

"Relax, there was no need – only a handful came, if that."

"What did they want?" Her voice rose and cracked. "What did they *do*?!"

"Nothing. They just sifted through the bodies and checked on us. They're probably planning another attack, but we will hit them first. Wake the others – I'm heading down with the gear," Phil said, grabbing his rifle and holdall.

She went to speak, but decided against it. Instead, she awoke Tom, and then Mike – both lads yawned loudly and stretched. Before averting her eyes, she noticed Tom had morning wood.

When Mike stood, he let out a fart as he scratched his privates and stretched some more. "Where's Phil?" he asked, yawning again.

"He's already gone downstairs – he's waiting for us."

Mike nodded, grabbed his stuff and moved out the door.

Tom and Vickie were a few seconds behind him.

Once they'd regrouped outside, they didn't bother sticking around long enough to inhale the God-awful stench that drifted over the town like a dark cloud. Instead, they moved back to the causeway where they crossed it and made their way up to Blair Long.

Vickie had half-expected an attack, but none came. They had more than dented the Dacchas' numbers; they were now like a wounded animal. Wounded and trapped in a corner.

Had the hunter become the hunted?

She didn't think so because now, they were heading into the home of the Dacchas – the white-skinned devils that guarded the hills of Invercurie, and they would fight to the death.

Good, she thought. *They are all going to pay for what they did.*

"How much further, Phil?" Mike panted, while holding his side.

"Not far," Phil called back over his shoulder. "Not another word, because I'm pretty sure those disgusting freaks have good hearing. Keep your eyes peeled."

Vickie had taken up the position of rearguard, with Tom a good ten to fifteen paces in front of her. In front of him was Mike, who was much further ahead again and practically nipping at Phil's heel.

When they reached the top of Blair Long, the caves came into sight.

"That's where they used to dwell," Phil told Vickie, keeping his voice low.

"That's where Jamie died..." she said to herself, but it didn't stop Phil from responding.

"Correct. I think we should detonate these caves too, just in case."

"I can make a start on that," Tom said. "I can't see a danger, especially if these caves have been abandoned. It'll save us time, too."

"Good idea," Phil said. "Try to go as deep as you can."

Tom looked at his watch. "Back here in two hours?"

Phil shook his head. "Make it three, just in case. But don't blow them until we get back here, got it?"

Tom nodded.

"Please, be careful! I'd like to have your children one day..." Vickie told him.

Tom took her hand in his. "That's news to me." He beamed. Before she could respond, he spoke again. "I'll be okay, promise." Within minutes, Tom disappeared into the nearest cave – his backpack in one hand, his rifle in the other.

"Don't panic, he'll be fine – those caves are long deserted," Phil said.

"Then why suggest blowing them up?!" she demanded.

"So they won't have a home to retreat to..." He let his words trail off. "Come on, let's get moving."

Once around the corner from where they'd said goodbye to Tom, it took Vickie and the others roughly forty minutes to get to the Dacchas' new home, which overlooked the sea – wild waves crashed against the bluffs below.

"Right, I'm going in first!" Phil stated. "I want you right behind me, Vickie. Mike, take up the rear. Once I feel we're in far enough, Mike and I will set as many explosives as possible. I want you to keep watch as we do so, Vickie. Okay?"

She nodded, seeing no point in trying to argue with the man, as he clearly had a plan.

"Do you think we'll encounter much resistance?" Mike asked, looking at the lightening sky.

"Hopefully we'll catch them napping, but there may be a few stray guards. They're bound to be on alert after yesterday."

"Agreed," Vickie said.

"Here, take these," Phil said, removing a pair of hunting knives from his backpack. "If you do see any, try and take them silently."

The others nodded in unison.

"Come on, let's get it over with!"

Without warning, Phil dashed into the cave ahead of him – he had a weak torch in his free hand, just like Mike did at the rear.

As Vickie walked the long, dark and damp passageway, which was rough and stabbing at her soles, she couldn't help but feel this was her last day on earth. That this was her end. Her fate had been sealed and she was going to check out in the same fashion as her brother.

No! I won't allow it. They are all going to fucking die for what they did.

They crept through the caves as quietly as possible. Now and then, they encountered a sleeping Dacchas. When they did, they slashed its throat where it slumbered.

They only came across one alert guard, which was duly bludgeoned by the butt of Phil's gun.

After walking for what felt like a week, Phil finally brought them to a halt.

"Right, this is perfect. We must be a good mile, mile-and-a-half in. We have enough explosives to bring the whole fucking thing down. There's some diesel in one of the bags, too. Vickie, start throwing it around the place as Mike and I get to work."

"Okay," she said, grabbing what she needed. The jerrycan was half-full, and so she worked on emptying it. The splashing of the flammable liquid was almost deafening, but she didn't stop. She just wanted it over with.

After ten minutes of prepping to bring the rocky home to its knees, they retreated up the passageway, with Phil holding a detonator. When the opening of the cave came into sight, Phil started shouting and yelling.

"What the hell are you doing?!" Vickie asked.

"Waking the sons-of-bitches up! The more that follow our echoes, the better. Yell!" he demanded.

And so Mike and Vickie did. They all stood still and shouted and cursed until they could hear an approach deep within the cave.

"Go!" Phil yelled.

As they made it outside, Phil detonated the explosives.

The thunderous blast almost burst their eardrums – a fireball came hurtling up out of the cave to meet them. Rocks cracked and crashed as the cave collapsed in on itself. The Dacchas screamed and screeched from within the rubble, flames and smoke.

Vickie, Phil and Mike didn't hang around long enough to see the whole hideout go crashing down. Instead, they ran back to where they had left Tom, who was waiting for their return outside his cave.

"Jesus, it sounds like you lot did a number on them back there!" he said, greeting them.

"Did you get all your explosives set?!" Phil yelled.

Tom nodded, offering his remote detonator to the ex-cop.

Vickie watched as Phil took the device in his hand. But before he could thumb the button down – which would blast the shit out of the cave – something unexpected happened, which took the wind from Vickie.

"What the hell?!" Phil said looking at the three huge figures emerging from the cave.

"*Jamie*?" Vickie said, watching as her naked brother walked towards them.

"Your *brother*?" Phil said, not taking his eyes off the huge men that stalked towards them. "It can't be – he's dead!"

Jamie stopped, which in turn caused his two goons to halt at his side.

"Well, I never thought I'd see you again," Jamie said.

Vickie went to run to him, to hold him, but Tom held her back. "Don't!"

"He's my brother…"

"No," Phil said. "He's changed."

"I see you've destroyed my people. My family," Jamie said.

"I'm your family! Mum, dad…"

"Please, mum and dad left me for dead. My people never harmed me. They took me in. Fed me, looked after me. When I was old and strong enough, I bred with them. In time, I became the one they looked up to. These are my sons," he said, pointing at the pair of half-breeds either side of him. They were monstrous in size, with a half-Dacchas, half-human look – their skin was deathly white, but they didn't have webbed fingers or stubby limbs. Their eyes, however, which were set deep inside their heads and burned red, looked ungodly.

"You can still be with me, Vickie," Jamie said, putting his hand out to her. "But the others must die!"

"No!" she sobbed.

"See you in hell!" Phil said, raising his gun. Mike followed suit.

"Don't!" she yelled, distracting the men.

This gave Jamie's offspring the upper hand, enabling them to grab the guns off Mike and Phil. Tom and Vickie watched on aghast as one of the burly Dacchas crushed Mike's head between its massive hands like a grape. His left eyeball popped out and blood gushed from his one good eye, nose and mouth. His final few screams were wet, high-pitched horrors.

Mike's killer then joined its sibling and helped in the tearing apart of Phil. Together they pinned him to the floor and ripped his stomach open, using their bare hands to punch through his flesh and tear the guts and organs from within him.

"Choke on 'em!" Phil screamed as they watched the Dacchas fill their faces with offal and blood. The slurping, sucking and squelching sounds caused Vickie's guts to flip-flop.

"Bastards!" Tom yelled, going for one of the dropped guns. He managed to get one shot off – his bullet caught one of Jamie's sons square between the eyes before the other one was on top of him, ripping, pulling, yanking, munching, chewing, slurping, devouring, licking, and sucking…

Then she did throw up.

The contents of her guts splashed against the rocks around her feet.

Some of her waste managed to get into her shoes and between her toes.

Jaime stepped forward and grabbed her by her hair.

All she could do was scream and kick as hot tears cut clear paths down her dirt-encrusted cheeks. He pulled her off her feet and hauled her towards the cave he had emerged from.

"Now that you've killed all my family, we shall have to start again!" he sneered.

As he took her deep down into the cave, all that could be heard was her loud shrieks, until it was replaced by the calming, crashing sound of waves.

Filial Cannibalism

Carla grunted with effort as she pulled the cork from the expensive bottle of red – the stopper made a satisfying *thunk* sound as it came free of its tight slot. She then threw the corkscrew with the skewered cork on its metal coil to one side before lifting the now breathing container to her nose. She inhaled deeply. The fruity fumes whizzed up her nostrils and engulfed her brain – the portent stench made her eyes water.

"*Phew*! Must have been a good year," she joked, putting the bottle back on the kitchen counter in front of her. "I do like a glass of red whilst cooking. Not that I'm a connoisseur, mind. Still… It's a special occasion!"

She smiled, then looked over at her hosts – mummy and daddy dearest were out cold, gagged and tied to their dinning room chairs, their chins resting on their chests.

"I do hope they don't end up wrinkling their fine clothes!" She tittered, almost filling her large glass to its brim with the fine wine. "Well, I can't start dinner until they're conscious – I wouldn't want them missing the unbeatable spectacle I have in store! Well, he can remain cold for now, but she *must* be awake for it."

The oven had now warmed and was waiting, the skillet and ingredients for her grand meal poised. The main elements, however, were yet to be fully prepped.

Carla looked down at the bruised and bloodied brats, now silent from being thrashed unconscious. The twin baby girls were less than seven months old, and oh, how they had screamed, cried and bobbed their little tongues whilst throwing their tantrums at being beat by her fist, bottle and everything else that had come to hand.

We could have had this... she thought, looking up at her host. *Could have been a happy family... But no, I wasn't skinny enough – I couldn't put my legs behind my head like Little Miss Bendy Hips!* Carla directed her gaze in the direction of her hostess. *The bitch thinks she's something cunting special by being a yoga instructor by day and a pro skirt by night. Fucking whore. No, not a pro skirt – a home-wrecking cunt!*

"He was *mine!*" she screamed, kicking the babies, causing them to grunt and whinge in their comatose state. "Good, then you little fucking shits are still alive!" She gave the hostess another look, eyeing the woman's extended belly. "Not enough that you already have two! Well, that will be another life snuffed out here today..." With one last burst of rage, she gave the babies another blast with her foot – they wailed with a bit more heart this time, suggesting they were coming out of their unconscious state. She smiled. *Excellent!* At first, Carla had panicked she'd beaten the infants to death in her rage, but that had all but washed away with their pitiful tears.

"It's possible they're brain-damaged," she uttered, looking at their battered, puffy faces – their eyes were barely visible beneath their inflamed folds of puppy-fat-like skin. "*Meh.*" She shrugged. "It isn't like it's going to matter if they're retarded or not. They'll be dead before the next couple of hours are out!"

After beating the children into their cabbage-like states, Carla had stripped them of their posh, highfalutin' clothes, accessories and nappies. The various articles had then been fed to the open fire before she'd sat down to start on her special sauce ahead of tonight's meal.

The sauce, containing a mixture of spices and condiments, had one vital ingredient: honey juice, which was extracted from her honey pot. *And there's nothing better than child abuse to get my honey churning*! she thought.

So, after dishing out some brute force to the little darlings, Carla had sat in a comfy chair, hiked her skirt up around her waist, pulled her lace knickers to one side, and then proceeded to rub her pussy until she'd squirted a mixture of honey and piss into a mixing bowl – she'd strummed her cunt to the sight of the babies' smashed, yellow-purple faces, crushed, minuscule noses and split, blood-encrusted lips. Their small bodies were black, blue, and consisted of cuts and weeping wounds.

"If you're going to cook traditional Welsh faggots, you need to make sure they have that extra bit of zip! Besides, they were *his* favourite at one time."

Since she'd lost her husband, her only God-honest cock to fuck and ride hard into a multi-orgasmic oblivion, to Little Miss Bendy Hips, Carla had had to rely mostly on her fingers or a wide selection of black rubber dicks that vibrated, spun and petted her pussy nub.

"She's welcome to the cheating bastard! No man walks out on me. No man!" she screamed at the unconscious couple. She walked up to the hostess, wrapped her hand around the woman's long black hair and yanked her head back. "We were doing well until you came along two years ago, you meddling fuckstick! Well, now I'm going to carve your happy little home up." Carla then moved her face close to 'Little Miss Bendy Hips'. "When he called me crazy, I guess he was right! And no restraining order was going to keep me at bay!"

She spat in the woman's face and moved over to the host. Carla gave her ex-lover a hard crack across his cheek, but he didn't stir. She put her hand through his hair and felt the weeping lump at the back of his head. "I bet that hurt, didn't it? Poor baby!" she mocked, pursing her lips and then licking his face. "Dean, you didn't think I was going to just let you walk out of my life and raise a happy little family, did you? Fucking clown. I was just biding my time – waiting for my opportunity to strike back and get my vengeance. They say revenge is a dish best served cold..." Carla looked over at the babies. "This will be hot! *Piping* hot!" She laughed at her little inside joke.

Carla moved back to the kitchen counter, scooped the babies up and dumped them in the sink. Their tiny heads made sickening smacks against the aluminium as they connected with the bottom of the basin. She then pulled open a drawer close to hand and looked inside. It was filled with a few implements she had been hoping to find: meat-pounding mallet, rolling pin, piping bags, knives, skewers, cleaver...

"All the tools of the trade!" she screeched, and then grinned like a crazy who had slipped her straitjacket. Her hands rustling around inside the drawer must have disturbed her hostess, as she was now groaning.

Carla looked up just as Little Miss Bendy Hips' eyelids opened – their eyes homed in on each other, and fused together in a mix of rage, fear and pleading. The woman started to thrash madly in her chair, sending her hair into a whipping frenzy. When she tried nudging Dean with her shoulder to no avail, Carla laughed.

"It's no use, ya dumb fuck! You'll never get loose, or wake him – I think I may have killed him when I smacked him with that frying pan. Whoops!" she said, shrugging her shoulders and raising her hands. "How's your head, by the way? I gave you a fair old whack. *Meh*, they say women are the stronger of the species."

Carla turned the sink's taps on and washed her hands as Bendy Hips continued to moan, rage and fight, only adding to Carla's amusement. Once her hands were dry, she proceeded in holding up the babies for Bendy Hips to see.

"I hope you're hungry!" she said with a playful tone. The sight of the battered babies was enough to set the woman off screaming and thrashing again. At one point, Carla was worried the woman would actually snap the ropes keeping her body, wrists and ankles strapped to the heavy oak chair.

But no. She soon became exhausted and flopped in her chair – tears streamed down her bright red cheeks.

"There, there," Carla said. "This horrible ordeal will soon be all over. And then you'll have learned your lesson, won't you? Never rub another woman's rhubarb!" She then placed the babies on the chopping block in front of her, grabbed the mallet from out of the drawer, raised it above her head, and brought it crashing down on the first baby's head.

When she retracted the mallet, baby brains, skin and flesh were whipped over her shoulder – the gore splashed one of the higher kitchen cabinets. But Carla didn't stop the butchering until the tiny skull was completely smashed open like an oozing egg. She then placed her hand inside split cranium and scooped out what was left of the baby's brain, which she dumped into the blender close by.

The atrocity had clearly irked the dead baby's sibling, as she started screaming until Carla thought her eardrums were going to burst. She hadn't planned on killing the second so fast, but she knew she could never prepare dinner with a screaming child.

So, she was forced to pick up the hammer once more.

"Tut! Look at the state of it," she uttered, staring at the crimson-coated metal – clumps of flesh and fine hair clung to the blood. "Well, I can't use that!" Carla tossed the hammer to one side and picked out the rolling pin from the drawer. Before using it, she inspected it. "Yep, seems fine."

She then proceeded to batter the skull of the second infant until her ears were filled by the sound of wet, sloppy smacks. Blood spattered her face, hair and evening dress, not that she cared.

She added the remainder of the second brain to the blender.

"Ah, that's better!" she exclaimed, looking up at Little Miss Bendy Hips – her eyes were filled with tears, which shimmered before falling. "Couldn't have been an easy thing for you to witness! To think, all this could have been avoided. Still, it's over now."

Little Miss Bendy Hips started another rampant outburst, but her words were muffled.

"Whatever you're trying to say or call me, it doesn't sound pleasant!" Carla admitted, chuckling.

She then started to hum "Whistle Whilst You Work" as she rooted through the same drawer for a good knife to take to the babies' bellies. Once she had a hold of what she needed, Carla dragged the first infant out of the blood-filled sink and stripped the flesh from its little fat belly.

The strips were then placed aside. She sliced the small trunk open and pulled the remaining organs out and placed them in the blender with the livers. All the while, Little Miss Bendy Hips screamed, cried, thrashed and tried her best to nudge Dean awake.

With the first baby skinned and gutted, she took the cleaver to it and chopped its arms and legs off before disposing of it all into a black bag. Carla then moved on to the second baby – she repeated the process until she'd stripped it of all its good bits.

"*There!*" She knotted the black bags and threw them into a bin. "I'll dispose of them later. Time to make my bacon and onion gravy – you're going to love it, Bendy. Just wait and see."

The blender was set to slow, giving her time to unblock the sink of bone fragment, skin and hair, which allowed all the blood and water to drain. Carla then disinfected the worktops, scrubbed all the utensils she'd used, and popped them back into the drawer. By the time she was done, the kitchen was gleaming.

"I hate cooking in a messy kitchen!"

When the offal had finished blending, she turned her attention to the skillet and filled it with the strips of belly before adding thirty grams of salt, thirty grams of sugar, ten grams of various dried herbs and spices and just zero-point-two-five grams of saltpetre.

Carla then rubbed it all into the meat before setting it to cook and adding her honey mix. Happy with how the bacon was coming along, she started her onion gravy.

Forty minutes later, with the gravy ready and the bacon waiting to be used, Carla set about putting her faggots together.

Dean was still unconscious, much to her annoyance.

I couldn't wait much longer! she thought.

Bendy Hips did nothing but glare, her energy spent from all her useless thrashing and crying.

A smile emerged on her face as she kept her concentration on the task at hand. She added the baby organs, breadcrumbs, milk, nutmeg, salt, and pepper to her bacon mixture and mashed it gently to combine it all into eight four-ounce balls. Carla then placed them on a large baking dish and added what was left of her wine.

As it cooked, she basted it occasionally with the pan juices until it was done.

Roughly twenty-five minutes later, the feast was ready to be served with her onion gravy.

Now, she knew her hosts were not going to eat, so Carla removed the piping bags from the drawer. Before filling them, however, she wanted the food to cool somewhat just in case the heat caused the thin bags to melt.

And she didn't want all her hard work to go to waste.

Hmm, what to do whilst I wait...? she thought, tapping a finger against her chin. And then her eyes fell on the skewer. "Aha!" After snatching up the large, spear-like item, Carla walked over to Little Miss Bendy Hips, who was snorting, glaring and shaking her head wildly. "There, there," she soothed, stroking the woman's face. "Food will be served shortly!"

She played the skewer in front of the woman's face for a few seconds, teasing her as she thrust the metal prongs close to her eyes.

"*Argh-ughh-umph!*" Bendy Hips screeched beneath her gag.

"What's that? Am I going to let you have a say? Hell no, bitch! You're going out the way you came into this world – kicking and fucking screaming. Cunt!" Carla spat in the woman's face before backhanding her. The vicious blow caused Bendy's head to snap back on its slender plinth. "Only whores wear these!" she yelled, yanking the woman's silk choker from around her throat.

Before heading back to the kitchen, Carla stepped over to Dean and gave him a few light slaps on his face.

Nothing.

He was out cold.

"Well, this might work!" she said, raising the pronged implement and ramming it into the man's crotch area.

Blood spurted into her face, causing her to titter. Dean sat bolt upright in his chair. He screamed beneath his gag so loud and strong that his neck turned a bright shade of red mixed with purple. Tears rolled down his face as he squeezed his eyes shut and tried to embrace the pain.

When he opened his eyes, Carla stared at him with a smile on her face.

He looked panicked.

"Hi, lover!" she said, twisting the prongs in a gentle manner, extracting more yells and whimpers from him. "Okay, enough of this torture shit – I'm better than that."

Carla filled the piping bags with her special Welsh faggots before pouring in the gravy and drowning them – the smell caused her to smack her lips together and her stomach to growl.

"Think I'll try some!"

She placed the bag's nozzle to her lips and pumped until her mouth was full. Some of the gravy flowed over her lips and drizzled down her chin and neck, and slipped between the crevice of her tits.

"Mm! That's tongue-smacking good!" she exclaimed, pulling the bag from her mouth. As she walked towards Bendy, an explosion of vomit erupted from the woman but was blocked by the gag. The strong-smelling spew found its way over, under and around the restraint, and splashed onto the woman's lap.

Carla ripped her gag off, then rammed the nozzle of the piping bag into her mouth and pumped. She didn't stop until the woman gagged and retched. She slipped the nozzle free and looked into the woman's eyes as she jammed the skewer into her baby bump and twisted it before retracting it to stab again and again.

Gravy mixed with lumps of mulched baby and onions exploded out of her mouth and ran down her chops as blood tangled with piss, shot down her legs and exploded onto the carpet.

"See you in hell, Bendy!"

"Argh! My baby!" she screamed when her throat was finally free.

Carla then poked both the woman's eyes, which popped like water balloons, sending yet more goo onto her lap. As she flopped in her chair, Carla moved on to Dean.

By the time she removed his gag, Bendy was dead.

"Please, you don't have to do this! Think of our children, Carla..."

"Oh, but I have thought of our little darlings, Dean!" she said, raising the piping bag. "If I couldn't have my babies in my car, you and that fucking whore weren't having them either! And no court was going to stop me from exacting my revenge, husband!"

"My God, what have you done?!"

She didn't give him another word; instead, she shoved the nozzle to the piping bag in his mouth and uttered in his ear, "'Why, there they are both, baked in that pie; whereof their mother daintily hath fed, eating the flesh that she herself hath bred. 'Tis true, 'tis true; witness my knife's sharp point.'"

Carla then pumped, and pumped and pumped until Dean's cheeks exploded.

FAGGOTS (WELSH-STYLE PORK MEATBALLS) WITH ONION GRAVY

The <u>Cwmcerrig Farm Shop</u> in Wales serves these hearty liver-enriched pork meatballs doused in a buttery onion gravy. The name derives from the old northern British term for uncased sausage.

For the Gravy
4 tbsp. unsalted butter
1 large yellow onion, thinly sliced
1 tbsp. flour
2 cups beef stock
$\frac{1}{3}$ cup madeira wine
$\frac{1}{2}$ tsp. Worcestershire sauce
Kosher salt and freshly
 ground black pepper, to taste

For the Meatballs
10 slices baby belly, finely chopped
1 tbsp. finely chopped sage
1 $\frac{1}{2}$ tsp. finely chopped thyme
1 small yellow onion, finely chopped
Kosher salt and freshly ground black pepper, to taste
1 lb. ground pork
4 oz. baby liver, finely chopped
1 $\frac{1}{2}$ cups breadcrumbs
$\frac{1}{2}$ cup milk
$\frac{1}{4}$ tsp. freshly grated nutmeg
$\frac{1}{2}$ cup dry white wine

Magic Beans
By
Sue Pass and David Owain Hughes

Jack opened her eyes and squinted. She had a sour taste in her mouth and her limbs felt as though she had taken a severe pummelling. *That was some trip,* she thought, pushing aside her regrets at the inevitable crash. Feeling horny, Jack rolled over and reached out for Dave. It was a sure-fire way to banish any post-trip low.

Instead of wrapping around a fat cock, Jack's fingers tangled in the cooling sheets. Where was Dave? He had been next to her last night. Not just next to her but on top and underneath. Poor guy had all but collapsed after she was finished with him. She smiled as she recalled the drug-fuelled sex. This new stuff that had hit the streets was amazing. Magic Beans. They looked like regular jellybeans, but these were seriously fucked up, causing the most vivid hallucinations she had ever experienced. The increased sensitivity accompanying the high meant they were having the most intense sex they had ever known.

Jack slammed her hand onto the empty space. Where the hell had he gone when she needed him? It was no good – a girl has needs. What the hell, she could always rely on herself. She withdrew her hand and started to stroke her breasts, pinching and teasing her nipples until they stood proud. Her touch sent shock waves across her skin to the sensitive place between her thighs. Moaning, she let her other hand wander lower, skimming across her flat stomach until she felt the slick, soft folds of her pussy. "Oh, yes," she mumbled, letting her fingers stroke and probe deeper. "Dave, if only you could see what you're missing." Jack's fingers plunged deeper. She rocked her hips as she imagined her latest boyfriend lying between her legs.

Bang! Bang! Bang! The bedroom door shook as a fist of iron pounded it. Jack's fingers slipped out from her and she sat up, frustrated at missing out on a morning orgasm. "What the hell do you want?" she yelled.

A disembodied voice rang back, "Are you getting out of bed yet? Jesus, Jackie, I swear you get lazier every day."

"For God's sake Mum, give it a rest. I had a late night."

"Don't think I don't know that. You and your good for nothing boyfriend kept me awake half the night."

Jack smiled at the thought of her mother listening to her and Dave screwing. *It must have been decades since the old bint had a good shag*, she thought.

"When are you getting up?" her mother continued. "If your father was still around, you'd have been out first thing looking for a job, not lying in bed sponging off your poor mother."

"Don't nag. I'm getting up." Jack pulled a face at the closed door. "Is Dave out there with you?"

"He went off with some men earlier."

Jack grabbed her bathrobe and shuffled to the door. She pulled it open and faced her mother. "What men?"

"How the hell should I know? Some of your dodgy friends, probably. You been getting up to your old tricks?"

"Get lost." She pushed past the old woman. "Did he say where he was going?"

"Don't be cheeky, girl. They left in a hurry. Didn't say where they were going. Oh…" She paused and rummaged in the pocket of the floral apron she insisted on wearing when doing the housework. "One of the men said I should give you this. Said it was important." She pulled out a crumpled envelope and handed it to her daughter.

Jack took the envelope in her sticky fingers and tore it open. She pulled out a sheet of black-edged paper bearing the logo of a brown cow cracking a whip. A wave of iciness engulfed her before she even started to read the hand-printed words.

"What's up, Jackie? You've gone as white as a sheet."

Jack ignored her mother and retreated to her bedroom, slamming the door behind her. She was vaguely aware of her mother shouting admonishments, but she paid no attention. She flopped onto the edge of her bed and forced herself to read the words that were already beginning to blur as tears leaked from her eyes.

The handwriting was strong and bold, just like the man who had wielded the pen. The words chilled her core. She reread them three times before they made sense.

I have your boyfriend. If you want him returned in one piece you'll hand over the money you owe me by midnight. If your debts aren't paid in full by then, he's going to be riding the cow in my club. The Giant.

Jack rubbed her tears away, aware of her own scent. How could she have been so stupid? The Magic Beans were amazing, but they weren't worth this. She'd never forgive herself if anything happened to Dave. Everyone had warned her not to deal with the Giant, but she had thought that she could handle him. Shit, if only she had sold the goods instead of using them herself. But they had been so good. Jack glanced at the plastic bag on top of her bedside table; there were perhaps half-a-dozen Magic Beans left. Even if she sold them, it wouldn't come close to what she owed the Giant.

Jack took a deep breath and made a decision. If she couldn't pay the Giant she was going to have to rescue Dave herself...

*

Rion "The Giant" Phipps, or Giant for short, owned and ran The Whip and Cow – a seedy, down-a-side-alley joint that every scum-sucking bozo from Tipperary to Timbuk-fucking-tu knew of. From within the confines of the sordid, overpriced fuck-station, the Giant operated a sex, drugs and arms trade.

The tall, fat fuck was rolling in money so soaked in blood that it had to go through three cleaners before it was usable.

But the Giant didn't care. He had the police and city officials in his back pocket. Hell, even the prime minister and chief of police were regulars at his club – they loved nothing more than being dressed in stockings and panties, whilst being whipped, abused and called faggot, sissy, slave or Nancy.

The Cow was the place to be seen. Even though there were illegalities going on behind-the-scenes, front of shop was a legal sex business – a joint where men of all ages, size and dick length could go to get abused, abuse or to indulge in any sick fantasy they wanted.

"I have the cleanest whores in town!" the Giant regularly boasted.

He was on top of the world. Had been for decades; nothing moved in the city, let alone The Cow, without his say-so.

The seven-foot-eight beast of a man feared nobody and life was good. Too good. Ever since the men running his drug lab had invented the hot new drug Magic Bean, the Giant's existence had become that extra bit comfortable.

No fucker is going to take the power away from me, he thought. On hearing soft moans behind him, he swivelled in his chair and faced the commotion. A smile spread across his face.

"Dave, Dave, Dave…" the Giant said, looking at the man on his office floor. The position Dave was in was an awkward one, not to mention humiliating and painful. He'd been placed on his knees and elbows, and then locked in old-fashioned stocks; his chin almost connected with the ground. His arse was skyward. It glowed like a beacon. His cock and balls, whilst not being abused by the Giant's imps, were shrivelled out of sight.

A truncheon had been imbedded in his arse – a ball-gag graced his mouth, meaning he could only grunt and groan.

His cock looks as though it's playing hide-and-go-peep, the Giant mused.

Being restrained meant Dave couldn't use a toilet – he'd been left to piss and shit himself. His waste mingled with dried jism about his knees – strings of it dangled from his shrunken bell-end.

The smell was intense.

I'm glad we're in the middle of winter, not Summer...

"*Ugh...*" Dave moaned. Saliva dribbled around the ball jutting from his mouth, slid down his chin and patted on the floor. Fresh tears rolled down his cheeks.

"I'm sorry I have to treat you this way, friend," the Giant said, getting out of his chair. He grabbed the big, eleven-inch black dildo off his desk. He walloped his open hand with it repeatedly as he walked around his desk. "But your pretty little Jackie, with her thick thighs and pigtails, owes me a lot of green. Green she won't be able to find, I dare say. I may have to fuck my money's worth out of her!"

Dave raged. He thrashed and bucked as much as he could, causing the police baton to waggle like a mother wiggling her finger at her naughty child.

From where he stood, the Giant could see trails of dried blood on Dave's backside.

Ooph, the imps can be rough when they want to be! Smiling, whilst continuing to belt his open hand with the massive rubber cock, the Giant bent in front of Dave and grabbed his face. The feel of his prisoner's rough, unkempt chin aggravated his palm.

Forcing Dave's head backwards, the Giant heard the man's neck crick as he looked into his eyes.

"Not to worry, though, *Dave*! I'll be quite happy to keep you around for my imps. I'm sure they'll happily abuse you until their cocks ring out with pain. Once they are bored, finished with you, I'll cut you into minuscule pieces and feed you to my pigs. Oh, how they have grown accustomed to human flesh, my pretty!"

As rough as he could, the Giant pushed Dave's head to one side, causing his neck to click again.

"*Argh!*" Dave groaned.

"Should I remove the baton?" The Giant smiled. "Then again, you look more than comfortable!" He wiggled the stick, causing Dave to cry some more.

Standing, the Giant looked at his watch. *She has plenty of time yet...*

Going back to his office chair, the Giant looked out his office window. The streets below were filled with dirty whores, junkies, flunkies, mules, and small-time gangsters with muscle around them that had seen too many Stallone movies and dirty coppers.

The high jinks of city life caused him to guffaw.

What a filthy, steaming, fucked-up cesspit – I love it. I love stirring it with my giant spoon!

*

Jack stared at her face in the mirror, her pale skin bruised from the smeared remains of yesterday's mascara. She didn't like what she saw. She looked fragile, weak, and that was not who she was. *Come on girl, you're going to have to do better than this,* she chastised herself.

Jack headed for the shower. She turned the temperature as high as she could bear, letting the scalding water strip away any doubts she had of getting Dave back safely. She dried herself and dressed her five-foot-two frame in skinny jeans and vest top and set about applying her make-up. She layered on mascara and drew thick lines of black eyeliner around her eyes. She finished with a slick of scarlet lipstick. Regarding herself again in the mirror, Jack was pleased. *A warrior needs her war paint.* Shrugging on her leather biker jacket, she grabbed the remaining Beans and left. Her mother's yells faded as she raced away. It was time to raise an army and she knew just the person to help her.

Twenty minutes later, Jack was heading into a rundown street in an area of the city earmarked for demolition. She stopped outside a mid-terraced house with boarded windows. The letter S was daubed on the door in red paint. This was the place she was looking for.

Jack pushed the door. It was stiff but gave way. She walked into a gloomy room that reeked of stale fags and sweaty bodies.

A deep voice called, "Stay right there." A dark form loomed from the corner and made its way towards her. "What do you want?"

"It's me. Jack."

The figure drew closer. "So it is. What are you doing here?"

"Is he here? I need to see him." Jack saw the man clearly now. His face was scarred and his nose had been broken numerous times. He was huge. Pure muscle.

"Go on up. I'm sure he'll be delighted to see you."

Jack walked through the darkness to the staircase in the corner and climbed. It was lighter upstairs. The windows were un-boarded, letting the winter sun in.

A tall, rangy man slouched on a chair next to a battered desk. He was counting through wads of notes and bagging them. He looked up as Jack approached. "Jack!" His voice was a mix of surprise and delight. "You're looking good. What brings you?"

"Hi, Stilts," Jack greeted her former fuck buddy. "I'm in some trouble. Think you can help me?"

Stilts rose from his chair. He had a rumpled appearance that Jack found endearing. "Tell me about it, Jack."

"I owe someone money. A lot of money. He's got Dave. If I don't pay by midnight…"

Stilts walked over to Jack and lifted her chin to look at him. "How can I help?"

Jack's eyes flitted towards the mountain of cash Stilts had been counting. "Well, if you could lend me the money to pay him off."

"No fucking way, sweetheart. I've got my own expenses. Anything else?"

She sighed. "Any chance a few of your guys could help me get Dave back? I need some muscle to back me."

"Now that I can help with." Stilts smiled. "But what's in it for me?"

"What do you want?"

Stilts' smile split into a huge grin. "Do you really need to ask? I can see you're wearing that red lipstick and you know what that does to me."

"What? Now? Then you'll help me?"

"Consider it a first instalment. We'll sort out the details later." Stilts took hold of Jack's hand and pulled her towards his chair. He sat down, reached his hands behind his head and nodded for her to kneel.

Jack hesitated, then knelt on the hard floor before Stilts. She wasn't surprised by his demand. It was one of the reasons she had chosen the red lipstick - Stilts could never resist it. She reached out and unbuckled his belt. His cock stretched the seam of his jeans, begging to be released. Jack unzipped his fly and reached inside. Stilts never wore underwear, so her fingers immediately coiled around his iron-hard cock and pulled it towards her. Stilts groaned at her touch and pushed himself back in the chair.

Looking up, Jack began to stroke her fingers the length of his shaft, watching his reaction to her touch. When she saw his eyes close she moved in closer. The familiar scents of Stilts' musk and habit of wearing the same jeans for several days filled her nose. Jack parted her lips and started to lick his long cock from root to crown, tracing the thick cord of vein. She was aware of

Stilts' soft moans as she flicked and licked, feeling him twitch beneath her tongue. Jack opened her mouth wider and engulfed his swollen head.

Stilts thrust his hips, grunting. Jack felt him strike the back of her throat and she almost gagged. He felt like stone encased in a thin layer of skin as he continued to buck his hips and batter her throat. She pulled back only to be halted by Stilts' hands twisting in her hair, restraining her. She wanted to be done as quickly as possible - she had forgotten how poor his personal hygiene could be.

Jack grabbed the base of his cock and pumped her hand up and down, simultaneously sucking and circling her tongue around his engorged head.

Stilts' grunting became more frequent, and his plunging faster and deeper. Jack had to hold him back with her free hand to stop him from choking her. Then with a final grunt and thrust he squirted hot, thick cum into her throat. She swallowed but more followed. *Shit, how long is it since he last had a fuck?* she thought. Jack sat back and wiped her mouth on the back of her hand: strings of cum mingled with scarlet lipstick. She wanted a drink to take his taste away.

Stilts relaxed in his chair. A grin spread across his sweating face as he adjusted himself and zipped his fly. "Fucking hell, Jack. I'd forgotten just how sweet that mouth of yours can be."

"So do we still have a deal?"

"Damn right. Fill me in on the details."

Jack pulled out the bag of remaining beans from her pocket and placed them on the desk. Stilts stared at the bag. His smile disappeared.

"Are those what I think they are?" He sniffed nervously.

Jack nodded.

"You get these from the Giant? Is he the one you're in trouble with?"

"Yes, but we ca-"

"You stupid fucking cunt, Jack. No one gets away with screwing with the Giant. You're not dragging me into this shit. Fuck it. You're on your own, girl."

"We had a deal. I kept my part. You were only too happy to stick your fetid dick down my throat."

"Yeah, thanks for that. I'll use it to remember you by when the fucking Giant shreds you."

Jack felt the blood rush to her face. She spat at Stilts, gaining a little satisfaction from seeing some of his cum, mingled with spittle, hit his cheek. She balled her fist and drove it as hard as she could into Stilts' crotch. He opened his mouth to scream in agony but nothing came out. His face whitened and he doubled over whilst clutching his balls.

Jack turned and ran down the stairs, past the thug who still lurked in the shadows. She ran into the street that was already beginning to darken. It was getting late and she was going to have to face the Giant alone.

*

The door at the Giant's back creaked open, causing him to stand straight and gulp in lungfuls of air. His breathing came in ragged rips as he fought to regain control over it; he was sweating profusely. It stung his eyes and caused his shirt to cling to his back and underarms.

He was huffing and puffing, and barely heard the tiny voice behind him say, "Boss?"

The Giant had his eyes transfixed on Dave. Before being disturbed, he had been whacking Dave across his face with the huge rubber dick – left, right, right, left, left, right. Some of the blows had been so hard that the

Giant had heard bits of shattered teeth ping off the office floor, desk and walls.

Strings of bloody saliva dangled out of Dave's mouth, reminding the Giant of thick strawberry lace. His lower lip sagged, exposing busted front teeth. On the floor in front of Dave, a chunk of his tongue could be seen.

He must have bitten down on when I uppercut him with my Johnson! he thought, slamming his open hand with the black, blood-stained cock. The sting of rubber lashing his palm felt good – he could feel his own cock becoming engorged.

"Fuck you!" Dave slurred, and then laughed. More chips of teeth slipped from his gob as he spoke. "I think you've broken my jaw, you overgrown fuckbag!"

Before turning to address the person behind him, the Giant got down on his haunches and roughly grabbed Dave's shattered jaw.

"*Arrrgh!*" Dave cried, fresh tears streaming down his face.

"You best be fucking nice, lad, or I won't give you the pleasure of becoming my imps' plaything!" He shoved Dave's head aside.

Dave faced the Giant once again before spitting in his face. "Pick up your fucking ears, prick – I said, fuck. You!"

Standing, the Giant smiled. *How deliciously stubborn*, he thought.

"Boss," came the feeble voice again.

"Yes, Muffet?" the Giant said, not turning.

"The Three Blind Mice are ready for you…"

"Thanks, Miss Muffet. Will you be joining myself and the Mice?"

"No, boss."

"Fine," he said. "Call the imps – I want this piece of shit to witness the Pigs…"

"I'll send them right in," she said, closing the door behind her.

She's a sweet thing...

Walking back to his chair, the Giant slipped his jacket off its back and whipped it on. He straightened his tie. "I do hope you enjoy the show!" he told Dave.

"*Uch...*" was all Dave could muster. His jaw had swollen and his left eye looked as though someone had put a boiled egg behind his lids – the skin around it was a purple-blue, with splashes of black.

Before the Giant could speak again, the door was rapped on.

"Come!" the Giant bellowed.

In walked his three imps. Their leader wore a short pleated skirt, fuck-me boots, stockings, suspenders and a tight t-shirt with *Punk is Dead* written across it in bright pink letters. Her small yet perky tits were visible through the thin material. Her hair was tied into three pigtails. She wore little make-up.

If it wasn't for the massive cock she carries between her legs and the plump Adam's apple, you'd never guess it's a he-she, he thought, looking at her silky smooth legs and soft, pretty face. .

"Tiffany," the Giant said. "Would you be so kind as to escort your squeeze to the dungeons, please?"

"Of course, boss man!" she said, snapping her gum and sidling up to him. She placed her index finger to his tie and slid it down to his belt buckle. "Anything you say!" Winking, she turned to her man-whores and ordered them to unlock their sex slave. "Will there be anything else?"

The way she lingered on the word "anything" made his dick pulsate. "No, thank you," he said. "When you get below, I want him taken to the Pen."

"*Huh!*" Tiffany gasped. "You're not going to..."

"We shall see. I want him to see first-hand what happens to the people who double cross me. Hopefully the experience will soften the stubborn motherfucker!"

Tiffany nodded, unclasped the bullwhip she had at her side, and lashed her imps (or imp-dogs, as she liked to call them) into action. "Come on, boys – you heard the boss! Get his sorry arse up."

The crack of her whip brought a smile to the Giant's face.

*

A few moments later, they were walking the length of the dark and dingy corridor to his dungeons. The passageway was filled with delightful screams of pleasure, pain and a bit of both. When they passed a man wanking in a corner whilst being whipped by a beefy dominatrix dressed in leather, the Giant couldn't help but smile.

"I see Mr. Horner is back in his corner. The dirty bastard!" he whispered.

Soon after that, they came across a solid-looking door. Begs of mercy could be heard from behind it.

Turning, he saw Tiffany's imps drag Dave along by his arms – his toenails raked the cobbled flooring and broke off. Blood trails could be seen into the distance. Behind the trio the Giant could see his faithful Tiff whipping her helpers.

"Move faster, you worthless fuck-slots. Faster, dogs!" The sound of her voice was followed by that of her cracking whip. Blood jettisoned up the walls to either side of her imps as they tried to obey.

The Giant opened the door and the corridor filled with the sounds of someone screaming, "*No, no! Please, God. No!*" Blood-curdling screams followed, by what sounded like a pack of animals tearing into flesh and bone. A horrendous racket of ivory disintegrating between powerful jaws caused the Giant to shiver, and then titter.

"Right, in with him!" he ordered Tiffany and the imps.

After Dave was dragged into the room, the Giant himself entered and closed the door. Turning, he was greeted by his hit men known only as the Three Blind Mice.

"Right this way, Boss," the leader of the Mice said with a whisper. "We have your package right over here."

*

Jack stopped at the off-licence for a can of Stella and a pack of gum. She slurped the lager, swilling her mouth of any remnants of Stilts' rank ejaculation. She flipped the empty can over a wall and popped some gum in her mouth to sweeten her breath.

It was full dark. Jack had paced the streets for the past two hours trying to come up with a plan to get Dave away from the Giant, but for all her thoughts she had come up empty. The only person she had thought capable of helping her was Stilts, and the bastard had deserted her. Above the city a bone-white crescent moon grinned at Jack's despair. She checked her watch. It was nearing nine-thirty. Less than three hours to either clear her debt with the Giant, free Dave or say goodbye to him forever.

She was in the seediest part of the city, not far from the alley where the Giant's club was situated. None of the street lamps worked in this part of town, so there were plenty of shadows in which the scum, deviants and syphilitic whores of the city could flourish. Jack stopped. The Giant's club was in the next alley. She peered around the corner. His heavies guarded the entrance to the club, which milled with low life. Drugs were openly exchanging hands and in one of the nearby doorways a pot-bellied, old man was getting blown by the skankiest prostitute Jack had ever seen.

She felt her heart race and her breathing came in jagged gasps as fear welled up inside her at the sight of the neon sign. It was a brown cow wielding a bullwhip. The same as the logo on the note she had received hours earlier. *Don't panic,* she told herself as she battled to bring her breathing under control. *If you lose it, the Giant will have you and Dave.* She didn't want to imagine what was happening to Dave right now and she didn't want to think about what the Giant would do to her if he got his huge hands on her.

Retreating around the corner, Jack realised she couldn't enter the club through the main entrance. The Giant's goons would grab her as soon as she drew near. She was going to have to find another way in.

The club was housed in a four storey, former factory. There was bound to be another way in. Keeping her head low to avoid recognition, Jack started to walk the perimeter of the building. Her search was futile. Jack slammed her hand against the wall in frustration and looked up at the dark, oppressive building. She saw it, on the top floor – a small open window. But how was she going to reach it? There were no fire escape steps leading to it and the drainpipe looked corroded and fragile.

Jack was at breaking point. The rush from the beans she had taken earlier had gone and she was getting twitchy. She needed something to take the edge off, something to help her think clearly. Something like the beans she had in her pocket.

Jack's hand searched for the bag. It wasn't there. "No!" she yelled before looking around to see if anyone had heard her. "You stupid cow," she scolded herself, realising she had left the bag of Magic Beans at Stilts' place. She didn't even have the remaining drugs to use as leverage. It was hopeless.

The night had turned chilly and Jack pushed her hands deep into her pockets to warm them. Her fingers nudged something small and smooth. She pulled it out. It was a single bean. It wasn't going to buy her any grace with the Giant so she popped it in her mouth, crunching through the shell to get a quicker hit.

Within minutes Jack could feel a heat and lightness traversing her skin. She closed her eyes and let the flickering colours and images soothe her mind and body. A calmness descended upon her, pushing aside the panic that had threatened to suffocate her. She stood for ten minutes, eyes closed, letting her blood absorb the chemicals and transport them to her organs.

She stumbled. A rumbling sound came from beneath and the earth trembled. Jack hit the ground and yelped. She opened her eyes and stared in amazement. The pavement had split and long green tendrils pushed their way through the fissures, twisting and climbing the walls of the old factory. The base of the monstrosity broadened until it was the thickness of a young tree. Looking up, Jack saw it had grown over the roof of the building, passing within inches of the open window.

I wonder... she thought, grasping a thick stem. It was cold like metal, and sturdy, flexing only slightly in her grip. Jack placed her foot at the base and pushed herself up. The giant plant bore her weight with ease, despite creaking and groaning at each step. Jack placed her foot at the base and pushed herself up. She climbed higher. *This might work.* Jack heaved her way through the flickering foliage. Every so often she swore a thick tendril wound itself around her wrist and pulled her a little further towards the window. Harsh fluorescent light spilled out. The vines seemed to grip her limbs and nudge her closer.

The gap was smaller than she had expected, but Jack was sure she could squeeze her slight frame through it. She grabbed the frame and pulled until her head was in the room. Bright light blinded her. Wriggling and slithering, she slipped through the space, landing face down on the stained tiled floor. The stench of stale pee burned her nose.

Her eyes adjusted to the brightness and she raised her head. She was in a bathroom. Turning her head to the side she spied someone gripping the side of the washbasin with one hand whilst the other pumped his crotch. The man suddenly realised he was not alone. Turning, he faced her and let go of his dick.

Jack gasped. She had never seen such a pathetic excuse for a cock in her life, and she had seen plenty. The stubby, pale appendage was no more than two inches long and, as far as she could tell, it was fully erect. She hadn't noticed it before as it had been completely engulfed by the hairy hand trying to squeeze spunk from it. It was a pale grub emerging from a forest of thick hair. Jack raised her eyes higher, and higher, and higher again.

She was lying face down on the floor before the Giant.

She scrambled to her feet and ran, but she was slow, exhausted by the climb. She gasped as a large hand gripped her throat, its fingers long enough to meet at the back of her neck. She was dragged from the floor and hoisted into the air. Her legs kicked wildly several feet above ground but connected with nothing. Jack was eye to eye with the Giant. She tried to hit out, but her arms were getting heavier every second. His face was the last thing she saw as the room darkened. Then, total blackness.

The Giant released his grip and Jack tumbled to the floor. Her only movement was the shallow fall and rise of her chest as she struggled to suck in the vital air she so desperately needed.

*

The Three Blind Mice were aptly named: triplets who were partially blind in both their eyes. However, they had exceptional skills and never let their employer down.

They were dressed entirely in black: suits, shades, shoes, raincoats and crumpled fedoras. They worked for the Giant as hit men, which meant they rubbed people out, captured, tortured or delivered their target to their boss.

"Here's your package, boss!" one of the Mice said, whipping an old brown cover off a whimpering female. She was young. Very young. No more than sixteen or seventeen. Her tits were mere bee stings, her twat bald. In the crux of her arms, needle pricks were visible. Her eyes were encircled black and bags the size of suitcases graced her lower lids.

Her pupils were the size of needle heads.

What a fucking Shakespearean tragedy!

She had been one of his best customers but had fallen way behind on her payments. For the past six weeks, the Giant's heavies had scoured every nook and cranny of the city – every rock and doghouse kicked over.

Nobody had seen hide nor hair of her, until now…

The Giant licked his lips.

When her eyes fused with his, she screamed a muffled scream beneath the dirty rag that was plugging her gob.

"Well, well, well…what do we have here?!" He beamed, bending closer to the girl. Her wrists and ankles were bound together by mower cord – it had been wrapped around her flesh so tight, it had bitten into her skin, causing blood loss. "Where have you been hiding, Jessica?" He put a hand out and stroked her cheek. "So young and pretty…"

With one forceful tug, he ripped the gag from her mouth.

"Please!" she gasped. "I was on my way to pay you! I've-"

"Shh-shh!" the Giant soothed.

"You must believe me, check my bag…It's all there…All five-grand…!"

"My poor girl, it's too late for that, but I thank you for getting my money together."

"Let me go!" she blubbered. Snot shot down her nostrils. Her lower lip bounced. "My mum will be worried sick…Please…Show mercy!"

"My poor girl, it's too late for that, but I thank you for getting my money together."

A cackle from behind made him turn – Tiffany stood there with her whip. Her cock was a rod of steel. "Give her to the cow!" she said, smiling. A glob of jism leaked from her jutting dick.

"Not the Pigs?" the Giant said, raising an eyebrow.

Tiffany shook her head slowly.

The thought of making Jessica ride the cow thrilled him. His own stiffness pushed at his trousers. *I need a release!* he thought. *Not yet. Take care of business first.*

"Mice," he ordered. "Drag her to the cow!"

"No! Not the cow!" she screamed. "Anything but-"

"Shut up!" one of the Mice said, punching her so hard in the mouth, some of her teeth rattled free.

The cow was a mechanical device, much like a bucking bronco people rode to win prizes. But this one was unique: the saddle had been replaced by a rigid, twelve-inch dick covered in razor-sharp barbed wire.

When a female was placed on it and the machine set to go, the barb rattled around inside them and made spaghetti strings out of their innards. Of course, if it was a male victim, then the giant shaft was forced into their anus.

There's nothing better than the sight of a man's virgin arse popping like a ripe cherry! the Giant thought.

And of course, the thing was never cleaned – chunks of decayed flesh and gore clung to the razor wire.

"On you go, girlie-girl!" one of the Mice said as he and his brothers hefted her onto the cow.

Her screams were horrific as her ankles were yanked and she was forced to sit – blood immediately shot down her inner thighs. Her eyes rolled like marbles. Her hands were lashed to the mechanical beast and it was activated.

"*Ugh*! It's fucking digging into me – let me off, fuckers!" she screamed and bucked madly.

"Pass me the controls!" the Giant said.

With glee, Tiffany handed him the remote for the massive fake phallus. Looking at the settings, he selected vibrate. This caused her to scream until he thought her throat would collapse.

He could hear his vicious toy rip her to shreds. Tiffany's imps moved closer and basked in the flying blood. They licked if off each other's leather suits, much to the Giant's joy.

Chunks of flesh spat free from Jessica, and soon a split raced up her stomach – the barbs ripped her open and exposed the fake, blooded bell-end. It looked eager for a slot to slam into.

When her pale form slumped forward, the Giant couldn't take his eyes off her. Seeing the death of another always transfixed him. Fascinated him.

"To the Pigs with her, boss?" one of the Mice said.

"Yes," he said softly, still staring.

"You cold-blooded bastards!" Dave slurred "You sick, murdering-"

A ferocious kick to his balls from Tiffany quietened him. He collapsed to the floor and clutched his sack.

"Drag him over to the Pen!" the Giant said.

Dave tried to protest, but was whipped and beaten by Tiffany and her imps.

"Do you mind if we depart?" one of the Mice said.

"No, you go. I'll settle up with you tomorrow."

"Farewell, boss. Enjoy!" Then they were gone, leaving the Giant and his imps.

When they got Dave and Jessica to the Pen, the Giant looked between the slats of wood that fenced the Pigs in. They were three fat, sweaty men dressed in nothing but tight leather shorts and gimp masks with open zips. They couldn't see - they had no eyeholes.

The Pigs couldn't be called human any longer, as the Giant believed they had no souls. The three deviants had come to his club one evening asking to be kept as pet pigs, and so he had obliged.

My three little pigs...

At the beginning, he had fed them slop, but had branched out into human meat. When the crossover had come, they hadn't cared, as they were too wrapped up in their fantasy. Now, however, they bayed for blood.

Or squealed, rather.

And, just like real pigs, they liked to snort and truffle, much to the Giant's amusement.

"Little pigs! Little pigs!" the Giant said, rattling their enclosure. This riled them. They scampered out of the darkness, squealing and screeching. They raked the wood and sniffed the air.

"*Jesus...*" Dave muttered.

"Get the bone saw!" the Giant said, removing his jacket and shirt. His chest was huge. A large tattoo of two brawling tigers graced his hairy pecs and an image of a Cajun queen was etched on his flat stomach.

"Would you like the hammer, too?" Tiffany said.

The Giant nodded.

Once given the implements, he started to pulverize Jessica's body with the hammer. He wanted the joints smashed to dust, which would make cutting through her with the saw easier.

When Jessica was as flat as a pancake, he started sawing into her. The noise turned him on, and made him think of leather being torn. The bits he cut off were thrown into the pen.

The Pigs tore into their snack.

Standing up to arch his back, the Giant looked down at the torso and decided to heave it over the fence. *They should be able to pick that apart...*

Wiping sweat from his brow, he looked at Dave and pointed at him with his hammer. He noticed the man had pissed on the floor. *Scared stiff! Well, he should be.*

As he approached, Dave started shaking his head.

"I was going to keep you," the Giant said, looking at his watch, "but because of your attitude and her being late, I think it's time to dispose of you!"

"*Nooooo!*" Dave yelled.

The Giant handed the hammer to Tiffany, along with the saw. "You can have the pleasure of taking care of this one. I will be upstairs if you need me," he said.

*

After leaving the dungeons, the Giant rushed upstairs to his office. Once there, he entered his private toilet and went to the sink. Without waiting a moment longer, he lowered his zip and grabbed his stiff cock.

With eagerness, he started stroking it. *Fuck! I need this so bad!* He couldn't bear to look down at his knob –

it was a complete embarrassment. *If the others ever found out, I'd be finished...*

A crash from behind brought him out of his musings. To his shock, it was Jack.

Before he could hide himself, he made a grab for her, before she escaped the bathroom...

*

It was dark and Jack's throat burned. It felt like she had swallowed acid. After a few moments she realised the darkness was due to her eyes being closed. Slowly she opened one, groaning as the overhead light dazzled her. As she grew accustomed to it, she opened the other and took in her surroundings.

She was no longer in the bathroom - Jack could see it through an open door. The Giant had dragged her into his adjoining office and dumped her in the corner. From where she lay she could see an oversized office chair tucked beneath a massive desk. A large filing cabinet stood against the far wall. Another door opened into the room, but it was closed. The Giant rested on the edge of his desk, his legs stretched out and crossed at the ankles. He stared at Jack and licked his lips. He looked hungry and she felt herself withdraw further into the corner.

"Well, well, Jackie. You finally managed to fucking show up." The Giant folded his arms. "But you're too fucking late, sweetheart. Hear that?" He cocked his head and paused for a few seconds. "If you listen carefully you might hear your miserable boyfriend's final screams. No? Well, you'll just have to take my word for it."

Jack whimpered, having no doubts that the Giant was being truthful. She had failed and now she was in his lair. What fate did he have planned for her? He wasn't known for mercy. Whatever was coming her way was going to be drawn out, humiliating, and as painful as he could make it...

The Giant pushed himself up from his desk and cracked his knuckles. The sound reverberated through the office. "You might not know this, little Jackie, but I've always had a hard spot for you. If you can satisfy me I might decide to keep you around. You could be my pet. I could walk you around wearing a collar and leash." He loomed over her before reaching down, grabbing hold of her vest top and dragging her to her feet. The thin fabric tore, exposing her lace-covered tits. The Giant drooled at the sight. "Why don't you lose the jeans and we'll see if you're up to the job?"

Jack shuddered at his closeness. With each breath she inhaled the stench of blood and death that emanated from his sweating body. Was the blood she could smell Dave's? She recoiled as his titanic hands pawed her breasts.

"Fuck yes," said the Giant. "Go on, resist me. Make me force you. I like it rough, you fucking whore!"

His words stirred something deep inside her. Anger, fury. Vengeance. She wasn't beaten yet. There was a game left to be played. "And what's in it for me?" she yelled. "I've seen that puny little worm you call a dick. Do you think I'm going to feel that grub wriggling inside me?"

The Giant roared and swiped her face, batting her across the room like a Ping-Pong ball. She bounced off the desk and crashed to the floor. He kicked her, forcing the air from her lungs and leaving her wheezing. Whilst she lay gasping, he picked up the phone on his desk and made a call. It was answered in seconds.

"Muffet!" His voice shook the glass in the window frame. "When Tiffany's finished feeding that slab of meat to the Pigs, have her bring my doppelgänger to the office. And if she wishes, she can bring her imps to watch the fun."

The Giant returned to Jack and squatted next her. "Tiffany and her playthings are going to be busy for a while, but she's going to bring you a special eleven-inch-long gift that's going to split you apart, I promise. But before she gets here, I think me and you should have a little fun. Don't you?"

Jack raised her head and stared at the Giant. She knew she only had one chance and couldn't afford to fuck it up. "What kind of fun do you have in mind?" she rasped.

"Starting to *come* around to my way of thinking, are you?" He winked. "I had a visitor earlier. Someone you know well." He reached into his pocket and pulled out the bag of Magic Beans Jack had left at Stilts' place. "He tells me you have a special skill. Nice boy, bit simple. I think he could go far."

Jack couldn't believe what she was hearing. She thought after Dave, Stilts was the one person she could trust. But fear of the Giant corrupted people. If she ever got out of this mess she would make sure he regretted betraying her. "What did he say I could do?" she asked.

The Giant ran his thumb across her lips, smearing her lipstick before slipping it into her mouth. She nearly gagged. It was far bigger than what lay inside his trousers. "Stilts tells me you have a very talented mouth, Jackie. Care to show me?"

She really didn't, but a plan was beginning to form, so she nodded.

"Good girl." He removed his thumb from between Jack's lips with a plop and started to unzip his fly. He grabbed her wrist and dragged her across the floor with him to his chair. He pushed her to the floor and grabbed her hair. "One more thing bitch. I own you. Understand?"

Jack nodded as best she could.

"Good girl. One wrong move and you'll go the same way as your faggot boyfriend." He sat down and directed Jack to his choad.

Jack settled herself in front of him. Never had she had so little to work with, and never did she back down from a challenge. She took hold of the flaccid flesh and began to work her fingers up and down.

The Giant was slow to respond but as soon as she closed her lips around it he started to harden. After the deep throat action with Stilts, the Giant seemed a less painful experience. Except for the taste - Jack could taste death even on his prick, which was starting to occupy a little more space in her mouth. She worked the Giant with her lips and tongue alone. He didn't have the length to accommodate a hand, too.

The Giant shifted position, urging his hips towards Jack. She responded by sucking and licking faster, encouraging him to lose himself in the moment. The Giant gripped the sides of his chair, his breathing ragged and fast. This was what she had been waiting for. Her only chance.

Jack bit down on the tough flesh as hard as she could. Her teeth pierced the skin, flooding her mouth with hot, spurting blood. She pulled back, letting it spill from her mouth as she gnawed through the Giant's dying root.

He screamed and sat up, punching Jack to the floor. She kept her teeth clamped shut and his dick tore away in her mouth. She turned her head and spat it across the floor as the door opened.

Tiffany looked down at the shrivelled piece of flesh at her feet and then at the dildo in her hand. "You said this was your doppelgänger!" she accused her boss. "Cast from your own..." She kicked the bloodied worm towards her fallen master. The other imps crowded behind her to see what was going on.

Jack was back on her feet, staggering towards the desk. "Who the hell are you?" she asked.

"I'm Tiffany. I serve...served him." She looked at her boss, confusion in her eyes at seeing her infallible master beaten.

Jack spat more blood from her mouth as she scouted around the desk looking for something she could use as a weapon. She tugged at a deep drawer. It wouldn't move. She tugged again and it gave a little. *It's not locked,* she thought. *But it's heavy.* Jack grabbed the handle with both hands and pulled, her muscles screaming almost as loudly as the Giant.

Slowly the drawer opened. The contents glowed. Gold bars filled the drawer. Jack reached in and withdrew one. Its weight was comforting. She placed it on the desk. "Tiffany!" she shouted above the Giant's wails. "What will you do to him," - she jerked her head towards the Giant – "for one of these?"

Tiffany looked at her master, then grinned. She turned back to face Jack. "Anything you want me to, boss."

That was the answer Jack had wanted to hear. She walked over to the Giant, who had slipped from the chair and was writhing around on the floor, trying unsuccessfully to stem the blood that gushed from his wound. She stood over him, blood dripping from her chin, and smiled. "Seems like you weren't quite the giant you liked people to believe." Jack planted a kick in his face. She relished the explosion of bone in his nose. "Tiffany, I think you and me are going to have a great working relationship. Your first job is to insert that dildo to its full length in every orifice he has. Including the one where his worm tail used to be."

Tiffany's face lit up. She turned to the other imps and flicked her bullwhip at them. "You heard the boss. Strip him!"

The imps descended on their former master like a pack of dogs. They tore and shredded his clothes with their hands and teeth until he squirmed naked before them.

"P...please, don't," he begged. "D...don't hurt me." Tears streamed down his face and he whimpered and wailed.

Tiffany seemed delighted. She grasped the dildo in both hands and turned to Jack. "Which one first, mistress?"

"Whichever one you want."

"Turn him over, imp-dogs," she said with a giggle. "I've been wanting to take him for a long time."

The Giant screamed and wrestled the imps, but he was overpowered. The pack flipped him over and pinned him down in a rapidly spreading pool of blood. Tiffany licked her tongue the length of the rubber dildo. Her eyes flickered with wild delight as she rammed it deep into the Giant's anus. She giggled as he screamed and begged for her to stop.

Jack sank into the office chair, exhausted but relieved. It seemed like she had a new job. Maybe this would keep her mother quiet. "Imps!" she yelled. They turned to look at her. "You work for me now. Understand?"

The imps nodded eagerly, then resumed their abuse of the Giant. His screams had subsided to a weak whimper as his blood drained from him and he began to fade.

"I have another job for you when you've finished that bastard off."

Tiffany left her imps to finish the work and walked over to her new mistress. "What would you have us do?"

Jack closed her eyes for a moment and thought of Stilts. She smiled. "This is what I want you to do…"

Sorry, No Service – Technological Disturbance

'Give a speech, I'm sure the co-operate fat cats will love it – they'll eat it up,' Tim mocked his assistant's 'pep talk'. "How about *you* give a speech, Gloria? How about that?!" he said, giggling as he powered his Mercedes around the quiet roads.

'You know I couldn't do that, Mr. Simms. I didn't invent the most incredible piece of technology...' he mimicked once again, looking at himself in the rear-view mirror. Damn, you're one handsome fuck. How does Gloria manage to keep her hands off me?! he thought to himself.

But she was right. On both accounts, of course...I *do* have to give a speech. Well, more of a presentation, to the big dogs. They're going to want to know the *full* capability of the Giff-8G before they take it to market. It'll be the most prestigious mobile phone out there.

Sure, his bosses knew its potential already, but they didn't know how endless its abilities were, as the phone could learn and grow with its owner. Not only did it have the usual crap installed on it, such as being able to surf the web, watch movies, access music, blue tooth, camera, play games etc, etc…but, with the Giff-8G, people would be able to control their TV's, music and light systems, along with any other household gadgets the average Joe may have at home.

How? Because the Giff-8G could also act as a universal remote.

It could also tell your children bedtime stories and hold conversations with the lonely. It was a companion, not just a tool. It was also age-specific, so children as young as five or six could operate and command one. Why? Because it could even act as a tutor. Your children could be home-schooled, along with many other things.

Forget self-help books for taking up languages or fixing your car. The Giff-8G would be there to help you with anything. *Anything* you could think of. *The Japanese would be slobbering like a big, hungry doggy over this one*, Tim thought.

Not only could it do all this, but the phone could adapt to any situation: protect itself from fire or water damage, along with being dropped or stepped on – it was virtually indestructible. How? Because it had built-in motion sensors and detectors. It would know if it'd been dropped or was around hazardous chemicals, liquids, fluids, water or extreme heat. If the phone were threatened in any such away, it would cocoon itself and shut its system down.

Pretty cool, right?

It would last the consumer years. No more upgrades. No more keeping up with the times, Tim thought, eyeing the test model on the car's dashboard. Its long, slender body almost brought a tear to his eye. Apart from Alex, his son, it was probably the most precious thing he'd created.

No, scrap that. It is the most beautiful thing I've created, he thought.

'*How's the thing so bloody impressive, Tim*?' he'd been asked by one of his superiors.

Tim had given the man a cock-and-bull story about his creation, when in reality, the phones had been fitted with military defence chips. It had all been done in the shadows, with a handshake and a couple of wads of cash here and there, which had gone a long way to securing the deal of the century.

All kinds of safety checks and tests had already been carried out on the prototypes, along with some having already been handed out to trusted sources to test. There had been no problems. No complaints, just rave reviews for Tim and his technological dream team at HQ. The bosses and fat cats were nothing but happy. Hell, they'd even given their children, wives and mistresses a phone as presents.

Cloud nine, here we come, Tim thought, looking in his rear-view mirror. The hookers he'd picked up from the dock were tongue wrestling again. Beautiful, he thought. "Cocaine, champagne and all the sex and food you want when I get you home, ladies," he said, watching the one named Cindy touch a hand to the other girl's massive tits.

Cindy and who? he thought...Jackson, that's right. Action Jackson...What a pair of names. Ah well, he didn't care what they were called when he was taking them from behind; or from any other position for that matter.

He found keeping a grin off his face hard, as he continued to watch them in the mirror. They may have had dreadful names, he thought, but they had seemed to be the cleanest girls at the dockyard. The most expensive, too – I hope they will be worth it, he thought.

Re-angling the rear-view mirror, Tim watched as Jackson shoved her hand between Cindy's legs and slipped it up her dress. You dirty bitch, he thought, smiling once again. The honk of a horn brought his attention back to the road, as a truck hurtled towards them.

Tim laughed as he swerved to avoid it and its blinding headlights. He blew his horn and yelled, "Fuck you!" as his Mercedes, with squealing tyres, edged past the huge vehicle. Both girls giggled behind him.

"You reckless son-of-a-bitch," Cindy said, laughing. She clamped a delicate hand to his shoulder, "Are you as dangerous in the sack?" she asked him.

This caused Jackson to titter like a schoolgirl.

His dick suddenly stiffened. Filthy cunts, he thought. "You bet I *am!*" he declared.

Both girls laughed and resumed their tongue match.

Eyeing them once again in the rear-view, he looked at Jackson's tits – they were proper bra busters, he thought. Those things had drawn him immediately, as he'd pulled up to her and a pack of waiting women. As soon as he'd flashed his cash, she was on board, with one condition.

"Cindy comes with me," she'd said. "She's my playmate…"

Having agreed, he'd started the drive home.

"Such tits," he mouthed, trying to forget about his rock hard cock. "Not much further – a mile or two, then I can unleash you!" he said, grabbing his dick.

Giving the road his full attention, Tim concentrated on getting them all home, when a fat drop of water hit the windshield, followed by another. Before he knew it, the rain started coming down in sheets. Flickers of lightning spread across the sky in front of him as thunder roared above.

"*Shit,*" he muttered, turning his wipers on to full blast.

After another five minutes of driving, Tim was at the foot of his driveway. A large iron gate blocked his path. Winding his window down, he pushed the buzzer on the wall, which alerted Harry in the control room inside the house.

Within seconds, the gates started to open.

"Ah, he's a good one," Tim uttered.

"*Oo*, you live in a mansion?!" Jackson said, sounding as thick as they came.

"That's right," Tim said, as though he was talking to his six-year-old son. *She didn't pick up on his condescending tone. Good*, he thought.

Pulling up to the drive and stopping the car, Tim was about to get out, when lightning struck the gravelled ground to the right of his car. A cloud of electricity washed over the Mercedes, causing the radio to burst to life. His Giff-8G suddenly started chiming and talking to Tim in many different languages, startling him and causing him to laugh.

Grabbing the phone, he turned it off and slipped it into his jacket pocket, before silencing the car radio.

"Was that little black box just talking to you?" Cindy asked.

God, he thought, *they're as thick as dog shit*. "Yes," he said. "It's a…" he started, but let his words trail off. "Never mind, let's go inside," he said, smiling at them in the rear-view mirror once again.

The girls got out of the car and dashed over to the main entrance to the grand house, which was surrounded by a maze garden, polo field, tennis courts, outdoor pool (which was covered at nights), stables and expensive cars.

The building was very new, as Tim had ordered the place built when he'd made his first few millions ten years ago. It had been impressive to start with, but now the structure bored him, and he spent most of his time filling it with gadgets, expensive art and relics of all kinds.

Beside himself, there was an in-house gardener, cook, butler and maid. Shutting his car door, he ran after the girls and into his home. He closed the door behind him.

Laughing, both women turned to Tim and started kissing him. Then they started to undo his tie and shirt. As Jackson started slipping his coat off, he managed to push them both off with a laugh. "Now, now, girls. There's plenty of time. Why don't you both go into the living room? Make yourselves comfortable."

"Anything you say, *sir*!" Cindy purred.

He smiled. "I'll get us some chilled wine," he told them, then watched both girls in their skimpy dresses, as they made their way into his lavish living room. Just as he was about to head off to the kitchen, his Giff-8G started rumbling in his pocket.

"I thought I'd knocked you off," he mumbled, digging the phone out of his pocket.

'*House secure*'...it blurted in an electronic voice.

"*Huh*?!" Tim said, looking at his phone. "What do you...?"

His words trailed off, as the sound of bolts engaging in the door behind him made him turn with a start. The alarm system then set itself. All around the house, Tim could hear bolts and locks activating themselves.

"*Tut*!" he said in annoyance. "Stupid bloody phone. The lightning must have done this...Giff, unlock home," he commanded, but the phone did nothing. It simply put itself into hibernation mode. "Fuck it," he said, pocketing the phone. "The place needed locking down for the evening anyway."

As he passed through the corridor leading to the kitchen, all the lights leading the way suddenly dimmed; some shut off completely. "That's weird," he said to himself, stopping by one of the lights that had gone out. He touched the bulb. Immediately, Tim retracted his scorched fingertips, "*Shit!*"

Placing his burned digits into his mouth, he moved into the kitchen. "I need to tell the guys down at the lab about this," he said irritably, picking up the phone that was mounted on the wall next to the fridge. He punched in a series of numbers with his other hand.

The phone rang five times before it was answered. Raucous music pumped through Tim's ear – it was clear Roger was having a celebration party, too. And why wouldn't he be? The Giff-8G stood to make the company millions upon millions.

"Roge?!" Tim yelled down the phone, "I think I've discovered a problem...*Roger*! It's me, Tim...Yes, a problem...*Roger*?!" Turn the fucking music down, he felt like yelling.

As if Roger had read his thoughts, the music went quiet. "That's better, I can hear you now. That's right, yes. I think the phone may have a glitch..." he started, then realised he was talking to nobody. "Hello? *Roger*?! What the...?" Tim said, before replacing the receiver back in its mounted cradle. He picked it back up, only to discover the phone was dead.

No dial tone.

No dead air.

Replacing the receiver once again, Tim made his way out to the phone in the hall. That one was also dead. The one in the smaller living room, too, along with the one in the dining room and billiard room, as well as, the one in the large living room the girls occupied.

"Power must have knocked them out", Tim said, as he slipped his phone out of his pocket. He looked at the screen – it was still sleeping. "Odd..."

"Everything okay?" Cindy asked in a sultry tone.

For the first time, he noticed she was now naked. Jackson, too. His eyes were immediately drawn to their shaved pussies.

"*Oo*, is that for us?!" Jackson asked, pointing at the bulge in his trousers.

"*Uh-huh!*" he said, nodding his head. Before unzipping his fly however, he told them that he would be right back – that he needed to check something first.

Going to the staircase, Tim halted, and eyed the armour suit at the foot of the stairs. Did the helmet just move? he asked himself. Tut, get a grip on yourself, he thought, placing a foot on the first step.

On hearing a faint groan, he looked up at the armour, which held a gleaming axe at its side. The lid to the helmet was perforated – two slits formed peepholes for the warrior's eyesight.

Warrior? *The bloody thing is empty*! Tim thought, smiling to himself.

Putting a hand to the banister, he lightly jogged to the top, where he was met by another suit of armour. This one was much older and held a sword and shield – the defensive tool was coated in Celtic colours. A plume of feathers jutted from the top of this one's face, covering it.

Again, he heard another faint squeak.

He turned around and noticed the helmet on the armour at the bottom of the staircase had moved its head. "*Impossible…*" he mouthed, backing away until his back met the armour behind him.

He placed his hands against the cool steel. A whimper escaped him, as he turned on his heel and looked up the warrior. It hadn't moved.

"Get a hold of yourself, will you! Your mind is running amok!"

"Is everything all right, sir?" an aged voice called out from behind him.

With a yelp, Tim turned to see Geoff standing at his bedroom door. He was wearing a nightcap.

Putting a hand to his thumping chest, Tim smiled. "Yes, everything is fine, Geoff. The storm has put me slightly off-kilter," he said.

"Oh, good," the man said. "Anything I can do for you before I turn back in?"

"No, thanks. Have the rest of the staff finished for the evening?" Tim asked.

"Yes, sir."

"Good. That's great. I have company, so I'd like not to be disturbed," Tim said.

"Very well, sir. Good night," Geoff said, closing his door.

Tim eyed both sets of armour before moving to the master bedroom.

Going to the phone, he picked it up – no dial tone. Slamming it down, he was about to walk out of the bedroom, when suddenly the radio alarm clock started blasting out music, causing him to jump, then the TV burst to life as all the lights in the room started flashing on and off maniacally, followed by the shower and sink taps gushing water.

"*Fuck!*" he yelled, rushing around the room to turn the appliances off. Thunder rumbled above him, as lightning flickered outside the bedroom window. "What the hell is going on?!"

'*Intruder...Intruder...*' Tim's phone started blurting.

"What...?" he gasped, taking his rumbling phone out of his pocket.

'*Intruders will be killed on sight...*' the device intoned. The word 'kill' appeared in capital letters on its mini-screen.

"No! Shutdown. *Shutdown!*" Tim demanded.

Then he heard Geoff screaming from his bedroom, as the sockets in his room burst apart – sparks and flashes of azure light filled the large room, as the TV's screen cracked and caved in.

Next to go was the main light above the bed, which blew apart, showering Tim in tiny shards of glass. Some of the pieces nicked his face as he ran from his room.

"Geoff?!" he called, "*Geoff*?!" Tom could hear the pensioner's garbled screams as he entered onto the landing. To his shock, the massive suit of armour was missing. "No…it *can't* be…" he said, edging closer to the old man's room.

"*Heeeelp!*" the old man croaked out, "They're killing me…"

Plunging the door handle down, Tim threw his weight against the door. What he saw before him almost made him laugh. Had he not been so terrified, he probably would have.

Geoff was pinned to his bed by snakes that had slithered out of the jungle portrait above his bed – their massive, Boa-like bodies were multi-coloured and spotted, their tails were unseen and they were still inside the oil-painted jungle. Tim could hear, but not see, monkeys screeching and lions roaring.

As Geoff struggled, the mass of steel that had been standing in the corridor only moments ago now moved closer to him – it raised its sword as it stood above the entangled man. "*Nooo…*" Geoff gurgled, as the large, metallic blade punched through his guts and pierced the wooden floor beneath the bed.

With a few fierce rips and tugs by the knight, Geoff's steaming, hot guts splashed the floor.

Finished with Geoff, the snakes slid toward Tim.

The knight turned on its tinny heels and stalked towards him.

Falling backward, Tim managed to catch himself before hitting the deck. He scurried out of the room and closed the door behind him, just as the blood-tarnished sword came through the middle of it.

Wood chips rained over Tim, as he fell onto his arse.

"This can't be happening. Have I already taken drugs speed? Did the girls drop me something...?"

As Jackson and Cindy came to mind, he heard them shrieking from downstairs. "*Shit!*" he yelled, getting to his feet. He flew down the steps, failing to notice the missing suit of armour standing there.

When he entered the living room, he noticed both girls were trying to avoid a giant axe, which was being wielded by the second knight. Sparks were coming from all the electric sockets, with the lights in the room flickering on and off.

He'd noticed the same things happening in Geoff's room.

Something's fucking with the power, he thought. It has to be the phone. *Must be.* But he didn't have time to check it then, as he looked about himself for a weapon.

The women threw tables, vases, and anything else that came to hand, at the knight, but it did nothing to slow the armour-clad warrior down...

"Help, Tim!" one of them yelled, but he was unsure which, as he continued to frantically search for a weapon.

"*Argh*, I'm trapped!" Jackson yelped.

As Tim looked up, he noticed vines and tree branches coming to life from paintings dotted around the room. "Get out of there!" Tim yelled, but it was too late for her, as the vines held her in place for the knight to do its thing.

It smashed its axe through her head, cleaving it open like a melon. Cindy yelled, as blood and brain matter plastered her naked body. With the head gone, the knight continued its dismantlement of Jackson by firstly cutting off both her arms, followed by her legs.

"Run!" Tim told Cindy, who managed to dash around the lumbering metal man.

She crashed into his arms, but he didn't hang around to cradle her and tell her everything would be all right. Instead, he made a bolt for the front door, whilst dragging her behind him.

'*Kill intruders...Kill intruders...*' he heard his phone say.

"Shut up!" Tim yelled, as he smacked the flat of his hand against his mobile. On the phone's instructions, all the lights popped in the hallway. Electric sockets burst into blue flame.

Cindy screamed, as Tim tried desperately to open the front door, which wouldn't budge.

"Quick, to the back of the house!" he yelled, just as Geoff's door burst into wood splinters and the second knight shambled out of the living room.

Only just avoiding the axe, Tim led Cindy into the billiard room.

"We haven't got time for a game of fucking *snooker*!" she yelled at him

"Fuck up!" he told her, as he closed and locked the door to the room. "This should give us some time. Grab anything you can!" he told her.

The room didn't just house two snooker tables, but also a mini arsenal – bows and arrows, axes, maces, swords, knifes, spears, kukris...the list was endless.

"What the hell is all this?" she asked, looking at the weaponry.

"Shit I collect," he said, digging his phone out of his pocket. He tried throwing it against the wall, before stamping on it. When that failed, he grabbed a war hammer off the wall and started hitting the Giff-8G.

Nothing put a dent in it.

When he tried to turn it off, it powered back up.

'*Kill intruders*!' it barked.

Before Tim knew what was what, a kukri thunked into the door by the side of him. Snooker balls hurled themselves at Cindy, as spears came at Tim like darts. He threw himself to the ground and could only watch in dismay, as red and coloured balls pummelled Cindy's face and body. He heard her bones breaking over her cries and pleas for help, before four cues dismounted and started taking turns in trying to cave her head in.

Again, all the sockets in the room burst into blue light.

Just like a commando, Tim started crawling along the floor. His destination was a second door. Once there, he counted to three, before leaping off the floor and scrambling through it.

Once it was closed, he stepped back from it, as axe heads, knifes and other deadly stabbing weapons punched into the wood.

"Jesus!" he breathed out, then placed his head against a safe part of the door. He could do nothing but sob, on hearing Cindy gargle out blood-soaked cries of help, before finally succumbing.

When he heard the knights approaching the door, he turned and ran into kitchen. He skidded to a halt on seeing a whirlpool of blue light at the centre of the room. All the appliances were going, from kettle to food mixer.

Pinned to the back of the kitchen door was Mrs. June, Tim's elderly cook. Five butcher knives had clearly propelled her against it. Skewers, corkscrews and cleavers could also been seen jutting from her body, turning her whites far from white…A lake of blood had gathered at her feet.

"What am I going to do?" he screamed, as tears filled his eyes.

Looking at the backdoor, he went for it, only to find he couldn't budge it. Getting his phone back out, he tried a few more commands. "Giff, power down. Giff, power down!" Nothing. "Giff, the house is safe. The house is *safe!*"

The phone continued in defiance.

Unlocking the keypad, he was shocked to learn he could still dial out. "*Yes!*" when he got an engaged number with the emergency service, he tried Roger again. No answer. Hanging up, he tried again. After the twentieth ring, he gave up.

"You've got him too, haven't you?!" he screamed at the phone. "Bastard!" '*Intruders must die!*' it told Tim.

"Fucking bastard!"

Then it hit him. "If I fry the phone's circuits, I bet I can kill it!" he thought aloud.

When the door he'd entered burst open, Tim grabbed a small knife from the knife block and made for the door Mrs. June was pinned to. Opening it, he ran to the stairs. The second knight was nowhere to be seen.

Taking his chances, Tim ran upstairs.

Getting to the top, he made for the room his son used when staying over. Ploughing through the door, he slammed it shut before falling to the floor.

"They won't be able to find me that fast!" he uttered, then tried desperately to regain his breathing. "Shh-shh…" he told himself, as he gasped for air.

Once he was calm, Tim started searching for what he wanted. Alex, being a little boy, had taken a keen interest in electrics and building stuff from scratch, even though he was only six.

Finding one of his son's electronic sets, he opened it up and pulled out a mini soldering kit. "Got you now!" he said, laughing at the phone.

As he tried to remove the phone's back casing, Tim heard the knights climb the stairs. "Come on, open!" he said, as his fingers kept slipping off the shiny black plastic. "Open, damn *you!*"

The phone flipped out of his hand, as an axe and sword penetrated the flimsy bedroom door. All Tim could do was sit and weep...*It's over*, he thought.

His mind filled with Alex and how he would never see him again.

"*Alex!*" he blurted. "I need to warn him..."

Before the knights could burst through the door, he managed to dial his son's number.

"*Sorry, the number you have dialled, is incorrect...*" the woman said on the other end of the line.

"Fuck, *fuck!*" he yelled, then heard a strange noise to his left.

On turning, he saw his son's Bucket O'Soldiers tip over. The lid popped off, as Tim was rushed by a number of green and red berets. They had their bayonets fixed and locked onto him.

From the gloom of the bed, he heard someone yell, "*Charge!*"

The soldiers were followed by tiny pro-wrestling figures, Ninja Turtles and toy clowns. He whimpered as they closed in.

Tim dialled the correct number the second time, just as the first wave of soldiers scaled his body and punched their rifle knives deep into his chest and belly.

Then his phone connected to Alex's phone.

"Alex..." he said, before four bayonets were stabbed into his voice box. "*Ugh...*" he tried to speak further, but more and more berets joined the fray, and helped sever the cords in Tim's throat.

"*Hello...?*" Time heard his son say.

"G...e...o...f...he...Hous...e", he gargled and spat as the wrestlers hammered away at his legs and knees. He felt more bayonets punch through his lower back, sides and feet.

"*Dad?!*" the boy asked, "*Is that you?*"

Then all Tim could hear was Alex screaming, as the boy called his mother for help. "*Mam...My phone...It's attacking...*

The line went dead.

'*Sorry, No Service – Technological Disturbance*', Tim's phone said, which was the last thing he heard.

Sleigh Sisters

Kevin stood in the pouring-down snow, basking in the pink, red and purple neon lights of the strip joint called Pole Pussy. The garish glow was more than inviting; it was warming, causing a storm of emotions to swirl through his gut, head and heart – mainly because of Mandy, his fiancée of three years and their one-year-old twin girls, Megan and Molly.

They'd thought having a baby would have helped solve their marital problems, but a child had made things worse. Much worse, considering two had come along instead of one, not that a solo baby would have made much difference. They were doomed, the divide between them growing just like their mountain of bills and debt.

Kevin, as always, started burying his head in the sand when things between him and Mandy crumbled. He avoided grown-up conversations and heated discussions with her. He was a child trapped in a man's body.

I've never been good with confrontations; *a trait inherited from that weak-arse father of mine*, he thought.

As a child, he'd witnessed his mother push his father around – watched as she'd beaten him black and blue with a rolling pin, frying pan, wok, or anything else that came to hand. Eventually, she'd killed him by way of electrocution: when he'd been taking a bath, she'd thrown a toaster into the water, frying him.

To this day, Kevin could smell the charring of his dad's flesh.

From that day forward, he'd promised himself never to get stuck in a dead-end relationship, where the children end up suffering.

It's just like that poem, he thought. *They fuck you up, your mum and dad...* He couldn't remember the rest, continuing to stare into the eye of the neon club sign – his jaw lolled, and drool trickled over his lips and down his chin. Kevin could hear the faint excited buzz coming from inside.

The strip joint had been his sanctuary for the past three years, as his marriage and life fell to rack and ruin. And, just like the last two Christmas Eves, Kevin had come here and blown his work bonus, which could be his last due to his mediocre ways at his supermarket job.

Pfft, fuck it – let's make this my best Christmas ever, if it's to be my last!

Depression and thoughts of suicide had taken hold a few weeks back, after he'd had a warning from his supervisor. It had caused Kevin to devise a plan, should he lose his job. To him, that would be the final nail in his coffin. And so, if it came to it, he would take a dive off the local bridge, which had a drop of more than eighty feet.

When I hit the barely water-covered rocks below, my body will explode. The fuckers will be able to sweep me into a crisp packet! The thought made him smile, and then a shudder rolled down his body as snow found its way beneath the many layers he wore. *If I don't hurry up and get my arse in there, I won't have to think about taking that medal-winning dive because this fucking blizzard will have done the job for me!*

With that, Kevin walked over to the door and gave the familiar bouncer a season's greeting.

"Yo, Kev – how's it swinging?"

"In this weather?! It's shrivelled to the left!"

"*Ha!* Well, I'm sure the girlies inside will help you out in that department," the six-and-a-half foot gorilla said.

"Well, we ain't all blessed with a dick the size of a didgeridoo like our nigger kin!"

"Get your skinny white ass in there, blood, before I give you a yuletide hiding!"

Both men laughed as the bouncer held the door open for Kevin. "Take it easy, Austin," Kevin said, walking through the door and into the club's foyer.

He was met with Gloria – a middle-aged, well-past-her-dancing-days old boot who glared at him from behind her glass that helped make up the reception booth. She always gave him the evils. Kevin was unsure why, but he knew deep down that she hated him.

"You *again*?!" she snapped. "What's 'a matter, boy – can't get your worn-down pencil hard at home?" Gloria tried passing her comment off as a joke with a grizzled grin – her fake teeth almost popped out of her withered, whiskery chops.

At first, Kevin had thought the sourpuss was a friend or an acquaintance of Mandy's via her family, but she was neither. When that worry had popped up, he'd been quick in tactfully asking Mandy if she knew of a Gloria.

"No, why do you ask?" she'd asked.

"Oh, she's this old bag that's started working in our wages department. A right nightmare – thought you may have known her, or vice-versa, since she likes busting my nuts!"

The thought made his bollocks shy away further as he wiped the snow off his donkey jacket and stomped his work boots free of the white stuff. When he looked up and saw her horrified expression, he couldn't help but smile within.

Suck it up, you sour-mouthed bastard! he thought, knowing he'd never have the nuts to say it to her face.

For good measure, Kevin wiped his feet on the clean, expensive-looking carpets before removing his coat and tossing it over her glass window.

"Keep a hold of that for me, Gloria – there's a dear!"

"I—"

Before she could finish, he walked away from her counter and through the main doors to the dance lounge.

She'll probably end up pissing inside my coat with her wrinkled cunt, but I don't care. Let her. For tonight, I drink, relax and wank like fuck in paradise. With that, he rotated his wrists, satisfied when the joints cracked. *Time to get my fucking freak on!* he thought, removing his wallet and heading towards the bar.

Just like every Christmas Eve, the place was packed with drooling, lusting fellas – he could almost hear their dicks rising in unison. The thought made him smile as the pushed his way through the throng of horny men, feeling their large, small and stubby erections rub against his thighs as he went.

Even though he grimaced, he couldn't help but chuckle.

They can probably feel my *throbbing hardness!* he thought, pre-come trickling out of his excited love truncheon. *As long as no fucking fruit reaches out for a squeeze!*

A laugh escaped him, causing some of the men close by to look at him in an odd fashion. The others, however, ignored him, either not hearing him due to the loudness of the dance music or their intense interest in the showgirls on the various stages.

When he finally managed to get served at the bar, Kevin bought two bottles of beer and paid with a fifty-pound note.

"Can I get all the change in single one-pound bills?" he said, raising his voice.

The pretty girl with a smile-for-all gave him a curt nod, but he didn't really see it as he was too busy looking at her knockers.

How in the fuck is that t-shirt keeping her milk churns in?!

He smiled, and then chuckled once again.

Life at this particular moment was good, just like it always was when he visited the Pole Pussy.

"Ho-ho-ho, Merry Christmas!" he bellowed as his beer and singles were placed down on the bar in front of him. "Here's to Saint Nick!" Kevin took a large swallow from his first beer, and then bopped his way through the crowd.

Destination: Stage One.

"That's where all the new fanny perform," he uttered. "Some of them are barely legal…"

Behind him, an announcer for one of the other stages addressed the crowd. "And now, please welcome onto the pole… Chaos! This ball-busting domme will tear. Your. Soul. Apart…!" The lights flickered, and fake lightning lit up the inside of the club – distant thunder rumbled throughout the joint.

Kevin paid little heed and continued to plough through the crowd. Stage One was now in sight, and unusually quiet: ninety percent of the tables and chairs were empty, with nobody loitering up the sides of the runway.

"Oh well, more fun for me!" he said, taking up his spot at the very foot of the stage – he was close enough to the action that his lolling tongue could have *Brasso*'ed the pole, had he been inclined to do so.

When he looked over his shoulder, he noticed some of the other men staring at him. They whispered to one another. Some giggled and elbowed each other in a banter kind of way. On noticing Kevin peering over at them, they all looked away, not that he could hold eye contact with any of them for too long.

A chill snaked its way down his back.

His rock-hard cock faltered.

"What the *fuck* is their problem?" he practically whispered.

"Looks like we have a brave soul at Stage One!" a low, rasping and almost comic-book-like villainous voice boomed over the speakers that loomed over the area he stood in.

Kevin's smile returned. *This is new...* The confident stiffness returned to his manhood, settling his unwarranted jitters. *Those clowns probably weren't even looking at me!* he thought, casting a nervous glance in their direction.

Nobody was looking at him.

"Please welcome onto stage... the Sleigh Sisters!" said the same, sly-like-a-fox voice from somewhere behind the stage.

Kevin stepped back a tad, unsure of what to expect, but he needn't have worried: out from behind the curtain stepped two girls who could have passed for sixteen, maybe younger. They both had long, down-to-their-arse raven-coloured hair, with a black Santa hat atop their shocks of curls.

Their stockings, which were pull-ups and reached the bottom of their arse cheeks, had a red and green stripe pattern going on – much like elf socks – and both wore red, lacy Basques that matched their flimsy g-strings and crimson lipstick.

They looked like twins. They had the same facial features and body type: short stature, small tits and tiny backsides.

His dick almost lost its load then and there, but he quelled his horn as one strutted closer to him by body popping and rotating her hips and arse, whilst her 'sister' worked the pole with an expert fashion.

I wish the lights would go down! he thought, flirting with the zip on his jeans. Every time he'd visited the place over the last few years, he managed to strum one out to the girls on stage – the ones who had caught him playing with his dick had said nothing. They'd just danced harder for him, much to his delight.

Of course, they hadn't gone unrewarded. They had been given the biggest share of his wad of ones.

If this pair is anything to go by, they are going to love seeing me play with my cock! He beckoned the closest one to him with a couple of singles. When she was close enough, she got down on her knees, arched her back, and thrust her lace-covered pussy into his face.

Kevin made sure nobody was looking before shoving his nose against her cunt and smelling it. She didn't seem to mind; she rubbed herself against his beak and squealed.

He drew back and shoved ten ones down her knickers with glee – he allowed his fingers to linger, and then slip beneath her folds. She didn't protest, yell or lash out.

Fuck, I can't believe this! These bitches are hot to trot, his mind screamed. Kevin was all but jumping up and down whilst clapping his hands together like an excited child in that proverbial shop.

And then she did something totally unexpected. She leaned forward and sucked his fingers into her mouth.

"I'm a naughty little schoolgirl!" she breathed into his ear in a low, sultry voice.

His prick ejected his hot muck inside his underwear, but he was hard again within seconds.

"Are you going to spank me?" she continued. "My sister, too?"

"Why…?" he croaked.

"Because Mummy caught us eating each other out! And if we're not corrected come Christmas, then Santa won't be bringing us any pressies… No new dollies for me and my sister." She pulled back so Kevin could see the pout on her face.

"Yes! Daddy will correct you!"

She smiled, and then strutted off.

The other sister stepped forward, saying something into the ear of her sibling before snake-hipping her way to Kevin with a massive grin on her face. Over her shoulder, he could see the first sister stripping out of her Basque as she continued to dance – her small, almost neon pink nipples stood at attention, reminding him of erasers on pencils.

Oh, fuck… She looks so young. So cute. Her tits, so child-like. Not fully formed.

But he didn't have time to think things through, as the other sister had her lace-covered tits in his face – her hand low and searching. He suddenly felt her dainty fingers stroke his dick. It wasn't long before he blew his load again, making her smile and bite her lip.

"I can smell your dirty seed, you naughty man!" she whispered into his ear.

He gasped; his eyes rolled.

As much as he tried, he couldn't get his dick hard again – it stayed at a semi-stance as he watched the sisters dance, use the pole, kiss, play with each other and then roll into a lovers' knot on the floor.

They tossed their g-strings at him, which he recovered from the floor at his feet and stuffed into his jacket pocket – he had a secret drawer at home filled with such trophies.

"Go on, girls!" he yelled, leaning across the stage as much as he could and then showering their young, naked bodies in crisp one-pound notes. "Take the fucking lot, you dirty bastards!"

And then the most bizarre of things happened, causing Kevin to burst out laughing: a troop of disfigured, disgusting elves shambled onto stage and shuffled to the music. Clumps of what appeared to be their flesh dropped off them and shot crimson in all directions when they hit the stage floor.

"What the...?!" He was down with the whole fucked-up Santa, Christmas theme, but this was taking it a level too far. Kevin had never been one for horror or sick shit. "Erm, girls... Can we get back to the whole sexy dancing? I feel as though I've walked onto the rehearsal set for *Thriller*!" he quipped, and then laughed.

"But don't you want to spank us, daddy?" the one sister said.

"Yeah, because Mummy will be cross if you don't..." the other said, fingering her sister.

"Ooh, sis!" the first said.

"And there will be no pressies..." said the second.

All the while, the freaky elves danced around them.

"Yes, I want to spank you. Both of you!" he said, forgetting the weirdness of the situation.

They beckoned him with their red-tipped forefingers "Come!" they purred. "We have such pleasure to give you..."

As he clambered up on stage, jaw swinging, tongue lolling, and drooling like a rabid bulldog, the gang of elves threw themselves on him. The covered him like a net, pinning him to the floor. The more he struggled to free himself, the more intense the resistance became.

"What the fuck… Help!" he screamed. "*Heeelp!*"

Something foul-tasting was rammed into his mouth.

I'm in a club full of people… What's going on?

And that's when he felt something hard and heavy smash across the top of his head, sending him into a pool of deep blackness.

He stirred in his sleep to the feeling of someone sucking his cock. The further he rose to the surface of the dark pool, Kevin also felt his balls being squeezed – pleasure was being fused with extreme pain.

He tried to scream, but his mouth was gagged – all he could do was yell beneath it, which sounded muffled and pathetic.

Tears trickled down his face.

When he was finally able to open his eyes, he stared into nothingness. The world around him was blacked out. *Why can't I see?!* His mind screamed, and then he was shouting a muffled cry once again as his balls were twisted and yanked on viciously.

His body spasmed.

The surface he lay on felt soft. It yielded beneath his weight – springs crunched as he thrashed his body.

"*Stop!*" he yelled, but it sounded distorted.

Kevin cried uncontrollably. Then the fabulous sensation of the hot mouth on his throbbing dick returned. His nuts tightened, and he forgot all about the pain he had gone through only moments ago.

It's the sisters… dirty bitches! he suddenly realised. *It's some form of game. A sex game. But why attack me? Knock me out?*

Then he felt teeth nibble at his helmet.

He squirmed at the delicious sensation – a shiver cut a path down his back.

His bollocks were left alone, which he was grateful for.

As he grew close to orgasm, his hands balled up the material he lay on into his fists.

"Oh, God! Don't stop...*Please!*" he gasped, feeling the mouth pull away. He wanted to cry – never had he been teased so badly. Kevin slammed his fists down at his sides in frustration, noting that he had rope or some form of rough material wrapped around his wrists.

He couldn't move his legs either, due to them being tied.

"Hey, what's the big idea, ladies?!" he snapped, the fear in his guts making him brave. Kevin heard them giggling. It made his dick bob. "Why not untie me, and I'll show you exactly what I can do with my hands and tongue!"

"Oh, we have special plans for you, Kevin!" one of the girls said.

"Yes, *very* special plans!" the sister said, whipping the hood off his head to reveal his location. She then pulled the gag free from his mouth.

"Jesus *Christ!*" he yelled, sitting up as much as possible on the bed. He was devoid of clothing. The bedposts and frame were made from snakes, which writhed and spit at him – the snake-posts closest to his head had their forked tongues close to his face. "Get them away from me!"

The girls giggled.

And then he noticed it was one of the elves that had been sucking his dick. A breath lodged in his throat. He didn't scream, just stared in wide-eyed wonder – the elf appeared to be a zombie. The flesh around its face and neck was peeling, revealing maggots beneath. Blood trickled out of its mouth and Kevin could see its teeth through its cheeks, which had holes in them. It too had a serpent-like tongue, but stank of soggy earth and death.

The elf-zombie looked up at Kevin and snarled before bending over and deep-throating him once again – he felt the thing's thick, bloody-saliva plaster his cock, making bile leap up his throat and flood his mouth.

"Please! Get it the fuck…" Kevin let his words trail off. His mouth sagged. "What the… Where am I?!" he shrieked, seeing a lake of fire behind the amorous elf – waterfalls of molten lava crashed into it, causing its banks to spill over. Bodies of dead children were being fed to the roasting, bubbling lake.

For the first time since coming around, he heard the continuous, torturous sounds of others about him. He spotted more and more zombie elves shuffling in the cavernous shadows. The air reeked of charred flesh and ash.

His eyes stung. Fresh tears poured out of him.

"Am I in a volcano?!" The question sounded even stupider aloud.

Both girls laughed.

He couldn't see them; they were behind him.

"No, you fucking pervert!" one of the girls said, stepping into view. "You're in Santa Klaws Hell!"

"*What*?!" he blurted, almost laughing.

"Santa Klaws Hell, dickhead!" the second girl said. "This section of it is run by us, the Sleigh Sisters. We take care of all the naughty grown-up men: cheating husbands, unfaithful partners, thieves, rapists, killers, muggers… You name it, we've ticked 'em off the Bad Boy List."

"Of course, there's more than just the two of us," Girl One said, circling the bed like a vulture with a large, wooden ruler in her hand – she wore her red Basque. "There's a whole division of us – Santa Klaws created us. He and Mrs. Klaws are too busy dealing with the children to handle the adults, too."

"But...but... I've always been a good bloke, sort of. I've never broken the law..."

"No, but you've broken your wife's heart. A faithful one at that!" Girl One said, smacking his hard dick with her ruler.

He cried out in agony.

She chuckled, as did her sister.

"Yes," Girl Two said. "We don't feel the need to drag all the men like you down here. The unfaithful – we only do that if we get a request. I mean, if we pulled all you dirty, perverted fuckers down here, we'd have no room left!" she quipped, holding a hand to her mouth to titter behind.

"A request...?" He was almost too scared to say the word. If this really was Santa Klaws Hell, then Kevin knew where a request for his naughtiness had come from.

"Yes, dear – your wife!" Girl One said, confirming his fear. She smiled. "Don't worry, you'll get to see her very shortly. Even though we drag you pesky, naughty fellas down here, we don't do the punishing. We leave that up to the injured party."

"Yeah, that's their present, see!" Girl Two said.

"I don't believe a fucking word you bitches are saying," he said. "And get that fucking thing off my dick! Enough with this Halloween shit. Did you fuckers slip something into my beer? Am I tripping?!" Kevin tried kicking out at the elf, but it was futile. He started laughing hysterically.

"How cute, he doesn't believe us!"

"Well, maybe we should drive the point home," the second girl said, and then clapped her hands.

Kevin lifted his head off the pillow and watched on in anticipation. A section of rock to his left slid to one side, much like a patio door, and out walked Gloria. His mouth sagged and he tried to speak, but his words kept tripping over themselves.

Gloria walked up to him. Behind her shuffled six zombie elves. In her hand, she held a letter.

"Dear Mr. Klaws," she read after clearing her throat, "I have come to fear that my husband may be breaking his marital vows by visiting strip joints and screwing the dancers. I want him punished for Xmas. Can you help? Signed, Mandy Hopestead."

"Bullshit! What is this? I demand you tell me, now!" Kevin said, finally finding his backbone. "I'll have your fucking guts…"

"It's not bullshit, Kevin," he heard a familiar voice say.

He turned his head and saw his wife walk through the door Gloria had.

"I thought Santa Klaws Hell was a load of shit, until I heard some of the other mothers discuss it at baby group."

"And that's how you know Gloria? You told me you didn't know her!"

"I didn't. I was told she was the postmistress for Santa Klaws Hell. You poor, dumb bastard – you picked the only strip joint in town to have a portal to this place!" Mandy laughed. It sounded cruel.

"I… We can make things work!" he pleaded. "I was desperate. Lonely. I couldn't help myself."

"All I want for Christmas is my two front teeth!" one of the girls said, walloping him in the mouth with a ballpoint hammer.

"Ugh-*argh*!" he cried, flying backwards on the bed. Teeth and blood popped from his smashed mouth and sprayed the horny, dick-sucking elf. Kevin was dazed, but he managed to stay awake. With one eye on Mandy, he watched her. "Please…" he slurred. Broken teeth surfed out of his mouth.

"You should have thought about the girls!" Mandy said, revealing a pair of shears from behind her back.

"No..." he pleaded. "I can change."

"I can change!" the second girl mocked.

The zombie elves closed in on him and, on the click of the first girl's fingers, bit into his arms, legs and torso. They tore great, bloody chunks from him before Mandy moved in to deliver the deathblow.

Kevin, whilst screaming, felt the coolness of the blades press against his prick, which he willed to shrivel. But it didn't.

"This is the best Christmas present ever!" Mandy said. She eased the blades together, which cut into him at a painfully slow pace, causing his blood to seep and then gush.

As he jigged and choked on his blood, Mandy stuffed his cock into his mouth and said, "Merry Christmas, baby!"

For the Love of Shakespeare

Edmund lay there awake, eyes burning as if he had grit in them. He stared at the ceiling, praying the noise had come to an end. Edgar, Edmund's brother, was in the attic, rattling his chains and stomping his feet.

"*Chum!*" Edgar wailed, which sounded faint through the floorboards. "Chum, Edmund. Please!" the half-man, half-monster, and completely fucking insane Edgar pleaded; some people had speculated that they were illegitimate siblings, but it had never been proven.

"The doctors should never have agreed to your release from Castell Hirwaun – the nuthouse was too good for you, brother!" he said, between gritted teeth. "Having said that, you should have been drowned at fucking birth, just like all the other runts and cunts of this world."

"Edmund..." came the groany, moany voice once again.

To be fair, it has been the best part of a week since I fed him last... he thought. *What would Mum think, old Juliet dearest, if she knew I was mistreating her ever-so-beloved Edgar, her first born?!*

"Never did find your Romeo, did you...?" he uttered bitterly.

"*Please*, Edmund!"

He grabbed the broom from by the side of his bed and started jabbing the non-bristle end at the ceiling. "Shut. The. Fuck. *Up!*" he yelled, lowering the brush.

"*Chum!*"

"Shut up! You fucking freak!" Rapidly and repeatedly, Edmund hammered at the ceiling with the brush once again. This time, however, he didn't stop until he could feel the heat in his face and his forearm ached. Sweat burst from his forehead like a ruptured dam. "I won't tell you again, *brother*! Shut it! Or I'll have to come up there... You won't like that, will you?!" Edmund threatened. In that moment, he looked at the cricket bat he had on the other side of his bed. "You know what will happen if I do, don't you?!" He tried to make his voice sound as strong as possible, because he knew if Edgar detected the slightest hint of fear then he would lose the upper hand.

And that could never, *ever* happen.

For the past six years, ever since their mother died, Edmund had ruled his monstrous brother with an iron fist.

Someone had to, for if the six-foot-eight, child-eating Edgar ever slipped his chains and escaped the confines of the family home, he would kill and destroy everything in his path. There would be no stopping him; he would be like a Rottweiler on steroids.

Why the hell did the doctors agree to his release? They knew how much of a threat he is! Because our mother was terminally ill at the time, that's why. Fucking idiots. They must have been crazier than Edgar!

"'We can't deny a dying woman her final wish,'" he mimicked the doctors. "'If Edgar goes on to cause trouble after his release, then we will have no option but to bring him back and keep him under our supervision for good, Mrs. Speare…'"

Of course, Edgar's doctors at the home for the criminally insane had not been aware of his habits of killing and devouring babies, teens and children in general. Edgar had never been tried for such crimes because Mother had covered them up.

All he'd been charged with were acts of insane violence, leading to the grievous harm of many; it had been imperative he was taken off the streets. However, the courts had found him to be sick in the head, and psychiatric treatment was for the best.

"My Edmund here will help me take good care of him, Doctor," he heard his mother say. "We have a *special* room in the house for him."

While reminiscing, he continued to stare at the bat. In the light cast by his candle, which burned in a sconce on top of his bedside table, Edmund could see multiple trails of dried blood on the smooth surface of the cricket implement, along with strands of hair that were stuck to it.

From above, silence, bar the faint rattle of Edgar's chains.

Thank fuck, he's settling down! Edmund thought, looking away from his bat and returning to glaring at the ceiling. He could still remember what the awful sanatorium looked and felt like: the long, drawn-out halls were icy-cold, matching the cheerless décor. Every footfall, light or heavy, reverberated around the building with a deafening sound.

The cold inside the old castle-cum-nuthouse wasn't the worst part. The screaming of patients and the buzzing of the electrode machines the doctors used to fry the brains of the insane were.

On getting too close to a window of a door looking in on a room, Edmund had watched as a group of nurses and a doctor set to work on a female patient. Whilst the nurses strapped the frail-looking woman's arms and legs to the bed and pumped her veins full of juice, the doctor had zapped her head.

He could still see the scorch marks on her temple and smell the burning of her flesh; the hospital garb she wore soaked through with piss and excrement.

"You get used to all the joyous sights and sounds," a pretty young nurse with big tits and a lopsided nametag had told him. "Now, why don't you run along and find your mummy and demented brother!"

At the time, Edmund had been young – eighteen, nineteen – and not the man of thirty he was now. Even though he'd been a teen, he'd still wanted to smash her face in for demeaning him in such a way.

But he hadn't.

God, that was one long, fucking visit! he thought, rolling onto his side after blowing his candle out. *I don't think I'm going to get any more trouble out of Edgar tonight.*

A few weeks after Edgar was turned over to the care of his mother and brother, Juliet passed, leaving them alone. Her dying words had been for Edmund to take good care of his brother, who she loved more than anything, even him.

He'd always known where she stood on the scale of care for her sons, but he was okay with it.

Edmund had been one for his father, until he ran off with a woman half his age. Still, he'd never resented him for it, knowing full well what he'd had to put up with: a wife who was a complete bitch and a monster for a son.

Edgar may have been grotesque to look at, but his craziness stemmed from his mother's obsessive love for all things Shakespeare: she would spend hours, days, weeks, even months on end reading and rereading the Bard's plays, stories and poems. When she wasn't reading William's plethora of misery, she was acting it out in the house, on the streets, in the pub or anywhere else she could get away with it.

On many occasions, she'd been carted off to a prison cell for disturbing the peace. Juliet was so mad on Shakespeare, she legally changed her name to Juliet Speare in the year her first son was born, naming him Edgar after the son of Gloucester from the play *King Lear;* Gloucester had two sons, and so, a couple of years later, Edmund came along.

From the moment they'd been born, Juliet had spoon-fed them nothing but Shakespeare. She didn't just read it to them all day and night, but preached it. After suffering many years at the hands of their mother, Edgar finally snapped, and it wasn't long before babies, toddlers and teens started vanishing from around town.

The bodies of infants and alike were found with their heads chewed off. In some cases, arms and legs had been savagely ripped from the children's' trunks and they had been beaten to death with them. Gruesome scenes were found daily, in and around their hometown, with Mother coming to her beloved son's rescue on every occasion.

Dad was much better off out of it! Edmund thought, closing his eyes and willing himself to sleep. But sleep wouldn't come. *What the hell is wrong with me? You know what...*

The thought made him squeeze his thighs tight together in fear he'd lost the contents of his bladder. His anus squeaked.

Edgar wasn't the only one with blood on his hands. Nor was he the only one who belonged at the crazy farm...

Edmund pulled the covers tighter around him – a chill had found its way into the centre of his bed. A nest of ice-vipers settled in the pit of his guts.

A year after Edgar was placed in Edmund's care, Edmund met, fell in love with and married a girl he knew from his schooldays: Elizabeth. She had been the typical girl-next-door type, which Edmund had found most endearing, being a shy person himself.

Some would have called their relationship a 'whirlwind romance': living together within the first few months of courtship, engaged by six, and then wed after a year.

When it feels right, it's right...

Before he'd moved her in, however, the introduction to Edgar had to be made. Luckily for Edmund, she took it all in stride, not finding it too hard to live under the same roof as an attic-monster.

She even helped feed, wash and change him...

After all, she loved Edmund and saw herself as his wife.

From this day forward, for better, for worse...

But over the course of the years that followed, Edmund became jealous of Edgar because Elizabeth seemed to be getting closer to his half-man, half-killer-monster of a brother.

Sometimes, when Edmund had caught her feeding Edgar, he witnessed sexual attraction and activity between the beauty and the beast. Edmund would watch from the shadows, half out of his mind with jealousy and rage as she seductively fed and flirted with Edgar, thinking they were alone in the dark, shadowy attic.

Gently, Edgar would lick her fingers clean and she would release his arms from his shackles, which were bolted to the wall. This was a rule never to be broken – not even their mother had freed his hands.

Elizabeth would let Edgar's hands roam her body, to mould her tits and make him grab her snatch.

Her small, almost soundless gasps of joy would drive him to the point where he almost revealed himself from the shadows.

But he hadn't.

Edmund managed to bottle his rage, swallowing it down into the pit of his guts. He allowed their dirty little rendezvous to continue, until one day when he found them fucking and sucking and kissing and grunting and groaning and yanking hair… which pushed him over the edge.

****

Before he started to climb the old, rickety ladder leading to the attic, Edmund could hear their gratuitous sounds of bestial love-fucking.

Elizabeth had thought him away on a business trip – a façade made up to try and catch her out. And from where he was standing, the smoke screen could not get smokier.

She was indeed a cheating, good-for-nothing whore.

A dead as fuck one, at that.

"Oh, fuck – I'm *coming*!" she screamed. "I'm coming, I'm coming, I'm coming!"

From the shrill sound of her orgasmic pleasure, Edmund feared she would soak the ceiling through as he put his foot on the first rung, followed by the second and then third.

Never, ever has she screamed like that for me! he thought, clenching his jaw until it clicked and then ached. *"I can't have orgasms…"* he heard her tell his brother.

His hands turned white as he gripped the sides of the ladder with all the power he could muster.

I'll fucking kill them…

The closer he got to the hatch, the more intense her filthy, nauseating sounds of gyrating fulfilment became.

When he finally reached the top of the ladder, he poked his head through the opening and saw them rutting by candlelight. They were close to his chains, their garments flung about the room as though there had been an explosion at a clothes shop.

Edmund saw her small, sweat-covered tits jounce wildly as she rode Edgar's cock. Her back arched. Her long hair lashed out in all directions, as though a demented circus master sat atop her head and cracked a cat o' thousand tails made from her golden strands.

In that instant, the pearl beads he'd bought her for Christmas the previous year were torn from her exposed throat by his lust-filled brother. She squealed in excited shock, causing her to ride him faster. Harder. Deeper.

Again, she shrieked. "I'm coming! Oh God, I'm coming…"

The way she sounded, Edmund thought she was going to cry – her sounds of pure pleasure, at times, sounded like a wounded animal screaming.

As he watched on, tears slid down his cheeks.

His hard cock pushed against his zip.

Out of spite, he freed his erection and stroked himself to climax, all the while watching his brother destroy his wife's cunt.

Before his cock exploded a milky white stream, his eyes fused with his brother's – a smile pulled across Edgar's hideous face.

The solidness in Edmund's dick wavered, but not through ejaculation alone.

He ducked out of sight and raced down the ladder on shaking pins. As he stomped across the landing, putting his dick away at the same time, Edmund cursed them into a heap.

When he got to the living room, he went to the back door and looked outside, spotting his shovel placed against his garden shed.

Now it was his turn to smile.

"I'm home!" he called, opening and then slamming the back door. "Liz? Liz, are you here?!"

Edmund couldn't help but smile at the sound of rushing, stumbling thumps from the attic.

"Shit, he's back early!" he heard his darling dearest utter, as she walked across the landing towards the stairs. "I thought you weren't back until Monday evening?" Elizabeth asked. "Is everything okay?"

He caught glimpses of her fixing her hair, straightening her dress and then wiping the sex-sweat from her flushed cheeks and brow. Edmund moved to the bottom of the stairs and looked up at her.

She wore the summer dress he had bought her for her birthday last week, with nude-coloured tights underneath. The look had always driven him crazy, since the dress was rather short and exposed a lot of thigh.

Edmund felt his dick start to stiffen once again.

"Hey, Liz," he said, beaming. "The meeting got cancelled today so we came home early. Surprised?"

"*Yes*! It's lovely that you're home early."

I'll bet it is, he thought. *I'll just bet it is*... "Come out the back, I have a gift for you..." he said.

"From your trip?" A smile spread across her face as she rushed down the stairs and followed him to the back door.

"Yes," he called over his shoulder. He led her out to the garden and pointed at the shed. "It's in there."

"But why, dear?!"

"I had to put it somewhere, just in case you saw it as I entered the back. I love you," he lied, stroking her face. "I see you wore the dress... Anticipating my return?"

She blushed. "Well, let me see this gift of yours."

"Go ahead, Liz. Just open the door and feast your eyes!"

He saw her smile grow wider as she stepped towards the shed's door. When her back was fully to him, he grabbed the shovel and raised it high above his head.

"Cheating bitch!" he uttered between gritted teeth.

"*Huh*?!" she gasped, turning to look at her husband.

The shovel ploughed into her face, breaking her nose and jaw simultaneously – blood shot in all directions as she collapsed to the flagstones. Her hand instinctively went to her nose, trying stem the blood flow.

"Damn, you're one ugly cunt!" he said, spitting on her. Then his breathing came in ragged gasp – her dress had rucked up around her waist during her fall, exposing her stocking tops and jism-soaked bush. "You didn't even have the respect to put your fucking knickers back on!" he snapped.

"Ugh...uch-urgh..." she tried to speak, but nothing but a garbled mess and a fountain of blood came from her mouth. Tears spilled down her cheeks.

"Huh?" he said, cupping his ear with his hand. "I can't hear you!" He then chuckled and undid his belt. "I can't let my brother have all the fun." Throwing the shovel to one side, he slid his trousers and underwear down his bony legs, and then removed them completely.

His cock was hard.

Edmund got on his knees and roughly shoved her legs apart, ramming his tongue deep into her still-wet pussy.

"Mmm, you both taste so nice!" He raised his head to look at her – the disgust on her face only helped heighten his excitement. Edmund smiled and lowered his head, wanting to lick her snatch clean before fucking her. His hands stroked her stocking-clad thighs as he did so.

Once he'd satisfied his oral need, he roughly turned her over and shoved his dick up her arse – she screamed as he lanced her tight anus. Blood squirted onto his chest, but it didn't stop him. He grabbed her hair and smashed her face into the flagstones a dozen times; some of her teeth rattled along the ground.

When he was spent, he turned her over and shoved the tip of the spade into her mouth and pushed down on the handle with all his might.

"Die, bitch!" he screamed, then grunted and groaned as he leaned all his weight on the spade.

She gargled and thrashed as the tip of the digging implement cut through her jaw and separated the top half of her head. It rolled along the floor and hit the shed, leaving a bloody stump print on its slats...

****

After that, into the wood chipper she went, he thought, rolling onto his back.

But her death had haunted him for a long time after.

He couldn't get rid of the bloodstains on his hands. He could *see* the crimson spots dripping from them. No matter how many times he scrubbed them with soap and a wire brush, the stains would reappear, causing him to laugh hysterically. Fear would nestle in him. Tears would roll, but the chuckling would continue.

"*It's all in your head*!" a tiny voice would whisper at the back of his brain.

Often he found himself screaming, "Out, damn'd spot! Out!" However, he couldn't remember the words that followed the famous quote... No matter how hard he tried.

Oh, how mother would be bitterly disappointed.

"Fuck the old cunt! She's shuffled off this mortal coil." The saying brought a smile to his face.

After sorting Elizabeth out, Edmund had dealt with Edgar in a harsh manner: he'd taken the cricket bat to him and pummelled his brother into a state of unconsciousness. When Edgar finally blacked out, bleeding freely, Edmund had locked him back in chains, this time adding a metal choker.

Then he'd started starving him for days on end before finally feeding him – a practice which continued to this day. The longest he'd let Edgar go without some form of nutrition was eight days.

A chuckle escaped him. "Some would probably say the bitch had it easier. That her suffering was *relatively* quick..."

Right, I must *get some sleep,* he thought.

As he nestled deeper into his bed, happy that the chill had been dispatched, a starling crash from above caused him to sit bolt upright. His covers gathered around at his waste.

Thump, thump, thump, thump...

"*Chum*!" Edgar wailed. "Chum, chum, chum..."

"Fuck sake. Shut up, Edgar. I mean *it*!"

The thumping continued.

Edmund covered his ears, but the sound was so intense, it found its way beyond hands and into his brain.

Edgar's yelling turned into a high-pitched screech that only a girl or a sack-less male could make.

Panic enclosed him, but he shook it off when he caught sight of the bat.

"Right, that's it!" he screamed at the ceiling. Edmund tossed his covers to one side, relit his candle, and then grabbed the bat. He stalked out of his room and onto the landing. Once there, he walked until he was standing underneath the hatch that led to the garret.

Edmund grabbed the pull string and yanked it. When the lid flipped down, it revealed a foldaway ladder. He caught a hold of the legs on the steps and drew it out of its resting place. Once he'd clicked the ladder into place, he began his climb.

A keen wind whistled down the hole, causing the flame on his candle to waver.

"*Shit!*" he exclaimed, but his light didn't extinguish.

When he got to the top of the steps, he poked his head through the opening and looked at the area where Edgar was normally restrained.

His jaw sagged.

The chains hung limp. Edgar was nowhere to be seen.

Edmund boosted himself into the dusty room and made circles. All the while, he thrust the candle out in front of him. His brother was nowhere to be found.

"I know you're in here!" he yelled, walking over to Edgar's restraints. When he stepped on something hard, he looked down and saw piles of tiny bones. "I see you've been snacking on the rats. Well, at least you've solved that little problem for me – I won't have to call an exterminator now."

A flash of movement to his left drew Edmund's head in that direction. He was just in time to see a shape disappear behind a few towers of old, dusty boxes. Before he could step forward, another gust of wind caught his candle, bringing with it a foul stench of damp.

"Get out from behind those boxes, you son-of-a-fucking-bitch!" He made a move towards Edgar's hiding place. "Need I remind you, dear brother, that I have the bat... Get back in your restraints, or you'll be sorry!" He tried to sound as tough as he could, but he wasn't even convincing himself.

As he stepped closer, a board creaked.

Shuffling feet could be heard in the darkness.

"Don't make this any harder than it has to be, Edgar! I let you live, didn't I? I could have killed you, like I killed that wife of mine. She fucked—"

"You mean *my* wife," came a voice from the darkness.

"What are you talking about, Edgar?"

"You mean Edmund! *You're* Edgar, not me... Elizabeth was *my* wife, not yours. You killed her out of jealousy and then locked me in here. I was meant to be the one looking after *you*. What would Mum think?!"

"Have you slipped further over the edge?! *I'm* Edmund! Aren't I...?!" he said, doubt creeping in.

"Without your medication, you don't know what's what, brother."

"Stop trying to confuse me!" Edmund said, raising the bat. "Now, come out from behind those boxes and get back in your chains. Now, damn it."

"You're the one that belongs in the chains, you hideous freak!"

"Right, I'm coming in to get you," Edmund said, raising his candle and thrusting the bat out in front of him.

The wind picked up inside the room and whipped the cloth off a tall mirror to Edmund's right, causing him to look. In the cracked glass, he saw his hideously deformed, scarred face: a hole at the side of his head where an ear should have been, his nose nothing more than a flattened mess.

He dropped the bat.

"It can't be!" he screamed. "I'm Edmund, not Edgar!"

"No, brother. You're Edgar," the voice taunted from the shadows. "And you're going to pay for what you've done."

"But...but... It's all been in my head...*No*..." the true Edgar whimpered, unable to take his eyes off the glass. His teeth were nothing more than needles, all lined up in a crooked, misshapen mess.

"You see, *Edgar*, you managed to slip your chains one day and catch me off-guard. Once you had, you knocked me out and locked me in *your* chains. Once you had me, you forced me to watch as you raped and killed Elizabeth..."

"No! You lie!" Edgar said, twirling on his heel to face his brother, who had now stepped from behind the boxes, his face pure.

"Afraid not, brother."

"I caught you fucking *my* wife!"

"No, *my* wife, Edgar. Mine. Because you've been off your medication for so long, you've slipped into a state of denial. You're making up fantasises in your mind. You're Edgar! Look again in the mirror – the glass does not lie."

"I..." Edgar let his words trail off. "I won't let you take your identity back!" he raged. After he placed the candle by his feet, he then flew at Edmund with the bat held high over his head. "I'll kill you!"

"You should have done that when you had the chance," Edmund said, pulling a flare gun from behind his back. Edgar stopped dead in his tracks. "Say hi to mother, you cunt!" He pulled the trigger, which fired a burning shell into Edgar's left eye, turning it to lava.

The monster howled, dropping the bat and stumbling about the room. He crashed into the mirror and then the tower of boxes.

"The things you find in an attic!" Edmund said, throwing the spent gun to one side. He then picked up a poker he had by his side and took to his deranged brother, who was rolling about the floor, holding his burst eye.

Edmund stood over Edgar. "You should never have been released from the hospital, Edgar. I should have seen to you a long time ago." He raised the poker and was about to bring it down when Edgar sprang from the floor, jungle predator-like, and sank his piranha-like teeth into Edmund's neck.

With a vicious tear, skin, blood and bone came away with Edgar's bite.

Blood dashed up the wooden support beams on the ceiling and splashed the floor.

Edmund collapsed to the ground, holding a hand to his wound. Blood ran between his fingers. His body did the jig of the dying as he watched Edgar walk over to the hatch and make his way down the ladder.

"Nothing personal, brother, but I did warn you to settle down, did I not? Had you listened, you probably would have continued living out your life as Edgar..." he said, and then smiled as he disappeared out of sight and closed the hatch on the dying Edmund...

Diverted

He brought the car to a screeching halt, taking no note if anything was close behind him on the old, dark road. No horn blared as he looked up and into the rear-view mirror.

Nothing.

The road was a graveyard.

A relic of its time.

It had been replaced some years ago by the dual carriageway to his left. Looking over to that road now, the one he *should* be on, Pete caught glimpses of vans, cars and lorries, as they thundered past on the brightly-lit motorway – their blurred presence was barely visible through the trees that hampered most of his view.

"*Fuck!*"

Facing front, he looked at the passageway before him, and saw that his strong headlights barely exposed the now grubby cat's eyes. The streetlights were long turned off, making it feel like he was driving through a tunnel.

Debris lay scattered across the aged and cracked tarmac. It blew wild in the late evening wind: leaves, used packets of crisps and snacks, bags and all sorts of general rubbish was tossed about, reducing his visibility further. All that's missing, Pete thought, are tumbleweeds...

Branches from overgrown trees dangled low, and thickets either side helped narrow the road. Sitting in his heated car with the headlights burning, Pete considered turning around, even though it would add another hour to his journey. Looking at his watch, he knew he couldn't afford it. He had less than forty minutes to get to work, or he'd lose the whole deal – his company couldn't afford to take such a hit.

His boss would not only have his guts, heart and balls for breakfast he'd also make sure Pete would never get such a respectable job ever again; his career would be fucked.

It was this way, or no way.

Tardiness was not an option.

Not if he wanted to keep his job, his cushy lifestyle and his hot, yet pampered wife.

He thumped the steering wheel. "Stupid, stupid, *stupid*!" he raged.

Once again he found himself on the old road between Neath and Hirwaun. A road Pete said he'd *never* travel again. *Ever*! Not since *that* summer's evening back in July, five years ago, when the road had started to die off.

It was a road he used to use as a shortcut.

And that's where his mind had been at, when he'd taken the diversion back at the roundabout.

"Why the hell didn't I just leave earlier?" he elbowed the window at his side and winced at the sharp pain. Because Sue was polishing the end of your cock, that's fucking why! "I...I...can't," he whispered, his body shaking involuntarily. His mouth suddenly felt dry. His tongue seemed twice its normal size, as a cold sweat ensued. "No...*Shit*!"

Time ticked on.

Thirty-five minutes until the meeting with the Japanese took place.

Thirty-five minutes until Pete's company lost a quarter-of-a-billion pounds. Thirty-five minutes until his life as he knew it was over...

He put the car in gear, stepped off the clutch, and let it roll forward. Looking in the rear-view mirror now was like looking down a well, trying to seek out its bottom.

Obscurity.

Nothingness.

Was there even a road behind or beyond his lights?

He shivered, as the car gathered momentum.

What if I continue on and plunge into a bottomless canyon? he thought. *Now I am being stupid.* Pete shook the wheel with frustration. "Okay, okay. Let's just get this done, Pete," he told himself, and pushed down harder on the accelerator. *I'll be home and celebrating with Sue before I can say 'Multi-billion-pound-deal'*, he thought, smiling.

With the radio down low, Pete could hear his tyres crunching on glass, twigs, gravel, and other various bits and bobs as the car rocked and bumped its way down the road.

There was no cavern laying in wait, just a thick, gobble-you-up darkness, which his lights couldn't penetrate. Not even on full beam. None of the cat's eyes glowed at the touch of his headlamps. Pete realised that the reflector studs in most were actually broken, and not just soil-covered.

"It's going to take me all night to get to bloody work at this rate!" noting he was only doing twelve-miles-per-hour.

Thirty-minutes until the meeting with Mr. Ichikawa.

Pete had heard that the Japanese businessman was not someone you trifled with; he didn't hang around for you, either. It was well known that Mr. Ichikawa would get up and just walk out of meetings if he wasn't happy. Hell, he was that wealthy he could buy the UK six-times over! "I guess mentioning Pearl Harbour is out of the question then!" Pete muttered, letting a girl-like giggle slip, which helped ease his fear.

Grasping the steering wheel, Pete sped up as fast as the broken trail allowed. "I can't believe I'm back on this fucking road. I really should have turned back. I've got no business being here. What if someone...someone *what*? Recognises the car? Are you out of your mind?! It's been close to five years. There isn't even a road to speak of any longer. It's *dead*..."

His sentence trailed off, as a huge building to his left came into sight. The car's headlights found sections of it, one piece at a time. It was set back off the road, with a massive car park at the front. A burnt-out car, with a gaping hole in its windshield, stood motionless in front of the place; the smashed window reminded Pete of a mouth twisted into a vile grin, with jagged glass teeth.

Are you a child? You must be. Only a child would think of such babyish ideas, he thought.

The walls to the building were cracked and broken, with portions of the structure lying in a pile of rubble. All the windows were smashed, all the doors missing.

"I don't remember seeing this place the last time I was out here?" he asked himself, his words coming slow, his eyes transfixed. Pete pulled the car off the road and into the building's 'car park'. "Where did you come from?" he whispered to himself, intrigued by the place and its state of ruin.

Stopping the car, Pete rolled the passenger side window down so he could get a better look. He saw the words '*Hob's Café*' written on the only intact piece of glass.

A chill wind whistled out of the building and battered the car. In the dim light, he could just about make out overturned tables and chairs scattered about inside. Shivering, he made to leave, but heard something from inside. It sounded like glass being crushed under foot.

Chilly sweat trickled down the sides of his face. He thought he heard a whispery voice escape the skeletal building…"I *know*," it said.

The ghostly words, entwined with the cold wind, cut him to the bone. Putting the car in gear, Pete slowly chanced a sideways look toward the building, fearing the owner of the voice would be standing there.

Transfixed, he continued to stare, as a shape appeared.

It was wearing nothing but rags – rags that flapped in the stiff breeze. It raised its hand and pointed a bony finger at Pete. Pushing the accelerator to the floor, the car skidded and kicked up plumes of smoke and dust, along with stones and gravel.

He raced away from *Hob's Café.*

Twenty-minutes until the meeting…

Some distance from the Café, he eased his foot off the accelerator. For the first time he could hear the damage that the low branches were causing the car's bodywork, not to mention the grief the potholes were giving the suspension.

"Easy, Pete, easy," he told himself. His eyes were beginning to sting, as the sweat from his forehead found its way into them. "It was *him*. It was! Had to be!" he suddenly screeched, and started sobbing like a four-year-old child.

His erratic speed picked up once again as his heart galloped along like a bookie's favourite. All worries about being late for his big meeting were lost.

"Calm down or you'll give yourself a heart attack! It wasn't him. Couldn't have been. How could it be?" he asked himself.

His foot once again eased up on the accelerator.

Rational thoughts started to leak in, which helped soothe his nerves. "Calm down, it's just your mind playing tricks on you. That's all. It's dark, and the shadows were thrown by the headlights, that's all…" his bottom lip trembled. "N…N…*No!* This *can't* be!" he squealed like a pig with a slashed throat, as Hob's Cafe came back into view.

"What the hell *is* this?!"

The car's tyres screeched, as he hit the brakes viciously. Clouds of dust were thrown up along with the smoke from the burning rubber. Pete shook his head as rage took control. Clenching his teeth, he punched the accelerator to the floor and raced the car down the poorly lit road once again.

He tore past Hob's Cafe, only to end up back in the same place again, and again, and again…

After the tenth or eleventh time, he surrendered to the loop he was stuck in. "It wasn't my fault," he yelled, pounding at the side panel of his door. "It was dark, I didn't see him!" he cried. Snot streamed from his nose as he sat there, the engine idling. "The police called it an accident on the news – even they thought the driver may not have noticed you!" He wasn't even sure whom he was shouting to, as he was that frightened and confused.

It had also been a foggy night, he recalled, resting his head on the wheel and closing his eyes. But as misty as it may have been, Pete had still seen the man in his rags, seconds before he'd ploughed his car straight through him.

It hadn't technically been a hit-and-run.

Pete had got out of the car. He fully intended on calling the emergency services until he'd seen the victim. The body had been dragged underneath the car. One of the tyres had ripped most of the man's face clean off. The neck snapped. Bones were found jutting from skid-marked skin. Blood gushed out of the man's wounds like water from a toppled fire hydrant.

His left leg and right arm had been twisted into unfathomable positions – teeth and bone matter decorated the tarmac as though someone had come along with a box of morbid confetti. One of the man's shoes had launched itself into a hedge. His duffle bag, along with his sign, had been flung far down the road.

"Oh, *shit*!" Pete had gasped, raking clawed fingers through his hair before dragging the mangled body off the road. "I'm so fucking sorry," he'd told the body, before rolling it into the gutter.

Jumping back into his car, he'd fled the scene as fast as he could, without looking back.

A hollow knock at his window made him spring back into a sitting position and turn his head. His jaw dropped open as he took in the sight before him.

A hitchhiker stood there, blood oozing from his smiling mouth – Pete could see the muscles in the man's face pulled taught, something the missing skin would normally cover, as he continued to grin wide.

He had a board around his neck that simply said Hirwaun.

Pete refused to scream as he slammed the car into gear, and shot off down the road once again. Looking in the rear-view mirror, the man was gone.

"*Ha*!" Pete yelled, but then almost smashed his car into a hedge as the wreck of a man in the passenger seat spoke to him.

"I'm heading to Hirwaun. Didn't you see my sign?!" the thing said. Blood spilt from his mouth and dribbled down his chin. Some broken teeth slipped out, along with an odorous stench.

"But...but...you were just back *there!*" Pete screamed, going for the door handle. The door wouldn't open, as he rattled the shit out of it, trying to get it to unlock. "Open the *fucking* door!" he screamed in the thing's face, which looked as if it had been dipped in a vat of acid.

"Drive, son. *Now.*" It said. It's broken jaw barely able to form the words it spoke.

"It was an *accident.* You have to believe me. I didn't mean for it to happen!" Pete said, holding his hands in the air. "Please...don't kill me..." he whispered. Sweat burst from his forehead, as tears stung his eyes. "I'm sorry. I'm sorry I left you out there like a *fucking* animal. I was scared. I...you were beyond help. You were *dead.*"

"*Shhh...*" it hissed. A condescending smirk lay on what was left of its mouth. "If you had *really* checked me, then you would have noticed I was still breathing, son. Five hours I lay in that cold, wet ditch. Five hours of agony, as my life slipped away from me."

"But...but..." Pete stuttered.

"I've been waiting a long time for this, *Peter!*" it spat.

Blood and maggots trickled out of the thing's trouser legs, and soaked into the car's carpet. Every time the dead hiker moved its feet, Pete could hear a squelching sound that caused his guts to roil.

"Get this car moving. We have a long journey ahead of us, son."

Rank spittle plastered the side of Pete's face as he put the car into gear and trundled down the road past the dilapidated café and further. He feared to speak. To look at his passenger. To breathe, even.

"Please. I don't deserve this," Pete whimpered. Tears spilled down his cheeks. "I was running late. You have to believe me."

"You deserve everything I decide to dish out."

Seeing some movement in his peripheral vision, Pete turned to see two skin-stripped hands lunge for him. He was too slow to react, as they closed around his throat and started to squeeze the life from him.

His vision turned stark white as he choked and gasped for air. He thrashed and bucked in his seat, as he unintentionally pushed down on the accelerator.

The hiker sneered and laughed. "Die," the corpse said. "Die, die, die, die…" as its feral fingers dug into Pete's throat…

Pete awoke in his bed, screaming. His own hands were wrapped around his throat. Sweat dripped off him. He sat bolt upright, and found he was staring back at himself in his mirror that was placed on top of his chest of drawers.

The morning sun was coming in through the bedroom windows, soothing his frenzied panting and gasping, which dissolved into bouts of hysterical laughter, as he realised he had been embroiled in a very childish, yet lucid nightmare. "Jesus," he muttered, starting to lower his hands.

Within seconds, the fear and hysteria were back, as Pete saw the hiker's sign hanging from around his neck.

The gaudy red letters gleamed before him.

Hirwaun, it read.

"Thanks for the ride!" a voice boomed from beside him in bed. His sexy, blond bombshell of a wife had been replaced by that of the dead, rotting hiker. "Kiss me, beautiful!" it said, before laughing at the sight of Pete clutching his chest…

Techno Tendencies

Paraphilia.

That's the word Izzy had read online concerning her...*needs*.

It was the closest of the 'philia' words used to specify her kind of attraction –sexual need or affinity to something in particular – the love or obsession with *something*.

Her magnetism? Electrical equipment or 'buzz goods' as Izzy liked to refer to them.

Paraphilia: a term that describes sexual arousal in response to objects or situations that are considered abnormal or odd in some societies. Such as paedophilia or necrophilia.

Of course, there are other words similar to paraphilia to describe my unusual sexual behaviour, such as objectophilia and mechanophilia, she thought, pressing her mobile phone tight against her shaven, naked pussy in readiness and anticipation of the incoming phone call.

Mechanophilia and objectophila however, were not fitting words in her eyes. These words best described a person who had a sexual *attraction* to machines such as bicycles, motor vehicles, helicopters, ships, aeroplanes, robots, androids, computers, tablets, buildings, bridges, etcetera…

Izzy did not have a mere *attraction* to electrical goods. No. She had a *sexual* one.

She liked to fuck them.

Gyrate her hips and pussy against them.

Grind on them.

Push the smaller ones inside her.

Tease her G-spot with them.

To have their powerful buzz take her; to make her scream and beg for more. And if they didn't, couldn't, please her, or weren't up to the job she would threaten to take their batteries away or cut their plugs off. It was as simple as that.

You either do as I say or you're history. Fit for the scrapheap!

Izzy continued to press her mobile against her. Her pubic bone was starting to ache, but she didn't care. She was longing for a techno release. She bit her bottom lip and turned her head to look at the small clock on her bedside table. It was a few minutes-to six o'clock. On the hour, she expected an early morning wakeup call from the app on her phone.

But of course, her electrical goods were inanimate objects, and couldn't listen to her commands and demands. Izzy knew that. She wasn't totally crazy. Still, she liked to bully and put the pressure on them. To hold power over them. It made her sexual experience with a new device even more pleasurable.

Whenever a new machine she was capable of playing with entered her home, she would always give it a harsh, mistress-like dressing down before permitting it to please her. Allowing it enter her and to make her G-spot swell.

"Listen up, maggot!" she would say, circling the tool like a vulture whilst delivering her well-worn speech. "The washing machine and shower head are the number one and two around here! Don't ever think you can muscle them out of their positions. Got it? The best you can hope for is nestling yourself in between my favourites. The most yearned for spot around these parts is to become one of my 'go-to' items. You got that, *pal*? Am I making myself clear? Do I need to speak up, or do you need to clean 'em spuds out of your ears, darling?!"

The machine would never talk back.

Never.

But sometimes, just for shit'n'giggles, Izzy would put batteries into the item or plug it in, and when she spoke, she would operate that particular device under her spotlight as though it was answering.

It's like the Spanish Inquisition, she thought. *Only here, my captives get to fuck me and make their tyrant come!*

And come...

...and come...

...and come again!

"You'll get one chance and *one* chance alone, sailor!" she'd continue. "Now, I'm not asking for Niagara Falls on your first attempt, but I do expect a good session. A session that will allow you a second go at my pussy, maggot, and if the second effort is improved, then it will guarantee you a spot within my kingdom until you are spent. Until your components can give no more. And if you can't please, then you will be cast aside. I'll either rip your guts out or cut your plug off. Or I'll cast you down lower than the non-fucking dildos! Are we understood?!" This last bit was usual yelled into the 'face' of the appliance.

When her phone started to vibrate, thanks to the prearranged phone call, she was momentarily startled, but that soon turned to one of joy. Her cunt became juicy, a tingle jolted through her pleasure nub as the mobile continued to ring. Thanks to the app she had chosen, the call wouldn't stop until she answered or her voice mail kicked in.

Izzy had disconnected her voice mail months ago, so there would be no disturbance, unless Opie, her two-year-old son, was to walk in and catch her lying there naked and gasping. *If he should, he wouldn't know what was going on. Not only that, he normally sleeps until seven or eight. That is why I get up and play early...* she thought, trying to keep herself from reaching an early orgasm. Izzy loved delaying her first one, which came stronger if successfully postponed.

She clenched her jaw and ground her teeth – her tongue pushed at them. Izzy buried the back of her head into her pillow, her tits pointed skyward. Her nipples were erect and looking like eraser heads on pencils.

"*Oh-ugh!*" she gasped, desperately trying to hold her orgasm off. She clamped her free hand to her tit and teased the nipple, not that it did much for her. It was all about the pussy and her G-spot.

"Oh, fuck!" she whispered. Her thighs started to shake. Izzy pressed her knees together but didn't ease the pressure on her mobile, which was becoming slippery. Her fingers were saturated. She bit down on her lip so hard, she could taste blood – a small trickle of liquid drizzled down her chin and pattered against her chest.

She arched her back and pushed herself up off the mattress with her feet. When Izzy reached her bowed zenith, she looked like a humpbacked bridge, with her soles and the top of her head as her only support.

Her hands remained busy.

"Fuck! I'm...I'm...C-c-c-*coming!*" she gasped, snatching at breaths.

Her Richter scale was pushing an eight-point-five

She licked her dry lips. When the first orgasm ripped through her body like a bolt of energy, she felt herself turn to jelly – her legs, which were concrete-like pillars mere moments ago, turned to yielding masses of flesh, blood and bone.

"Ugh!" she quivered, her hand that had been grabbing, moulding and teasing her tit, shot to her side and clutched the duvet. Izzy's grip on the bedding was so intense she thought she was going to rip through it. Tears pearled at the corners of her eyes.

As the orgasm burned out, she collapsed onto the bed like in the scene from *The Exorcist* when the hoofed fella leaves Regan's spent, drained body.

But she didn't allow the ecstasy to stop.

A second, almost as powerful orgasm rushed through her, followed by a timed third and a fading fourth. Six was her record with her mobile. Apart from the washing machine and showerhead, Izzy's phone was the next best thing. It was also the device she had kept the longest. It had outlived a washing machine and two showerheads. It was also the gadget she kept on her at all times.

Izzy removed the phone from her snatch and looked at the juice-covered screen. She then put her thumb to the little green phone and answered the call. She didn't bother putting the speaker to her ear, but she heard the voice talking, which sounded tinny.

"This is your automated wakeup call. The time is now 06:18. Good morning..."

Izzy disconnected the call and pulled the covers over her. She had another couple of hours before she had to get up and sort Opie out with his breakfast and get him ready for playgroup.

She wiped the screen clean on her bedding, knowing she had to change it today anyway.

An extra few juices ain't going to harm it!

When she was satisfied the phone was clean, back and front, she popped it on her bedside table and closed her eyes. She allowed her mind to wander; to try and take her excitement off the arrival of the new household product, which should be with her later this afternoon.

Got the wine chilling in readiness, which will go well with the Indian takeaway I think I'll order, she thought. *Yep, it's just going to be me and my new* man! She smiled. *Of course, I'll have to wait until Opie has gone to bed before the pleasuring can begin...'Man'. That's a laugh!*

It had been three years since Izzy had been with a bloke. Since she'd had penetrative sex with a human, which had been with Opie's dad, Felix. He'd been a one-night stand. A drunken fumble. Izzy did not regret this. It had produced her beautiful son. She'd always wanted to be a mum but had never thought it would happen.

Felix, who she had thought would flip-the-fuck out and distance himself like a weak-kneed ass, had been, and remained, a magnificent dad. He pulled his weight, provided money, care and a home for their son on weekends. Regularly, he would turn up and take Opie out for her to have some alone time or to attend her part-time job as a barmaid.

Being a single, twenty-something mum was hard, but Izzy was determined to make something of herself. Twice a week, she went to night school to train to become a hair and beauty artist. She didn't want to remain on government benefits.

As much as Izzy tried to focus on life, her job, her studies and her son, her bizarre sexual need did tend to distract her. It didn't completely rule her world, as she had a strong hand over it, but still... it occupied a lot of her thinking, and did, at times, push all other responsibilities to one side.

When did it start? She wondered, feeling restless and turning over in bed. *A long time ago... longer than I care to remember!*

Izzy had tried to cure herself through meditation and medication. There was nothing the doctors could suggest. She'd tried classes, but nothing seemed to work. She needed the electrical buzz.

Sex toys did little. Just like men, they were a cheap imitation.

University, of course! There had been much experimenting.

From before her higher education had started, Izzy had a string of boyfriends and casual fucks, but none of them could blow her mind. At first, she'd thought she may have been gay, but that turned out to be a negative.

A human tongue did nothing. Man or woman.

Once, while at University and staying at a friend's house, Izzy had allowed her friend's bulldog to lick her pussy clean after discovering bestiality online. The unusual porn had stirred something within her, and she'd been game to try it. To see if she could finally find something that would get her off.

The act had occurred after stumbling home half-cut, to find the pooch lying on her bed. Izzy had coaxed the dog into tongue-fucking her by smearing chocolate all over her twat. Even though the experience had slightly thrilled her and made her come just the once, it didn't quite do it for her.

And then, just like that, Izzy found her *thing*.

After University broke for the summer, she invested in a phone so she could stay in touch with friends. When the thing had started vibrating in her pocket, sending shocks of pleasure through her pussy and triggering multiple orgasms, Izzy had been keen to test a new avenue.

Whenever she had a spare few minutes and wanted to get herself off, Izzy would use her phone. As soon as she realised that she was falling for what her mobile could do for her, she tried other objects, with equally stimulating results.

However, that summer her mother fell ill, her life as well as her plans to continue exploring her sexual awakening were put on hold.

Once her mother had finally succumbed to the cancer eating her from her inside out, and after Izzy had finished grieving, she got her life and sexual desires back on track. She didn't allow her pregnancy to stop her, either. With a new house came plenty of electrical goods to play with. She was finally happy as she explored her techno tendencies, and moved through life as a single mum. There would be no more men. Ever.

Every new electrical gadget that came through the door, she tested with her fanny, before putting it to work: toothbrush, razor (firstly, remove the blade), exfoliating machine, back massager, blender, hand mixer, oscillating fan, food mixer, handheld vacuum cleaner, screwdriver, whisk, tumble dryer, dishwasher, shower head; all can be laid against one's nether regions when in the "on" position. She'd pretty much tried everything there was to test.

Well, I can't just lay here all morning thinking about my pussy! Izzy rolled over and threw the covers off her body. *Once Opie's fed, ready for playgroup, and is sitting watching his cartoons whilst I get ready, maybe I can have a little play in the shower!*

Happy with that idea, she got up and crossed the landing to her son's bedroom door, which had bright coloured tiles on it spelling out his name.

"Opie, baby, it's time to get up!" she tapped on his door lightly and walked in to find her boy sleeping. She couldn't help but smile.

With Opie fed, dressed and playing in his chair in front of cartoons, Izzy had taken to the bathroom for her customary morning shower.

A girl can't have too many orgasms in a morning! She wiped the mist from the bathroom mirror and looked at herself. At her body. She didn't think much of herself, but plenty of men had lusted after her. Told her how gorgeous she is. One fella, with whom she had been friendly with, had told her that she had a "stripper's arse." That she "belonged on a pole".

The memory brought a smile to her face and she turned to show her bare backside in the mirror. It was ample: 'booty,' some would call it.

"Nothing wrong with a little junk-in-the-trunk, I suppose," she uttered, turning front and centre in the glass once more. "It offers a bit of cushion-for-the-pushin'! If only someone would come along and put some of that arse fat in my tits, then we'd be talking."

Not that her smallish breasts or size sixteen figure bothered her. Truth be told, she was happy within her skin. However, Izzy found her face and long red hair to be her best features.

She cast all thoughts from her mind and stepped into the shower. Hard, hot rays of water assaulted her body, making her groan. Her nipples instantly turned hard. She imagined the shower's water as a tongue: licking, lapping and caressing her body. It poked its watery organ into her bellybutton, flicked her nips and invaded her anus. The thought alone was enough to take her to the brink of climax, but she managed to hold back.

Izzy squirted shower gel into her hands and slowly massaged and stroked it onto her skin, causing a divine amount of lather. She gently glided her hand over her twat, not wanting to take the matter out of the shower head's hands, so to speak, as she cleaned herself.

That's your area... she thought, biting her lip. *It's all for you! For you to take care of.*

A shaky breath escaped her.

"Oh, God! I don't think I can hold off..."

Her skin prickled with gooseflesh.

"So, there's a new bit of electrical muscle coming home to play later today?" Izzy opened her eyes and noticed the shower box affixed to the wall had formed a mouth. It was talking to her. It sounded jealous. "Surely it won't replace me, your trusted shower head?!"

At that moment, the water seemed to hit her harder as it worked its way into all the desirable cracks.

"N-n-n-*no!*" she managed. A shriek escaped her. "You're my number two. *Always* will be. But you know you could never match the supreme power of the washing machine! He-h-h-he'll always be my number one." Izzy continued to soap her body slowly.

"Oh, I know that. I'm more than happy to be your number two, my beautiful Izzy. But I don't want to be overthrown by a new device!"

The water infiltrated the hood of her pussy and swirled around her G-spot.

"*Ugh!*" she gasped at the unexpectedness. "You are a rude boy!"

"Take me off my hook and press me against your cunt, Izzy. Please."

In her mind, the showerhead had a smooth voice, soft like blended chocolate. "And if I m-m-make you wait?!" her lip was starting to hurt from where she had it clamped between her teeth. She loved it when her electrical friends got jealous of each other.

"Then I will keep teasing you."

"Oh, you bad, *bad* boy!" Another yelp escaped her. Izzy put a hand to the shower wall to steady herself. Her legs felt weak, her thighs started to tremble.

"What is the new device?!" he asked.

"That's for you to find out! Now, satisfy your madam!" Izzy said, slowly removing the showerhead and pressing it against her pussy. Instantly, an orgasm pulsed through her, and she juggled the showerhead, almost dropping her man and collapsing to the floor.

As she lowered herself to the shower floor she huddled into a ball with her legs jammed together, crushing the showerhead against her privates.

"Oh!" She screamed and panted, hoping Opie wouldn't hear her over the gush of water. She writhed and thrashed her legs – her right knee struck the wall but she didn't notice in her moment of euphoria.

Her mind swayed and bobbed like a ship lost in a storm. Whilst the showerhead did its thing, buried in her twat, she thought about the new machine she was expecting. It was like cheating in her mind: as she was being fucked by one gadget, Izzy had another on her mind.

It was delicious.

A second and third orgasm tore through her body, followed by a powerful fourth – it was like being struck by lightning.

Yeah, ride the thunderstorm! she screamed inside her head.

After a fifth climax racked her body, the showerhead slipped from her relaxed hand. Her body spasmed as she lay there catching her breath and trying to recover. She felt on fire. Her cheeks were flushed and burning. Her forehead, too. Sweat poured from her.

"You're so good to me!" she wheezed.

The shower didn't respond.

"Maybe I'll come back later today before I try out the new electrical device. Maybe I'll allow you to warm me up ahead of my romantic evening. You'd like that, wouldn't you? It would make you feel some form of manliness, wouldn't it? You dirty bastard!"

"*Yes!*" it said.

"Oh!" she exclaimed. "You're such a dirty motherfucker!" Izzy smacked her fist against the wall in pure joy, before getting to her unsteady legs and turning the shower off. She got out, wrapped a towel around her body and stepped out of the misty room.

Before crossing the landing to her room, she popped her head around the banister. Izzy could hear her son laughing and playing.

Thank God! Izzy felt guilty when she left Opie on his own so she could pleasure herself, but she didn't dwell on it. *I'm a good mum. He wants for nothing and is loved.*

That evening, after a long, tiring day of looking after and playing with Opie, cleaning the flat, making them food and running errands, Izzy was finally able to relax. She lay on the sofa in her pyjamas feeling spent and limp-like. And then her eyes fell on the large box that had been delivered earlier in the day. They lit up – a surge of fresh energy engulfed her. A tingle of pleasure shot through her.

Izzy felt instantly rejuvenated.

She sat bolt-up right. "I'd forgotten about *you!*" she purred, slipping off the sofa and onto all fours. Slowly, Izzy slinked over to the huge box, sashaying her arse as she went. "I'm sure I can make my rudeness up to you…"

When she got within touching distance, she seductively ran her index finger down the mass of cardboard. It reminded her of a fortress, with its sharp edges and reinforced industrial tape.

"*Impenetrable*!" she mouthed, taking her finger back and then running her tongue up the box. "Your size is impressive." To Izzy, her drawl sounded sexy. "Would you like me to dress up for you? Shave my legs and make them soft? I bet you'd like that!"

She pressed her tits against the box and threw her arms around it. Izzy gave it a bear hug. "You smell so nice. Fresh. Factory fresh. Maybe I should rip you open and roll around in your padding first? Would you like that? Your bubble wrap will go pop, pop, pop, pop," she teased, "like staggered machine-gun fire! I won't need to give *you* my speech. I already know you're going to be impressive. I was going to let the showerhead warm me up first, but I don't think I'll waste my time. You have my attention."

Izzy then pressed her mouth close to the box, as though whispering in its ear, "My knickers are wet."

She then tittered, and continued, "Before I get ready, I'm going to take you out of the box."

After spending the next fifteen minutes unpacking the new electrical item and disposing of its wrapping, she'd slipped into a pair of sexy black stockings, complete with suspenders and garter.

She didn't bother wearing knickers or a bra.

To conceal her nakedness for the time being, Izzy had slipped into a thin robe.

"I'll reveal myself once I'm good and ready!" she'd said to herself.

The plan had been to eat and relax with a few glasses of wine before jumping straight into the sex games with her new fella. But she couldn't wait.

Her pussy was snapping and foaming at its entry for the electro buzz that it knew was coming. *Not even a lion tamer could keep my girl in place at this point!* She'd thought, patting her privates.

When she got back to the living room, she stood before the new gadget with her legs apart. "So, you think you're man enough?! I've got a lot of faith in you."

The machine didn't answer.

"Going to do your talking with your mouth, hey?! I like the strong, silent type," she teased, letting her robe hit the floor. Izzy then hurriedly plugged the machine in and brought it close to her. Before lying down, she grabbed all its impressive extensions. "My, what a lot of toys you come with!" she exclaimed excitedly.

All around her, she felt the other various appliances had their jealous eyes on them, giving her that added thrill. "I hope you boys enjoy the show!"

Before Izzy started her new wet-and-dry vacuum cleaner, she removed the nozzle that could have an assortment of different heads attached to it and placed it against her G-spot. She then hit the on button. The robust machine snatched at her, teasing her into an immediate, powerful orgasm. Her eyes rolled. She didn't think she would be able to withstand another, and so switched the machine off.

"Jesus Christ!" she huffed. "You're incredible!"

Izzy heard a few unimpressed groans from around the room – even her mobile phone sounded inferior. "Now, now, boys – there's no need to pout. You'll still get your chances!"

She giggled, whilst she sorted through the numerous heads: brushes, scrubbers, extensions... The list went on.

Before the night is out, I plan to go through them all!

As time ticked by, Izzy tried and tested the variety of heads and made a mental list of the ones she liked and didn't.

When she came to the last attachment, she felt a slight sadness. Her heart sank.

Our time has almost come to an end. Probably a good thing, because I don't think my mini can take much more!

The final interchangeable head was long and slender, reminding her of a bamboo shoot. When she clicked it into place, it added a good foot to the nozzle.

It must be used for reaching all those awkward, hard to get to places. Plus, with it being slender, it could be slipped into tight gaps. Or...up tight gaps!

A smile spread across her face as she lowered the pipe and put it to her pussy. In her eagerness to feel pleasure, Izzy failed to notice the sharp, jagged edge at the top of the pipe where a piece of its plastic had snapped off.

It looked like a spearhead.

"Ooh! A turbo button!" she squealed at seeing the function on the vacuum. When she hit the button, the pipe was viciously sucked up inside her cunt. Izzy felt it rip into her walls and tear through the flesh as it snaked its way inside her.

"Ugh...*No!*" she screamed, collapsing onto her back. She tried to rip the pipe out of her, but it had gone too deep and was attached to her insides. "The off button..."

She tried to get up, but the agonising pain in her stomach pinned her to the floor. She felt a wetness puddle out from between her legs. She guessed it was blood. Izzy became faint. The room started to spin. "Get out!" she screamed and kicked at the machine.

Her outburst did nothing but help the attachment slip further up inside. An excruciating pain ripped through her, and she felt something in her rip open. Her stomach rippled. Blood trickled from her mouth and nose.

Izzy's uterus prolapsed and the pipe gobbled it up, wheezing and choking with the effort as it tried to swallow it down to its bag.

"*Help!*" Tears flooded out of her. She screamed and screamed.

Finally, Izzy managed to sit up slightly. Her hands fell off the attachment and found a pool of blood between her legs. With nothing holding the pipe back, it pushed further up inside, impaling her. She felt like one of Vlad's victim's.

Her abdomen split open, the structures ripped. Soon her bowels and everything else inside her would be sucked up, hollowing her out like a Halloween pumpkin.

She tried to hit the off button, but the vacuum slipped away from her reach as Izzy laid her slippery fingers on it.

"Opie!" she screamed. "Opie!" A faint hope arose in her when she heard her son's feet come rushing down the stairs. "Help m-m-m-mummy...!" She was starting to faint. Something was being forced free in her. The vacuum was beginning to make a choked, blocked sound. Smoke funnelled out of it.

Before she fell onto her back again, she watched as her son rushed to the pipe and pulled on it.

"*Aaargh!*" she screamed, witnessing Opie's face being splashed by her blood. She started to spasm.

Her son yelled as yanked on the vacuum's extension.

Then, the pipe came free.

"Look mum! There were sausages inside you!" Opie said in amazement.

Izzy felt a moment of supreme disgust and embarrassment as she watched the powerful machine claim her intestines and other parts of her guts. She felt everything split away from inside – her blood was pumping out from between her legs.

"Ugh...uch" she gurgled, her head hitting the floor as her life was sucked out of her.

Thighs Maketh the Woman

Not tonight, please. Not ever *again. I can't...* he'd argued with himself on his way home from work, but the sight of so many women in short skirts displaying their tight-clad legs had driven him crazy. Businesswomen, college sluts, mums, women out shopping, grannies, fatties, skinnies, curvies – they were out in force for the perverted world and its gimp to see.

Now, parked up, his body shook violently from the horn coursing through him. He yearned for sexual release, even though he'd had one in the men's toilet at the office. Glory, his supervisor, had been wearing the shortest skirt he'd ever seen, and when she sat at her desk, which was across from his, he could see up it and had spied her pink knickers.

Dirrrrty bitch was wearing stockings, too!

Come dribbled out the tip of his cock – the front of his pants were slowly gluing themselves to his bell-end and nut sack. When it came to removing them later today, Anthony knew his pubic hairs would be a matted, knotted mess. The thought made his cock pulsate and ache. His hardness pushed with such force, Anthony thought the elastic in his underwear would snap, but it held firm.

The various sights up Glory's skirt and of her bending over in it had initially stirred his lust, but he'd quashed it. Anthony had thought by doing this, his journey home would have been uneventful, but he'd been wrong. And, thanks to his change in shift pattern, it meant he was leaving work at three in the afternoon at the height of summer – there would be weeks of torturous drives home and he'd already been a bad boy on more than one occasion.

His eyes flicked up and landed on the newspaper lying across the top of the dash – his hard-on wavered.

It's not my fault! Why was I cursed with a leg fetish?! He hammered his fist against his steering wheel. *Just drive off. Go on, do it*, his mind niggled. *Put the turn signal on, and pull off... I dare you!* Anthony put a shaking, hovering hand to his car's indicator, but he couldn't do it.

Tears welled in his eyes.

A knotted tightness developed in his gut.

"Just one more to add to my collection," he muttered. *"One!"* He looked up and out the car's windshield through glassy eyes – a stray tear splashed onto his cheek and slid down to his mouth. "I don't mean to hurt them, honestly..." He licked his dry, cracking lips and tasted the salt from the single tear. Another beaded his cheek. "Things tend to turn rough, that's all."

The headline on the paper caught his eye: *Stocking Strangler Slays Sixth*! But his gaze didn't remain. A cackle from across the road caught his attention. A bevy of beauties had gathered outside The Turntable pub, which was located down by the terminal ending for trains. It was a deserted site where the ladies of the night gathered, even though it was only four in the afternoon.

"Get yourself down there, mate," Gary from work had said. "Those dirty slappers will allow you to do anything to them. Fuck 'em in the arse, *anything*! They'll even gobble your gravy pipe for a fiver!"

However, Anthony was looking for a special kind of lady to add to his collection. He'd bagged a skinny, a fatty, a curvy, a college slut, a suit and granny. Now he was on the hunt for a chick with a dick – a pretty boy with a shlong looking to have a hot load dumped up her arse.

"What about boys?" Anthony had asked Gary on the quiet, not wanting to be overheard in the office. Gary had pulled a face of confusion, and Anthony had quickly added, "You know, with tits!"

"You dirty little man!" Gary had grinned. "Look out for a woman wearing pink fuck-me boots. Her – or his – name is Francesca." Gary had then winked and walked off.

Thinking about it now, it hadn't just been Glory's ridiculously short skirt or the sight of so many tight-clad legs on the streets whilst driving home. No. Gary's information had been the catalyst. It had bubbled at the back of his brain since their conversation that morning, and had clearly chewed away at his sub-consciousness.

And then his mind emptied, his eyes clapping onto a tall woman wearing pink, thigh-high boots as she exited the pub. When she strutted, he could see she was wearing tights under her boots and a petite, flaming cerise-coloured skirt. Her make-up and hair was immaculate, and from this distance, Anthony would never have been able to tell she was a man in disguise.

Gary never said if she's had her cock cut off or if her magnificent looking tits were real... It didn't matter about her knockers, so long as the dick was there, rubbing itself against the gusset of her tights and knickers. *A new one for my collection,* he thought, rubbing his hard-on.

He started his car and pulled down to the pub where she stood. Anthony used the buttons on his door to operate the passenger-side window.

"Hey love, fancy a good time?" he asked, digging a fistful of twenty pound notes out of his wallet.

Her eyes seemed to light up, and she bent over and leaned on the door. She poked her head in and addressed him. "Sure, lover. What you looking for?"

"The works!"

She smiled and got in.

He drove her to a dark, secluded spot where the trains used to pass – but the rails had gone cold decades ago.

"Are you wet, baby?"

"Uh-huh," she said, biting her lip but not looking at him.

"I'll give you extra if you take your tights and knickers off and give them to me for my collection."

She looked in his direction and gave him a cold stare. "It's *you*, isn't it! You're him." She grabbed the paper and threw it at him. "Some of the girls have been talking about you, the way you get them to peel their tights off..."

Fuck! He'd made the paper a few weeks ago after beating a woman and taking her tights by force. *The game's up...* Anthony thought. But, to his surprise, she rucked her skirt up and took her tights and knickers off.

"It's okay – I can play rough with the boys!"

Anthony's eyes were instantly drawn to the woman's cock growing between her smooth, muscular thighs.

"You want to touch it baby? You like the boys? I thought it was legs... That's what the papers and other girls say about you."

God, I want to run my hands up those thighs so badly. He nodded like a bobble-headed toy and reached out for the woman's penis. "You are Francesca, right?"

"The one and only." She smiled, pulling him closer. "Go ahead, put your mouth around it. You know you want to."

Anthony bent forward, his tongue protruding. "Thank you, Francesca."

"That's okay, hun..." she said, and then forcefully wrapped her tights around Anthony's neck and pulled with all her might.

As he bucked and thrashed against her, she rubbed her cock against his flip-flopping body to a pulsating orgasm. "Oh, I'm coming..." she gasped. Her thick, pearly-white jism splashed his face and found its way into his mouth.

Anthony tried to get his fingers beneath the material constricting his breathing, but Francesca's hold was too tight.

"*Please...*" he chocked, spitting phlegm-like come onto the dashboard. His fingertips clawed at the silky-smooth tights to no avail. His mind scrambled, to try and think of a way out of his situation, but failed. In an attempt to elbow her in her guts, Anthony found he had no leverage, and so his blow to her midsection was weak, causing little to no damage.

The stranglehold intensified.

He then made an attempt to slam his hand down on the car's horn, but he couldn't reach it. His feet acted like flip-flopping fish out of water, and couldn't be used to stamp down on the accelerator. His eyes started to flicker and roll in his head. Dizziness set in and black spots danced before his off-kilter vision. He coughed and spluttered as the last of his air escaped him.

"Lucky number seven!" she whispered down his ear.

End

Recognition

"There is nothing to writing. All you do is sit down at a typewriter and bleed."
— Ernest Hemingway

Julian's fingers glided across his PC's keyboard with frantic, yet accurate, movement. The clack, clack, clacking sound of the keys acted as a background score to the shifting images, sounds and voices inside his head.

He braved a glance up at the clock above his computer, but didn't dare stop his enthusiastic typing as he did so.

"Eleven-thirty," he mouthed. "I have until midday, right? That's what the guidelines had said in my editor's e-mail. I'm sure of it. Bloody *deadlines*!"

Julian muttered and cursed to himself as he averted his eyes from the keeper of time to his monitor. His lips moved with rapidity as he read over the last few sentences he'd constructed – his chain of thought had been broken by the clock's distraction.

A smile developed on his face, and he fought the urge to laugh like a schoolgirl. The story he was working on, a noir novel called *Neon Ice*, was coming along better than he'd wished for.

It would be his best creation yet.

The critics will love it!

Not only would it be his unsurpassed work of fiction to date, but also his fifth novel – a landmark he'd thought unachievable when he'd first started writing some twenty years ago. This would also be his first crime story.

Horror fiction was all Julian had ever known, had ever created, but of recent, crime had taken his fancy. And when an idea for a noir novel had started forming in his head, he knew he'd have to undertake it – to push himself and explore different avenues and genres with his writing.

For the first few years at the beginning of his journey, Julian had practiced his craft by pumping out short stories, one after the other. The ideas had moved around inside his brain as though they were on a conveyer belt. All he had to do was write them down. Back then, Julian had thought his mind was incapable of running dry. Thankfully, it hadn't.

Julian put this down to the love of storytelling and the admiration he had for the horror genre itself. When he wasn't writing stories, he was speaking them. He told strangers, family members and work colleagues various lies and fabrications. Why? To garner reaction. Also, he got a kick out of it.

He lies and tells tales.

It's what he does.

He's a writer, so he spins yarns.

It makes him smile.

Julian also thrived off deadlines and ate them for breakfast.

To this day, he saw submission closing dates and timeframes for work to reach editors as motivators, or drill sergeants, as he liked to refer to them. Julian loved having them lined up on his calendar like little soldiers on parade. When one objective was finished and scrubbed off his schedule, he liked having another two or three jotted down for later in the year to replace the fallen troops.

Like some kind of Greek mythical monster, he thought. *When you cut one head off, six more grow back!*

Deadlines get fingers tapping and creative juices flowing. They leave you with little time to think about anything else. A writer does not take a holiday. They are incapable of having such a luxury. When a writer is away from his desk, they are still working. Committing unsolved murders and dreaming, scheming and plotting sex scenes, monsters (real or otherwise), dark places, creepy hangouts, sex-starved maniacs, real-life situations… The list is inexhaustible.

Their mind *never* shuts off.

When they are with you in a room or on a date, they're not really there. They might be in body and soul, but not in mind and heart. They're in their own little world, cheating on you with a person you will never know.

Ever since his schooldays, Julian had thrived off such organization. He found at the time, and to this day, that being governed by a date and time drilled and dieted his creative mind. It kept him trained, primed, focused and the cogs in his creativity machine turning.

That, and the amount of reading he devoured week in, week out.

"Stories to a writer are important. It doesn't matter if the tales are trash, good or ugly! We need to understand and analyse the use of language and grammar to appreciate and recognize how professional wordsmiths use their tools of trade," one of his creative writing tutors had told him at University during a semester. "As King points out, 'If you don't have time to read, you don't have the time (or the tools) to write. Simple as that.'"

An impressionable Julian had lived by those words upon hearing them. King's quote, along with two from Kurt Vonnegut – "Here is a lesson in creative writing. First rule: Do not use semicolons. They are transvestite hermaphrodites representing absolutely nothing. All they do is show you've been to college" and "We have to continually be jumping off cliffs and developing our wings on the way down" – were pinned to his wall for inspiration.

The first quote by Kurt always made him smile, as it had enraged many people he'd told it to over the years.

Success had soon followed in the wake of Julian's hard work. His short stories found their way into online magazines and physical ones, along with local anthologies and compilations from reputable publishing houses.

Money flowed in dribs and drabs, but what did that matter? Being published and recognised were the only concerns. The house and Ferrari would come in due course, not that he was a materialistic person in the least.

As long as I earn enough to keep me writing I'll be happy!

Soon after it started coming together for Julian, he gave up his full-time cleaning job and married the girl of his dreams. The blocks of life started falling into place. All he had to do was sit and wait for recognition to register – to push him up the publishing charts and make him a household name among the big guns.

Yeah, but it wasn't all champagne and caviar! he thought, continuing to smash away at his keyboard as though intended to destroy it. *No, there were a lot of... dark days.*

On his path to success, Julian had suffered from depression, confusion, self-doubt, self-loathing, and mental blocks, and had found himself lost on the road to glory. All the aforementioned were crippling. When the infamous 'black dog' showed up, it would shut Julian's creativity down for days, weeks or months at a time.

The black dog, whom he'd lovingly named Morose, would attack without warning. He'd set on Julian with a snarl of its flashing fang and robust body, enveloping him in a world of misery and inner pain.

The coffee pot got me through most of it!

A smile creased his face.

But it wasn't the caffeine alone that aided him.

At his lowest it was Jack Daniels and his good friend Gordon that got Julian through his black spots and banished Morose to his hellish kennel at the back of his brain. When it wasn't the booze, it was cocaine and pills. It didn't take long for things to fall apart. His wife and house went, followed by his reputation as a stand-up writer and person among his peers. Some of the bigger publishers washed their hands of Julian when his addictions and wife's vilification hit the newspapers.

Luckily, his agent stuck by him and steered him back onto the straight and narrow.

Julian had found the fall from grace hard, but got through it.

Recognition. It was the thing he needed. *Craved.* Without it, he'd seen himself as a failure. A flop. Julian and his agent had tried all the marketing gimmicks to push him into the limelight, which had worked, but not enough for Julian's liking.

The local rags, as much as they spouted about 'supporting local talent', turned a blind eye to Julian and his work.

"We hardly see blood and guts as *intelligent*, Mr Griffiths," he'd been told by one journalist. "Our paper will not be associated with such drivel."

After years of little appreciation, a meagre fan base and a bunch of hit-and-miss reviews (after decades of hard work), Julian had been driven to the brink of obliteration.

His mind had started to come away at the seams.

"Why don't you leave it there, baby?" his wife had cooed.

His response, after smashing the kitchen up, had been, "How the *fuck* do you expect me to do that? It consumes me, woman. It *is* me!" He'd refrained from slapping her.

A cold shoulder is the worst thing you can give a writer! he thought, flashing the clock another fleeting look. *I should have this book wrapped up and sent off with time to spare. It's not like me to let a deadline get so close. I never did agree with that Adams fella. "I love deadlines. I love the whooshing noise they make as they go by." Such a juvenile way of thinking.*

Once he'd knuckled back down to his work, cleaned himself of drink and drugs, and cleared his name of wife-battery in court, his fortune started to turn for the better.

Sales picked up. His fan base grew.

"Even bad press is good for business!" his agent had said.

His money stack started to grow, along with his dream, and it wasn't long before Julian had it all, and more: dream house by the beach, a horde of readers who gathered outside his home daily, interviews and guest appearances on TV shows.

I have to keep it up. Stay focused, continue to crank the work out – my editors, publishers and fans expect nothing less! Who knows, maybe I'll get film rights one day?

"Maybe," he muttered, adding the last few sentences to his novel. "I could see this being played out on the sliver screen!"

He wrote 'The End' under the last paragraph.

Looking up, Julian noticed it was ten to twelve.

"*Perfect!*"

He opened his e-mail and created a new message. In the address bar, he typed his publisher's address and added his agent's in the 'Cc' section. Once he'd written in the body, Julian attached his novel and hit 'send'.

"*Ah!*" he huffed, collapsing in his chair. He felt spent, drained, but also relieved, as though a huge weight had been lifted off his shoulders. "Good to have the bugger finished."

Now for the waiting game.

It would take Paul, his publicist, a few days to reach the e-mail, what with it being a bank holiday. However, it didn't matter. Not to Julian. Now that his deadline was filled, he could spend the next few weeks relaxing and writing return e-mails to his fans.

Before getting up from his roller-chair, Julian rotated his head, stretched his arms and arched his back – everything seemed to click into place. *I need to see my chiropractor next week,* he thought. *I don't know. Who'd be a bloody writer?!*

He then busied himself by organising his workspace and replacing his notebooks, pens, pencils, eraser, Tip-ex and sharpener. If it was one thing Julian hated, it was a messy desk.

Slowly, he stood. The joints in his knees cracked.

"*Ooh*! That's better," he said, turning to look out the window. Sunlight slanted in through the glass. "A room with a view. No. An *office* with a view!"

Julian walked over to it and looked outside, seeing Alejandra tending the flowers. "I have it all, right down to the female Mexican gardener," he uttered, his eyes darting from her arse to her tits. "Mmm, my buxom burrito!" He smiled and waved at her.

She didn't return the greeting.

"She's a moody one, all right! Maybe a pay rise will perk her up? Or possibly a threat to deport her Spanish–speaking arse?" he said, laughing. "No, I kid…"

Julian placed his hands behind his back, stood on tiptoes and cast his gaze across the plush garden. He half expected to see copies of his books littering the lawn and neatly trimmed hedges: Some of his fans had thrown their editions over the wall in hopes he'd sign and toss them back over.

"Madness," he mouthed, his breath fogging the glass before him. Julian glanced over his shoulder and saw it had gone midday. "What about a bite…"

His words slurred and trailed off.

A bout of dizziness washed over him, causing him to stagger to his left, pinball off a wall and stumble to his right. He collapsed to all fours and closed his eyes. His thighs trembled.

"What *the*?!" Julian put a hand to his face. "Jesus!" A fog clouded his brain. "No, I *don't* have it all," he muttered, removing his hand before standing up and turning to the window again. "There is *one* thing in my life I'm missing."

To his amazement, there were now more than a dozen people wandering around the garden.

"Who are these people?!" he yelled, and slammed his fists against the glass. "Get off my lawn! This is private property. Where in the hell is…"

What's the one thing we're missing, Julian? his mind asked, startling him.

"I can't remember! Why are all these people in my garden? Who are they?"

Think, Julian. It's important you remember. Think!

He turned from the window and faced his desk, but there wasn't one. All that remained was a small plastic toy in the shape of a PC. His writing equipment – pens, pencils and the rest – was nothing more than a stack of safety crayons. Their once fat nibs had been shaved down to needlepoints.

"What's going on?!"

Julian rapped his knuckles against his head as he rocked back and forth. "Whose white gown am I wearing?" Tears rolled down his cheeks.

Information dripped into his drug-addled mind.

Julian had been a writer, but wasn't any longer. He had been tried and convicted for the murder of seven people, two of whom had been his publicist and agent. When he had crashed into his black hole the last time, he had taken on a more sinister personality. He'd killed in the name of recognition.

He had slaughtered people in ways he'd killed characters in his novels in an attempt to garner him a bigger readership. The idea had meant to look as though he had a crazed fan on the loose, one who had a deranged obsession with Julian's novels and other works of horror fiction. It had worked too, until the police had finally linked the murders to Julian.

"Whacko Wordsmith Slays Seven!" one newspaper article had read. "Writer Wrecks Havoc for Ratings!" said another. A third: "Modest Author Murders Many."

Julian brought his trembling hands to his face. "Who am I?"

Catherine Tramell, a voice inside his head whispered. It was the name Julian had started penning stories under.

"*Who*?!" The name rang a bell. "I got it from a TV show. No, a film! But why?"

Because we thought it was funny, Julian!

Julian shook his head.

He was more scared and confused than he'd ever been in his life. The walls around him were padded, and closing in.

"As long as he thinks he's still a writer and dosed up on his drugs, we shouldn't have a problem with him," he remembered someone important-looking saying.

"We could give him this? When he's up to his eyes on meds, he won't know any different!" another had said, displaying a Fisher Price toy in the shape of a computer.

"I killed my ex-wife!" he blurted. "Oh, God!"

Focus, damn it! What's the one thing we're missing?

Julian's eyes frantically flicked from left to right, right to left. "*Freedom...*" he whispered, his gaze coming to rest on the crayons with the vicious ends. "I sharpened them with my thumbs." He looked at his digits – there were coloured filings underneath his nails. "I remember now! When the drugs wore off the last time and I was free to think in a rational state, I'd planned to kill my nurse and make my escape the next time my medication wore off..."

By pretending he was not a danger to himself or anyone in Castell Hirwaun, home for the criminally insane, Julian had got them to move him to a less secure part of the hospital.

When he heard the turn of a key in his lock, Julian grabbed the crayons and hid them behind his back. As the door edged open, the young nurse greeted him with a "Good morning", to which he calmly replied.

She had with her a tray filled with needles.

You're not making the rational-thinking Julian go night-night this time, bitch!

"I'm telling you, my characters came to life! They're roaming the real world! You have to *do* something!" a bearded man screamed in the hallway as he was dragged off by two male nurses who looked as though they ate bullets for brunch.

"Calm down, Mr. Hughes," a female said soothingly.

Then the door closed.

Julian pounced, raising the crayons high. She dropped her tray. The needles and bottles of serum smashed against the floor.

"Whore!" he bellowed, stabbing the children's playthings into the young woman's neck. When he retracted them, blood sprayed up the pristine walls. As she gargled and held a hand out to him, he stabbed again and again. The crayons ripped out one of her eyes and slashed and tore the flesh from around her mouth, nose and cheeks.

Gore showered Julian.

"Die, die, die!" he screamed in her face.

Breathless, he stood over her. A pool of blood spread rapidly beneath her.

"My keys now!" He sniggered, plucking them from her pocket and making his way out into the corridor…

A Box Full of Kinks

"Hope's the rope that keeps you tied in knots."
— W.A.S.P

When she was a child, her parents and teachers had considered her a normal, healthy girl. She liked to play with her tea set, dollies, mock kitchen appliances, and Hetty Hoover, and dress up with her mother's clothes, shoes, jewellery and make-up.

Throughout her lower and upper school years, Jodie had good friends and bagged solid grades that indicated she would become a professional, career-driven woman with an outgoing personality one day. This notion was later solidified when she gained access to a leading university and joined a law programme.

During her teenage years, Mother Nature blessed her: Jodie transformed from a sweet-looking girl into a striking, dark-haired beauty. Her body became tight, slender and sported an ample bust that had all the boys in her class hounding her for a date. Even the older lads bayed for her attention.

To add to her perfection, Jodie didn't drink, smoke or eat unhealthy foods. She liked to keep her mind sharp and her figure taut, which had filled out a tad by the time she'd started her degree. So, three times a week, she took to her campus gym, where she'd enrolled in kickboxing and yoga classes. Jodie also liked to use the pool and thought herself a strong swimmer.

"You're like a bloody fish!" her mother would say. "You could be an athlete."

Her peers and a handful of female tutors envied her; even the girls who considered themselves Jodie's 'besties' tried their paramount to bite down on their acidic tongues and hide their green faces in her radiance which cast shadows over them.

Jodie was destined to have it all. She knew it, and, more importantly, the people around her did, too. She was sure to find herself a rich husband that liked to spoil her; the type of man who drove a Jaguar, had a platinum membership to the local gun club and liked to play golf on the weekends with his poker-playing mates so he could spend time away from her.

However, beneath her glory and Little-Miss-Perfect, butter-wouldn't-melt-in-her-mouth ways, there was something about Jodie – in her make-up –, which nobody knew about. It was a secret that could have held her back as a child or, more disastrously, ruined her adult life with her ending up in jail or dead.

But she'd learned to control and hide it, once it reared itself, and she knew it wasn't going away.

It had started as an itch, a fire between her legs, when she was ten years old. Of course, Jodie had been far too young to realise and understand its workings and what it all meant. At such a tender age, she could have told her mummy and tried to explain what she'd felt, but something inside had told her that Mummy, and her 'imaginary sky fairy' called God, would not like what she had done, or the excitement that had coursed through her. Also, Mummy had no idea Jodie liked to secretively mock her strict religious beliefs. She played along with it and attended Sunday school and church only to appease her.

So, going to her was out of the question.

Not only that, she'd liked the thrill of what had happened to her, even if it had brought her great shame.

Mummy would probably get Daddy to take his belt to me, she'd thought, looking down at her wet, pissed-through bottoms and soaked carpet. Her cheeks had burned. *He'd probably enjoy it!* Jodie hadn't really known what she'd meant, but had giggled nevertheless.

The urge to go to the toilet had come over her as normal, but instead of going to the bathroom as she would have, it had come from nowhere and demanded her to leap up and run to the full-length mirror in her parents' bedroom. Once there, it had told her to wet herself. At first, she had shaken her head and bitten her lip, her bladder pinched.

"No," she'd whispered, trying to move but not allowing herself to do so.

And then she'd released and watched the wet patch at her crotch grow into a large, dark patch; her urine had flooded her knickers and run down her legs and splashed against the plush carpet at her feet.

Butterflies had fluttered in her guts, a strange thunderbolt of pleasure running through her as though she'd been struck by lightning. Her eyes had rolled, and her legs had turned to pillars of wibbly-wobbly jelly.

The blame for the pissed-on carpet had been laid at the feet (or paws) of Mr. Ruffles, the family hound.

"Well, he is getting on," Jodie had heard her father say to her mother. "Incontinence is probably kicking in."

She hadn't understood the word her dad had used at the time, but soon came to learn of its meaning when she asked her teacher. This had then given her freedom to keep on wetting herself and getting her kicks from doing so.

Finally, after twelve months of scrubbing piss out of her expensive shags, Jodie's mother had ordered the dog's execution, which had sent a new wave of excitement through Jodie. She'd acted sad for the dog, but inside, she'd loved every treacherous second of it. And, when she'd put on the crocodile tears, her parents had showered her in lavish gifts.

"Maybe we could buy you a bunny?" her dad had suggested.

By the time her periods started, which was a year after her dog's passing, Jodie found multiple new ways to appease her gratifications, now that she was limited to wetting herself outdoors or when standing in the bath. Some of these new methods involved: telling lies and getting people in trouble; bullying children younger than herself and humiliating them by sticking gum in their hair, pulling the trousers and underwear of boys down and raising the skirts of girls; putting vile substances in people's meals and drinks; shaving defenceless animals and sticking her parents' toothbrushes up her bum, which was her favourite.

When the other children threatened to tell on her, she would threaten them with violence or more of the same. She ruled the playground and schoolyard. The ones she couldn't break or keep in line, she had the older boys handle by promising them a glimpse of her 'special place' and a kiss.

After her mid-teens rolled around and Jodie had developed into a swan, masturbation kicked in and she learned more about what it was that dwelled inside her and pushed her buttons through online research.

"I'm a pervert," she'd muttered. It had disappointed her, because she was a normal young woman with a good head on her shoulders when the urge to do racy things didn't kick in. "I'm ninety-per cent perfect, and I will go far in life."

Whilst a lot of what she was doing was normal and healthy, most of her practices were unusual and detrimental to her state of mind.

Still, she found it liberating.

When the boys gave her the eye in school, Jodie liked to play the attention off as though she didn't notice. However, the thought of how her sexy body drove their dicks wild with mad frustration delighted her.

What would Mother think? she'd thought at the time.

And, to add to their flustered, prick-teased ways, Jodie hiked her skirt enough for the lads to notice, but not the authority around her. She'd also invested money in make-up and stockings, which she would adorn before school and remove after her last class so as to not get caught by her parents.

Throughout her days at her comprehensive school, Jodie developed more kinks, some of which were normal, like the arousal of female feet, men's legs, being spanked and tied up… But when her first serious boyfriend had refused to beat her and then throw her down a flight of stairs, she'd got angry and lashed out at him.

"I get turned on by it!" she'd screamed.

These outbursts normally resulted in her becoming single. And, when she thought they'd tell their friends how kinky, disturbed, and fucked-up in the head she was, Jodie threatened to make up lies about them to destroy them.

The crackpot look in her eyes had told them how serious she was.

Not only that, but she took knives and scissors to them and their clothes.

"I'm your worst fucking nightmare, pencil dick!" she'd told one boyfriend after he'd refused to play dead for a second time as she rode his cock to the tune of multiple orgasms.

Playing-dead fantasies turned into voyeuristic ones, as she crept around her campus so she could peep in windows and watch people fuck, pleasure themselves or undress late at night.

When she couldn't get her own way, she hurt small animals or violated someone vulnerable on the streets, such as a homeless child or an old person.

Jodie was as cunning as she was horny.

She kept her tracks covered, and her movements in the shadows.

Anyone who tried or thought they could get in her way, she stepped on. And, when someone was brave enough to call her out, she fluttered her eyelashes or turned on the tears. Either way, she always looked clean.

Her shit didn't stink.

"Don't tell such lies!" others would say in her defence. "She's nothing but lovely."

When one lad had blabbed about how she liked to get fucked with various household objects, she'd spread rumours about him having a tiny dick, and how he couldn't get it up unless he was bedding an underage girl.

The masses believed her.

He became so ridiculed, he left the university.

Of course, nobody knew where the rumours had started – Jodie hadn't told anyone. Instead, she'd scribbled it on walls around campus, along with his phone number.

"You'll get your comeuppance one day, *whore!*" had been his parting words to her.

"No idea what you're talking about," she'd said, winking and smiling after making sure there was nobody around.

Voyeurism turned into Nasophilia (a sexual attraction to the nose). This was followed by an exploration into licking and rubbing herself against doorknobs and unsuspecting people. Farting against random folk also thrilled her. It wasn't long before she had men and women pissing on her, and she found pleasure in turning people into human furniture by tying them in place with bondage equipment.

Most of the fetishes came with names.

However, it wasn't normal to have so many.

"You're like a box full of kinks!" one of her many fuck buddies had quipped after she'd told him she liked exposing herself and walking around a crowded city in a coat with nothing on underneath.

It reached a point where being fucked or having her pussy eaten did nothing for her, as her perversion matured.

One evening whilst bored, Jodie had taken a stroll through the park and surrounding woods. She soon found that she liked being out in the dead of night, especially on cold evenings.

It became a new avenue of filth for Jodie to explore, which excited her. The students had been told never to leave the site after a certain hour, as the crime rates for violence, rape and muggings were at an all-time high.

Of course, this only added to her excitement.

When out and about, she liked to play Fight or Flight whenever she saw someone walk out of the darkness towards her – it gave her unlimited thrills.

Ah, the endless dangers, she thought, sitting on a park bench, ready to play her next game. The seat she had chosen was situated beneath a single light, which drenched her in a weak orange glow. Beyond the circumference of luminosity in both directions, Jodie couldn't see much, apart from two other lampposts: the one to her left was out, and the right displayed the same level of feebleness as the bulb she was seated under.

Shapes shifted in the gloom.

Bushes rustled; twigs snapped.

Branches groaned to the might of the wind.

The sound of footsteps carried on the stiff night air, along with distant laughter and conversations, which came from the town nearby. When Jodie looked behind her, she could see the glow of cityscape.

Safety, should she need or want it, was a mere heartbeat away.

I live for danger! she thought. Nobody's a match for me.

Tonight, however, she would need to be quick on her feet if she planned to play Flight or Fight, as she wore a tight mini skirt, heels and stockings – the black, racy garments that encased her legs displayed their tops, due to the way she was sitting .

I feel like Audrey fucking *Hepburn – all I'm missing is a cigarette.*

But she was getting restless. The park was unusually quiet for a Friday night. She hadn't even come across the resident bums, who'd she'd found splayed out in various positions on benches, in bushes and along the path over the time she'd been visiting the area at night. Some had even stank of piss and shit – the front and backs of their trousers stained.

Jodie fucked with the homeless she found sleeping. The previous Friday night, she'd stolen their clothes and thrown them in a pond, which she'd found highly amusing.

And it wasn't just the winos she messed with. In the daytime, when she passed through the place, she'd like to make little ones cry by shoving them, breaking their toys or popping their balloons – anything that would get a reaction out of them. She was even prone to punching, pinching and kicking them.

The thought made her smile.

Her laugh tore through the night.

"Ugh, how much longer?" she muttered, looking at her watch and then all around her. It was dead. "Maybe If I walk to the bandstand? There's always little fuckheads there smoking crack and drinking cheap cider. I really want to play—"

A healthy-sounding snap of a twig cut her dead.

Her ears pricked.

It wasn't unusual to hear such sounds.

More crunching – someone was definitely approaching. Sneaking; using the darkness as cover.

A tingle sparked in her pussy, hardening her nipples.

Time to play...

"Who—who's there?" she stuttered, trying to sound as scared as she could. Jodie fought hard to keep the smile off her face and the laugh down in the bowels of her guts.

Shrubbery rustled violently to her left, causing her to jerk her head in that direction.

Someone was definitely close by – she could hear their harsh, raspy breathing.

Standing on bowed legs, with a hunched back, Jodie squinted. "I have *mace*!" she lied. Again, she battled the urge to laugh.

An orgasm built deep within her core.

A snigger escaped the bushes. "You ain't got shit, slut!" a voice snapped. "We're going to cut you into tiny pieces."

"Yeah, we been watching you, cunt!"

Suddenly, she didn't want to play, as two faces emerged from the bushes before her. They looked familiar. Over their shoulder, three more people appeared.

"Thought it was pretty funny to fuck with us down-and-outs, didn't you?" the first one challenged.

A glint off something bright flashed in her eyes. *Knife*! her mind screamed.

"Gonna rape your twat," threatened the second one, who was practically hidden behind his comrade.

"Yeah, that's the fucking bitch!" a faceless person affirmed from somewhere behind.

"Tear her knickers off and stick it to her," another random homeless blurted.

"Ha! You said 'stick it to her'," a fresh voice said. "Rango has a knife," they continued, attempting to explain their poor joke.

Jodie gasped, turned and was about to flee in the opposite direction when she saw more of the homeless crawl from beneath bushes and slip out of the darkness.

"Slice her open, Rango," a female yelled.

"Rip her juicy cunt apart," a man slurred.

A scream lodged in her throat. "No, please!" she begged, collapsing to her knees. And then she gasped when the one with the knife, Rango, stepped out of the gloom and towered over her.

"You're going to get it, tramp!" He spat on her, and then bent over to show her the sharpness of his seven-inch blade. "I'm going to ram this in your twat, once I take what I want."

She tried to get up to run, but Rango held her in place. His breath reeked of whiskey and tobacco. In the poor light, she made out a large scar running from his eyebrow to his jawline. And, when he smiled, she noticed an impressive array of gold teeth.

He was terrifying and brutishly large – his hands were the size of shovels.

Rango gripped the front of her dress and ripped it open, taking her bra with it and exposing her ample tits.

"No!" she pleaded.

The thug then threw her legs apart and reached a rough hand up her measly skirt and tore her knickers off. Before sniffing them, he licked them, and then undid his belt buckle and lowered his jeans and underwear.

"Hold her arms and legs!" he bellowed at his lackeys.

His crew pinned her to the floor. She tried to pull away but stopped when she saw the size of his pulsating cock, which leaked pre-come. It was veiny and lacked foreskin.

A deformed snake, she thought, which also brought to mind the image of a Sphinx cat. "Don't you dare touch me with that...that *thing!*" Jodie screamed. Tears ran down her flushed cheeks.

Whoops and laughter tore through the crowd gathered around her – they were baying for her destruction.

"You want a taste, fuck?" he said, brandishing his knife. She whimpered at the feel of his hard prick pushing at her pussy flaps. "Firstly, I try you... The terror in your eyes turns me on," he said, giggling.

He gasped as her hand smacked against his arse. "What are you waiting for? An invitation?" With that, she pushed on his buttocks, forcing his cock deep inside her.

He groaned at first, but when he pulled back for a further pump, he screamed in pain, causing a hush to fall over the crowd.

"My *prick*!" he squealed.

"Come on, fuck me," she insisted, a laugh escaping her.

"*Aragh!*" Rango screamed, dropping his knife.

Jodie thrust her pelvis back and forth, back and forth, causing her would-be rapist to scream more – tears ran from his eyes as he tried fruitlessly to disengage from her vagina.

"Got ya, big boy! Now, fuck me but good, ya black son-of-a-bitch," she whispered into his ear, and then wrapped her arms and legs around him before burying her face in his chest so he couldn't head-butt her.

"Get this crazy—*Argh!*" Rango screamed as he bucked, thrashed and tried pulling away and out of her once again – she could hear his foreskin rip and tear; her pussy was drinking his blood.

"W-what's going on?" a nameless, faceless from the crowd asked.

"She's killing him!" another replied.

"That bitch is crazy. I'm going before she works her hoodoo-voodoo on me."

Soon the sound of rushing feet filled the air around her and Rango. Not that Jodie was paying much attention – she was wrapped up in the throes of orgasm, as she continued to pump her hip.

"Yes! I'm coming, I'm coming!"

His macho mask slipped, his hard, violent talk of threats and yells turning to that of a five-year-old's blubbering ways when they lose their mummy in a supermarket.

"I—I *sorry!*" he squealed. "Get. It. Off!" Tears spilled down his cheeks and splashed her face, along with his stringy snot, which found its way into her mouth.

"Yes! Yes! *Yes!*" she screamed in response like a pig with a ripped-open throat.

And then she felt a gush a fluid between their melded hips and private parts, which she knew was a mixture of his spurting blood and her rushing juices. In the pale moonlight, she could see the colour drain from his face, which, ten minutes ago, had been flushed red with excitement.

His struggling lessened.

"You're going to die in"—she bit her lip as another wave of ecstasy trembled through her—"inside me..." Jodie panted, her orgasm coming, going and building towards another.

Within seconds, he collapsed on top of her.

Dead.

"Oh, shit!" she heard someone say, causing her to turn her head in that direction. One of the homeless had stayed to watch the whole sordid episode. "What you done, miss?" he asked.

"Not me, my Rape-X." She tittered. "It's like a cock-shredding condom that fits all nice and snug in my twat. The inside of the device is covered in small barbs. You see," she continued, rolling onto her side and pushing the dead Rango off her so she could get to her knees and grab the knife, "my kinks have evolved..."

She saw him look at the knife as she slowly turned it in her hand.

"Please... I didn't see—I won't say *anything*! Oh, sweet Jesus."

"Ooh, are you going to run? I might just enjoy playing Hunter and Hunted." Jodie jumped to her feet with eerie rapidity and lunged at the man, who was turning to flee. She landed on his back, taking him to the ground. With one vicious swipe, she drew the impressive blade across his throat and rolled around in his spurting blood, getting herself off once more.

By the time she was finished playing in the pools of cold, congealed blood, three hours had passed.

I better get up and go after the rest off them, she thought. With a concerted effort, she dragged herself to her feet, stretched and yawned and then looked around her. She heard bushes rustling, voices whispering.

They were watching.

Ooh, how fun!

"I'll give you fucks until the count of ten, and then I'm coming." Her grip tightened around the knife. "One, two, three..."

Her smile widened when she heard the sound of rushing feet.

"Nine, ten... Ready or not, here I come..."

END

About Your Author

David Owain Hughes is a horror freak! He grew up on ninja, pirate and horror movies from the age of five, which helped rapidly instil in him a vivid imagination. When he grows up, he wishes to be a serial killer with a part-time job in women's lingerie…He's had multiple short stories published in various online magazines and anthologies, along with articles, reviews and interviews. He's written for This Is Horror, Blood Magazine, and Horror Geeks Magazine. He's the author of the popular novels "Walled In" (2014), "Wind-Up Toy" (2016), "Man-Eating Fucks" (2016), and "The Rack & Cue" (2017) along with his short story collections "White Walls and Straitjackets" (2015) and "Choice Cuts" (2015). He's also written three novellas – "Granville" (2016), "Wind-Up Toy: Broken Plaything & Chaos Rising" (2016).

www.hellboundbookspublishing.com/authorpage_hughes.html

www.facebook.com/DOHughesAuthor/?ref=hl

www.amazon.co.uk/David-Owain-Hughes/e/B00L708P2M/ref=sr_ntt_srch_lnk_3?qid=1458241417&sr=1-3

http://david-owain-hughes.wix.com/horrorwriter

www.goodreads.com/author/show/4877205.David_Owain_Hughes

twitter.com/DOHUGHES32

<u>Other HellBound Books Titles</u>
<u>Available at: www.hellboundbookspublishing.com</u>

Puckered

Percy is kinky.
Percy is perverted.
Percy is a loner.
Percy is sneaky…

…But most of all, Percy wants to be left alone.

Whether it be a nagging mother or something from his past, it feels like he is always trying to escape something.
Will he be able to find his own peace, or will the real world catch up to him?
There will be blood.
There will be s**t.
There will be unusual sexual kinks.
But most of all, there will be murder…

Man Eating F*cks

A dark, incredibly entertaining excursion into the delightfully twisted imagination of David Owain Hughes....

An average teenage girl and her father find themselves caught up in a brutal nightmare at their local recreational centre, when an age-old enemy comes stumbling out of the woods to crash a heavy-metal gig; a gig that has all the promises of being killer. This is one blood-soaked gig you won't want to miss!

Praise for Man-Eating F*cks from Ty Schwamberger (author of The Fields, Deep Dark Woods & The Death of a Horror Writer.)   "Man Eating F*cks is old school horror, but with a new, blood-soaked twist! David Owain Hughes effectively creates enjoyable and lethal characters in this tale that is sure to keep you up at night. This is the type of tale that you need to read with a light on...I'm serious. You better put your seatbelt on 'cause you're in for one helluva ride. Look out, Hughes might very well be headed to the major leagues after this twisted tale! Highly recommended!"

Worship Me

Something is listening to the prayers of St. Paul's United Church, but it's not the god they asked for; it's something much, much older.

A quiet Sunday service turns into a living hell when this ancient entity descends upon the house of worship and claims the congregation for its own. The terrified churchgoers must now prove their loyalty to their new god by giving it one of their children or in two days time it will return and destroy them all.

As fear rips the congregation apart, it becomes clear that if they're to survive this untold horror, the faithful must become the faithless and enter into a battle against God itself. But as time runs out, they discover that true monsters come not from heaven or hell... ...they come from within.

No Rest For The Wicked

A modern day ghost story with its skeletons buried firmly in the past.

From beyond the grave, a murderous wife seeks to complete her revenge on those who betrayed her in life; a powerless domestic still fears for her immortal soul while trying to scare off anyone who comes too close; and the former plantation master - a sadistic doctor who puts more faith in the teachings of de Sade than the Bible

When Eric and Grace McLaughlin purchase Greenbrier Plantation, their dreams are just as big as those who have tried to tame the place before them. But, the doctor has learned a thing or two over his many years in the afterlife, is putting those new skills to the test, and will go to great lengths in order to gain the upper hand. While Grace digs into the death-filled history of her new home, Eric soon becomes a pawn of the doctor's unsavory desires and rapidly growing power, and is hell-bent on stopping her.

The Amnesia Girl

Filled with copious amounts of black humor, Gerri R. Gray's first published novel is an offbeat adventure story that could be described as One Flew over the Cuckoo's Nest meets Thelma and Louise.

Flashback to 1974. Farika is a lovely young woman who wakes up one day to find herself a patient in a bizarre New York City psychiatric asylum. She has no idea who she is, and possesses no memories of where she came from nor how she got there.

Fearing for her life after being attacked by a berserk girl with over one hundred personalities and a vicious nurse with sadistic intentions, the frightened amnesiac teams up with an audacious lesbian with a comically unbalanced mind, and together they attempt a daring escape.

But little do they know that a long strange journey into an even more insane world filled with a multitude of perilous predicaments and off-kilter individuals are waiting for them on the outside. Farika's weird reality crumbles when she finally discovers who, and what, she really is!

The Cabin Sessions

The Cabin Sessions is a confronting, hard-hitting dark psychological thriller, told with an acid wit. Themes of domestic and child abuse are explored through minds distorted by fear, and corrupted by hatred and delusion. A tale where redemption is gained in unexpected ways.

It's Christmas Eve when hapless musician Adam Banks stands on the bridge over the river that cleaves the isolated village of Burton. A storm is rolling into the narrow mountain pass. He thinks of turning back. Instead, he resolves to fulfill his obligation to perform the guest spot at The Cabin Sessions. He should be looking forward to it, but fear stirs when he opens the door on the Cabin's incense-choked air.

Meanwhile, Philip's sister, Eva, prepares to take a bath. It's a ritual. She's a breath holder. At twenty-eight she's returned to Burton to finish the business of her past; business she must attend to, if only she could make sense of it. Memories begin to surface concerning the innocence of her brother.

Blood and Kisses

The definitive short story collecting from James H Longmore - an eclectic mix of dark horror, bizarro and Twilight-Zone style tales of the downright disturbing.

Welcome to the long awaited collection from the writer of horror novels *'Pede* and *Tenebrion*; a forword by Richard Chizmar (co-author of *Gwendy's Button Box* and author of *A Long December*), 18 short stories, 5 flash fiction and even a poem - all skin-crawling, soul-shredding tales of terror, of the darkest things that skulk amongst the night's inky shadows, and of the everyday gone horribly awry.

Discover the alternative implication of technology becoming self-aware, enjoy the acquaintance of a charismatic new pastor who promises his flock a brand new place in which to worship his God, and spend a little time in the company of a nice young man who is inexorably caught up in his home town's terrible secret. Then there is Cupid's revelation that personally he has never experienced love, yet we discover that very emotion alive and not so well amongst the ruins of a post zombie apocalypse world, and we bear witness to a childhood innocence forever destroyed in a war-torn city. There is more, Dear Reader, much, much more; for within these pages we have devils, demons and ghosts, lycanthropes and demi-gods, all rubbing nefarious shoulders with vilest of Hell's offspring who have slithered from the netherworld to doff their caps and wish us all the sweetest of dreams...

The Big Book of Bootleg Horror 2

The second volume in HellBound Books' flagship horror anthology - this one bursting at the seams with even more fantastically dark horror from the cream of the rising stars in today's horror scene!

Featuring: Tracey A. Cross, Elizabeth Zemlicka, Shelby Thomas, Matthew Gillies, Spinster Eskie, Stephen Clements, Ken Goldman, Nathan Robinson, K.M. Campbell, Cody Grady, Sebastian Bendix, Leo X. Robertson, David Owain Hughes, Timothy McGivney, Kane Gordon, Todd Sullivan, Mike Mayak, Edward Ahern, Rose Garnett, Jaap Boekestein, Brandy Delight, Stanley B. Webb, D. Norfolk, and Thomas Gunther.

A HellBound Books LLC Publication

http://www.hellboundbookspublishing.com

Printed in the United States of America